PROJECT KAITLYN

GRAYSON AVERY

FARCICAL PRESS

To my lovely wife,

Finally my dirty jokes are paying off for you!
Thanks for letting me test them out on
you for the last twenty years.

G.A.

1

Coffee. Kids. Clusterfrig. That was life for Kaitlyn Colby on most days, leaving room for the optional snot-bubbling cry beneath the covers to end the day (at least the floral pattern was forgiving). And this day would be no different.

Kaitlyn launched two paper plates across the kitchen island like a bartender in the Old West. The plates skidded to a stop in front of Ronny and Riley.

"Five minutes and we're outty like a belly button," Kaitlyn said, dumping a so-called non-stick pan in the sink that had half the pancakes still quite stuck. The char hung in the air like a foreign industrial zone.

"You're so weird, Mom," Riley said with a tongue cluck, an eye roll, and a toss of her brown hair off her shoulder, way too young to exude such mastery of teen 'tude.

"Almost ten and ready for the *Real Housewives*." Kaitlyn shook her head while continuing to clean up.

"Five minutes means no forks," Ronny said with hands in the air like a Viking conqueror, and then flashed a smile that reminded Kaitlyn of Aaron, except for the missing top tooth that Ronny sported with pride. It was what most reminded her of Aaron, the smile that used to make her melt, but in the year since he'd left, the feeling was closer to an ache. Both kids looked more like her with wavy, brown hair and peachy skin, which overpowered the green eyes they got from Aaron.

Ronny rolled his syruped pancake like a burrito and stuffed half of it into his mouth like a savage, or a normal eight-year old boy.

Riley looked up between bites. "Mom, do we have anything Friday night?"

Kaitlyn zipped up a backpack and looked around. "Yeah, by the look of this place, I think we're going to be on an episode of *Hoarders*." If only her life was occupied by more than work, kids, and binge-worthy television after the first two ran her into the ground.

"I want to go ice skating."

"We'll see." Would the ancient parental response work? She tore open a loaf of bread, the stupid plastic clamp thingy vanishing like David Copperfield. "Where the frig..."

With half a mouthful of pancake, Ronny mumbled, "Can I get a TV in my room? Dad said he was gonna get us one for our room at his house."

Kaitlyn searched the floor and muttered, "That's because your father's a douche."

Riley asked, "What?"

Kaitlyn straightened up. "Huh? I said, 'He's a cool dude.' Did you get a good night's sleep?" she asked, quickly.

Riley shrugged. "It was okay."

"And you, my little man?"

Ronny frowned and swallowed. "I'm not little."

"Big man?"

"I couldn't fall asleep. I heard that humming sound coming from the walls again."

"Umm, that's just your imagination," Kaitlyn stammered, and rushed to the den, a backpack in each hand. She made a mental note to turn the TV up three notches during her alone time with Buzz. "I feel like I'm sending you off to war with these backpacks."

"More like prison," Ronny said from the kitchen. "You never answered about the TV."

"You have an iPad. It's a personal TV. Shoes on in two," Kaitlyn said, grabbing her lunch bag and purse. She looked at her watch. "Make that one." She slipped on her flats, choosing function over fashion, as always. Fashion did little for a single mom of two. Except cost too much money. She didn't need the height, anyway, at five-foot-seven.

Kaitlyn and the kids hopped into the car. She turned the key. The aging, but usually-reliable Honda Civic groaned sickly. "I don't have time for this." Kaitlyn smacked the steering wheel and tried again. The groaning morphed into a hangover puke. "Dang it. Uncle Russ told me to get the spark plugs changed."

"Did you?" Riley asked.

"Obviously not," Kaitlyn said.

"Sorry," Riley said, obviously not sorry at all.

Kaitlyn popped the hood and stomped out of the car, the kids right behind her. "But he did show me how to clean them." She keyed the code into the garage door keypad then waited for a moment as the door slowly wobbled and squeaked higher. She held her breath. The last thing she needed was the garage door to become a floor. That was beyond her DIY power. She hustled in and grabbed a ten-millimeter ratchet and returned to the car. Kaitlyn lifted the hood and propped it up. She leaned in and removed the spark plug nuts, fantasizing about doing the same to her ex, and then removed the first of the coils.

Ronny climbed up on the bumper. "Can I help?" His hands grabbed for the ratchet.

"Yeah, just help me turn it. It's on there pretty good." Kaitlyn made room for Ronny's hand.

"I wanna do it myself," Ronny whined. "I'm a big boy."

All evidence to the contrary. They grappled over the ratchet until Kaitlyn finally let go. "Alright. Give it a shot. If it doesn't budge, don't force-"

He forced it. The ratchet slipped from the nut and clanked across the top of the engine, the socket catching a loose hose and tearing it from its rightful place. Ronny fell to the ground. The loose hose functioned quite like the male anatomy after a long car ride. Liquid exploded forth with an expression of relief. Filth and muck spewed every which way. Kailyn reached for the hose like some weird, blind-folded game played at a frat party after midnight, but quickly abandoned the effort. She decided instead to shriek, shield her head, and duck until the force of the blast petered out.

"Mom! Are you okay?" Riley asked, teen 'tude thankfully left behind.

Kaitlyn spat out what tasted like burnt oil before answering. "I'm okay. That wasn't exactly a smoothie, but I'm pretty certain I'm not gonna need breakfast."

"Why'd you let go?" Ronny asked, dusting himself off, and examining an oil blotch on his shirt. "Cool."

Kaitlyn ignored the question, instead focusing on damage assessment. The car was grounded until further notice, of that she was sure. She walked around to the side of the Honda and caught her reflection in the window. Her hair clung to her face like glue. Had she seen her new look on the cover of *Cosmo* recently? Definitely not. Nor could she claim retro status. No one would mistake that mess for 'The Rachel' made famous by Jennifer Aniston during her Friends days.

"Fabulous." Two showers before 8 a.m. She was sure that some parent somewhere had beaten her new personal record, but she took little solace in it. Kaitlyn peeled her blouse from her body and held it away from her skin. She looked down and said, "It looks like Jesus on a jet ski." At least that was her best guess for the impromptu Rorschach ink blot test blasted onto her person.

"You're not gonna drop me off at school like that, are you?" Riley asked, her eyes scanning Kaitlyn up and down.

"Umm, no. I can't go to work like this, honey. I'm a mess." *So, just a regular Tuesday, I guess.*

"What are we gonna do?" Ronny asked.

Kaitlyn looked at him. "Change your shirt. The hose caught you, too. And I have to shower." She turned to Riley. "Call your father and see if he can take you."

Ronny frowned. "Come on. I like it. And why are you calling Dad? Aren't Aunt Jenn or Shelly closer?"

Because he left us. "Because we're a family."

Riley stood with two fists on her hips. "Then why doesn't he live here?"

Kaitlyn took a deep breath and answered the easier question again. "Because Aunt Jenn and Shelly are already at work." It was probably true, but truer still was that Kaitlin wanted an excuse. An excuse to see him. An excuse to show him the mess he had left her in. An excuse to make him realize he was needed. Badly.

"Can he take the motorcycle?" Ronny asked.

"How would we all fit?" Kaitlyn asked. "And you're never allowed to ride on it, anyway."

Riley and Ronny glanced at each other.

Unbelievable. "Figures. He takes you guys on his motorcycle."

"Only up and down his street. It's quiet," Riley said.

Kaitlyn trudged back inside, kicking her shoes off. "Lock the door if you leave with your father before I'm out of the shower. I've gotta wash my hair. And tell him to come back after he drops you. I need him to take me to work."

"Do you want to just talk to him?" Riley asked.

"No," she lied.

KAITLYN SAT on the toilet in the master bath. The hairdryer whirred into her ears, further jumbling her scattered thoughts. She needed a plan. And to stick to it. That was her downfall. Aaron was too smooth, deflecting and downplaying her needs and concerns with precision. How could she get him to see what he was missing without beating and burning it into his beautiful face with a hairdryer? She weighed it in her hand. Maybe that *was* the answer. She tossed the hairdryer onto the counter and huffed. She had already hit her self-imposed daily limit on fantasizing about doing bodily harm to Aaron. It was one of her only hobbies.

What was her plan? She had to keep him at arm's-length, of that she was sure. The closer he got to her, the less willpower she had. But what would she say this time that she hadn't already said?

She pulled her hair back into a ponytail, still damp. It would have to do. He would be there any second. She shuffled into the bedroom and untied the belt on her robe.

"You still got it," Aaron's deep voice echoed through the room.

Kaitlyn shrieked and jumped back, her hand smacking against a picture frame on the dresser. "My God, Aaron! You can't do that." She wrapped the robe tight around her and retied it.

Aaron leaned in the doorway, peering into the bedroom, arms folded. "I called out to you, but the hairdryer was on. Then I heard the door open. I should've waited until the robe was on the floor."

"Very funny." She looked him up and down. *Damn.* He wore his dirty-blond hair long and tossed to the side like a surfer. His only imperfection was the crow's feet around his eyes, but Kaitlyn liked them. It gave her the false sense of security that he was actually maturing. And had he worked half as hard on their marriage as he did on his abs, which bulged out from his tight t-shirt, they would've still been together. And then that smile. A flush rushed throughout her chest and neck. "Thanks for helping out, but I have to get dressed. I'm gonna be late for work."

Aaron walked toward her and smiled. "I think I can be of even more assistance by helping you out...of that robe."

Her pulse pounded. Her stomach churned. *Be strong.* She stepped backward, but her retreat was halted by the dresser. "Aren't you still with that teen with the braces?"

"Veronique? She's twenty-three and it was Invisalign. But, no. It's over."

The pounding of her pulse intensified. Before she could blink, Aaron reached for the belt on her robe.

She grabbed his hand, keeping the knot intact, and whispered, "I'm not your plaything. We're not doing this...again."

"Of course not," Aaron said, nipping at her neck. "This isn't a game. You're the mother of my children. You'll always be special to me."

The fear slipped away. The locksmith had worked his magic. No tools required. Only words that inflated her self-worth. She couldn't resist him. She needed him. She needed to feel wanted.

Kaitlyn removed Aaron's hand from her belt and untied it herself. Aaron slipped his hands inside and around her. Kaitlyn's neck tingled as Aaron gently sucked on the tender spot just above her collarbone. Excitement surged through her body. She wrapped her arms around his neck, looked into his eyes, and then met his lips deeply and fully. He pulled her in, and she pressed forward to meet his body, pushing him toward the foot of the bed.

Aaron slipped the robe from her shoulders. She released him and let her arms fall freely behind, the robe slipping from her to the floor. She fumbled with his belt. Her hands shook. It had been a while. Buzz and Jaime from the steamy show, *Outlander*, had been her only companions in the past year. And neither wore pants. Buzz was just a mechanical wiener and Jaimie wore a kilt while locked inside her TV.

Kaitlyn lifted Aaron's shirt from his body and tossed it behind her, eyes closed, and then he lifted her. They stumbled and fell onto the bed, giggling, but never parting lips.

"Can you do a Scottish accent?" Kaitlyn blurted.

"What?" Aaron sucked in a breath and kissed her hard again.

"Nothing." Kaitlyn lay back and let go, pleasure coursing through her body.

2

Two minutes and seventeen seconds later...Aaron rolled off Kaitlyn and took a deep breath. "How was that, babe?"

"Umm, good. Very efficient. I mean, I'm late so..." *Would it kill you to waste a few strokes?*

Aaron, his chest still heaving, said, "Just like old times, Lynnie."

Ugh. She cringed. She hated when he called her that. It didn't matter how many times she asked him not to.

"Well, I'll let you get to it. We really should go. I gotta swing by the office before an appointment." Aaron patted her on the knee and then slipped off the bed.

Kaitlyn lay on her back, staring up at Aaron's shirt, which dangled from the ceiling fan. The void returned to her stomach as if she had been hollowed out like a pumpkin. Only messier. *The shirt most certainly hit the fan.*

Aaron laughed. "That was a good fling."

Is he kidding me? "What?"

Aaron pointed to and then tugged at his shirt before

freeing it from a fan blade, along with a herd of dust bunnies that had multiplied, well, like bunnies. Apparently, they had gotten a whole lot more action than she had in the past year, excluding Buzz.

"Oh."

He shook his shirt out. "Might want to dust once in a while, Lynnie." Aaron laughed, but it quickly morphed into a cough. He smacked a poor bunny as it floated down in front of his face.

"Maybe if I wasn't doing—" *Both of our jobs.* "So many other things." She could still salvage this.

Aaron stopped at the dresser, picking up the picture she had knocked down. He stared at it for a moment. "You still keep this picture out?"

Even though there were at least six frames on the dresser, she knew exactly which one it was. It was the four of them on the beach in San Juan. Better times. Much better. "Oh, that? Been kinda busy for the past year with the kids and all. Didn't even realize it was there." She sat up. She searched his face to see if he bought it, but he could always see right through her.

And the sheets, apparently. He nodded to her with a smile. "Your headlights are still on." Aaron zipped his fly and secured his belt while maintaining eye-headlight contact.

"They're high end. They shut off on a delay."

Aaron chuckled. "I hadn't realized you were a luxury model."

You and me both. The flush returned to her neck and seeped into her face this time. She turned her legs and, more importantly, her face, to the side and away from him. With the grace of Humpty Dumpty, she thrust her body forward in an attempt to exit the memory-foam crater that she and Aaron had formed. Had the memory foam remembered the last time Aaron had joined her there? She grunted and grabbed hold of the side of the bed. "I need a ladder to get out of this thing." She half-slid, half-fell, landing with a thud, and smiled at Aaron as if she meant to do it that way. She wrapped a blanket around herself. She didn't need any more headlight comments. "That was exhausting. I want to dive back in there for a nap." She racked her brain for something intelligent to say. Cute and funny was all well and good, but she needed more.

Aaron chuckled. "I see you haven't outgrown your klutziness."

Kaitlyn smirked. "Yeah, because people grow so much at thirty-nine." At least they each hadn't grown enough to stay together. The only growing they'd done was apart.

Aaron looked at her, but didn't say anything.

What was there to say? She glanced up at him and then away. "I'm glad you came." Definitely not that.

"Yeah, I did." Aaron flashed that heartbreaker of a smile.

Kaitlyn sighed. "That's not what I meant. We've missed you." She let the words out slowly, "I've missed you." She scanned his face, looking for a sign, chest pounding. Something. Anything. "We, umm, have game night on Saturday. Want to come over for pizza?"

He stared at the floor. "Ahh, don't think I can. I've got a, uh, thing."

"What? A meeting..." Her voice trailed off. She knew.

"Yeah, kinda. We should probably get going." Aaron walked out of the room without looking back.

Kaitlyn closed her eyes and pulled in a breath, slow and deep. *How could I be so stupid?* She was nothing more than a good fling to him, left hanging. She swallowed hard and barely got out the words, "I'll be out in a minute."

She picked up the San Juan picture and stared at it through blurry eyes. She grit her teeth and snapped the frame in two, the glass shattering into a dozen pieces.

3

Kaitlyn found Aaron where she always did when he was waiting for her. In front of the oversized mirror in the living room. At least he was wearing his shirt while admiring his appearance this time. She did like it when he made his pecs dance like he was the headliner at Chippendales. He turned to look at her and then back to the mirror once more for a final view. It was apparently too far a walk to the rearview mirror in the car parked at the curb. Kaitlyn never gave that mirror a first glance. Let alone a second.

"Let's ride like Bonnie and Clyde," Aaron said, heading for the door.

Yeah, right. Kaitlyn exhaled, grabbed her bags, and followed Aaron outside to the car. She slid into the passenger seat of the frostbite-blue Dodge Charger, ever so grateful that she didn't have to sit in the back. Although she wouldn't put it past him. Ronny was still using a booster seat, which would've been embarrassing for Kaitlyn to roll up to work strapped into one.

Kaitlyn broke the silence. "Since I'm gonna be late, I've

gotta stay late, so can you relieve Victoria at around 4:30? She'll get the kids off the bus and do homework and stuff. Shelly will give me a ride home."

"Yep. Should work."

Kaitlyn stared over at him. "No snacks. No sugar. Nothing."

Aaron smiled. "No problem. I don't even know why you're telling me this."

She scoffed, but didn't respond. "Can you fix the car? Russ says I need to change the spark plugs and Ronny had a mishap with a hose."

"Tell Junior that's nothing to be ashamed of. It's happens to the best of us." He laughed. "Well, not me, but he probably got that from your side. I mean, there's no way your dad is getting it up all the time without help, right? How else does he keep a woman half his age satisfied?"

Idiot. "Can you fix the car or no?"

"Yes. I can try to look at it later, but if the kids are all over me, you'll have to call Jimmy Green down at the shop. I'm swamped for the next few weeks."

"Thanks." *For nothing.*

They rode in silence until they arrived at the office building that housed her company, Sutton Advertising, and a dozen other small businesses and boutique firms.

Aaron slowed to a stop in front of the main entrance. "So, I'll swing by at six and pump 'em full of sugar before dinner, right?"

Kaitlyn opened the door halfway and stopped. "I know you're kidding, but it's 4:30 and don't mess with me right now."

"We messed around enough this morning, eh?"

Too much and not nearly enough. She stood up and was

able to say, "Thanks for the ride." She slammed the door and walked off.

"No way!" Taylor shrieked.

Kaitlyn glanced over to see Shelly and Taylor gawking at her.

"Good morning," Kaitlyn said, embracing the blotchy skin that surged forth for the nth time of the day.

"Umm, explanation, girlie?" Shelly's eyebrow arched so high it nearly blended into her hairline. Not many blondes could accomplish that without a good colorist. Shelly had a plain, but pleasant face that she rarely did much of anything to improve, and one that Kaitlyn was avoiding making direct contact with at the moment.

"What?"

"That," Shelly said, pointing at Aaron's Charger, which roared in the distance. "And that guilty look on your face."

"My car broke down." Kaitlyn kept on toward the entrance, Shelly and Taylor falling in on each side of her.

Taylor shrieked, "Did you stay over at his place last night? What'd you do with the kids?" Taylor was the youngest in their circle of friends, even though she technically wasn't a member of the Sweet Water Circle. She was a top-of-the-pyramid cheerleader type, short and thin, and still young enough to care about how she looked. Her heels, more than miniskirt and tight blouse, were well above her pay grade. She wore her straight, black hair long and loose.

"Shhhh! Not so loud. This is my place of business."

"So, it's true?" Shelly asked, her eyes bulging.

"I did not stay at his place." It was true. Not the whole truth, though. She flung open the door and walked through, leaving the ladies behind.

"But there's more to the *story*," Taylor sang.

They stopped in front of the elevator in the open lobby.

She should've taken the stairs. There would've been fewer questions. Plus, she could see that cute model. It was actually a cardboard cutout of Dimitri, the spokesmodel of Berlin, one of their European clients, but she had met him once, so he was real. Not to mention, she had made a few Dimitri withdrawals from the Buzz bank over the past few months.

Kaitlyn stared straight ahead, willing the elevator to arrive.

"Jedi mind tricks aren't going to open the doors any quicker on this piece of junk." Shelly took Kaitlyn's hand and said, "We've been friends for thirty years. I know you. You totally screwed the pooch." Shelly gently pulled Kaitlyn's chin toward her and looked into her eyes.

Kaitlyn looked down at the ground, her shoulders slumping. "I screwed the pooch. Literally."

"Aaron's definitely a dog, so that makes perfect sense," Taylor said.

"No! You and Aaron did the dirty deed?" Shelly said, just as the elevator door opened, revealing Kaitlyn's recent college grad hire, Carl.

Carl nodded without eye contact and then scurried away.

"I have to work with him." Kaitlyn shook her head as they entered the elevator.

"Was it good?" Taylor asked, apparently not grasping the weight of the situation.

"Why?" Shelly asked.

"Because who wants to have bad sex?" Taylor asked.

Shelly rolled her eyes. "I was talking to Kaitlyn."

Kaitlyn took a deep breath and looked up at the ceiling as the elevator shook to life. "It was great for the two minutes it lasted."

"Oooh," Taylor said. "That's like giving a starving woman one noodle when she needs a whole bowl full."

"Are we talking about real noodles or figurative?" Kaitlyn asked.

"Yeah, doesn't matter," Shelly said, as they exited the elevator to the main lobby of Sutton Advertising. "Why?"

"I don't know."

"Why?" Shelly said, forcefully.

"I...I want him back."

Shelly stopped, closed her eyes, and took a deep breath. "I'm calling your sister. This can't continue. You are to report to Seicho for a Sweet Water Circle intervention at 12:30."

"Sushi!" Taylor smiled and clapped.

Shelly shot her a look.

"My bad."

"I can't. I'm already late." Kaitlyn cut into the kitchen and held up her lunch bag. "Plus, I brought." She shrugged. "Sorry."

Shelly tore the bag out of her hand and threw it over her shoulder without looking. "Oops."

Kaitlyn's mouth dropped open as the bag soared into the hallway and connected with Carl's brown curly head with a fwop. He nearly spilled his smoothie.

"Ahhh," Carl said, rubbing the side of his head. "Are you on the brick diet or something?"

"Look out," Taylor said, just a tad too late.

Shelly turned to Kaitlyn. "You will be there."

Kaitlyn opened her mouth, but Shelly interrupted. "I'm driving."

Son of a...

~

Kaitlyn sat with Shelly and Taylor around the corner of a hibachi table to her right. Kaitlyn's knee bounced rapidly. "Do we have to do this at hibachi? Why couldn't we get a regular table? I don't want to talk about this stuff in front of the chef...or the strange little doll that pulls down his pants and pees sake on everyone."

"It's more fun. Plus, we might need a man's opinion," Shelly said, smiling.

"And the naked doll is kind of fitting, no?" Taylor asked. "Plus, Shelly hasn't seen a naked anything in forever."

"Hardy har." Shelly smirked.

Kaitlyn shook her head. "I don't need the chef's opinion on my love life. There are already going to be too many opinions around this table."

A waitress arrived with a smile and broken English. They each ordered their own meal while Kaitlyn chose for her sister Jenn, who was always late. The sound of heels click-clacking grew from behind them. Kaitlyn turned around to see Jenn, tall and thin with a killer blue power suit and matching heels, approaching. They looked alike, save for Jenn's blue eyes to Kaitlyn's hazel, but Jenn was everything Kaitlyn was not. Glamorous. Confident. Powerful.

"My loves." Jenn slipped into the seat to Kaitlyn's left. "This Sweet Water Circle intervention is called to order. I had to cancel a call with Billionaire Ben, so we best make it count. We need to make some progress on this poor soul. This morning was the final straw. The Circle can no longer stay quiet. She needs help."

"I'm right here." Kaitlyn rolled her eyes.

Jenn smiled at Kaitlyn and squeezed her knee.

"Am I in The Circle?" Taylor asked, excitedly.

"You're on the waiting list. You can continue to act as a

proxy for Donna," Shelly said.

"Doesn't her membership expire at some point? She moved away, what, like ten years ago?"

Jenn said, "It never expires. We made a pact to always be there for each other thirty years ago and that's not gonna change now. And this is not the time for that discussion, T. We have a crisis on our hands. I think we can all agree that this morning's events are unacceptable."

Total exaggeration. "I can manage. Plus, it's already done. What can I do now?" Kaitlyn fumbled with her chopsticks and a slippery piece of iceberg lettuce.

Taylor raised her eyebrows. "Why don't you just doink Carl? He's cute."

"I'm not gonna *doink* Carl. He's twenty-three and my employee."

"I might," Taylor said. "I'm only three years older and we don't work in the same department."

Jenn cut in. "Okay. Send him a calendar invite. This is about Kaitlyn."

"She wants him back," Shelly said.

Kaitlyn bit her lip. Despite that morning's event, she couldn't argue with Shelly, and that multiplied the shame.

"She wants Carl back? Carl's mine," Taylor said, pounding the table.

"Can we get serious, ladies?" Jenn looked at Kaitlyn. "Answer me this. How do you feel when you're with Aaron, assuming you're not in the midst of carnal pleasure?"

"I don't know. I just know how I feel when I'm not with him." *Broken. Alone. Unlovable.*

"That's just loneliness," Shelly said.

The three women all stared at Kaitlyn. "Think," Jenn said.

Emily Page. Kaitlyn hesitated. "I guess...I've always felt second best. I always felt like he wanted to be somewhere else. With someone else."

Jenn huffed. "Emily Page?"

Kaitlyn nodded.

"He chose you," Jenn said, firmly.

"Because she moved across the country after college. And then he left me."

"Fifteen years later. What else? The Emily Page issue is nonsense," Jenn said.

Not to me. All eyes were on her, waiting. Kaitlyn thought for a moment. "I guess I've kind of always felt he's held me back a little. He put his business over my career. Kept me from getting my MBA."

Shelly raised her eyebrows. "Now you're only holding yourself back. I hear Sutton is looking for someone to take over the beverage vertical. Rumor has it that Mark is on shaky ground after the Pulse Energy disaster. The explosion graphic looked like an orgasm. Sales plummeted. You should go after it."

Kaitlyn nodded, but didn't say anything. *I want it, but I'm not good enough to have it. Just like Aaron.*

"Ooh, I totally want to try that. It's called Pulse?" Taylor asked.

"I guess Mark should've recommended they go after the sorority girl demographic," Kaitlyn said.

"Sis, ever since we were young, you've cut yourself short. You are so much better than what you see in yourself," Jenn said, shaking her head. "But when you're with *him*, you shrink even more."

"I just don't understand—why doesn't he want me? To be with me? Our kids?" Kaitlyn sucked in a shaky breath. Her eyes filled with tears. *Why am I not good enough?* She knew it was true. She just didn't know why.

"That's on him. When has he ever shown devotion or responsibility?" Jenn looked like she had just tasted bad sushi.

Ouch.

A squeaky cart approached, pushed by a short, mustached man with a chef's hat. "Hallo! My name is Reo." He slipped in front of the grill and took out a piece of paper.

Reo looked at Jenn. "You filet mignon."

She nodded.

"You prime cut, baby," Taylor said, chuckling.

Reo moved to Kaitlyn. "You have scallops."

Kaitlyn whispered, "Is he talking about my boobs?"

Jenn laughed. "No, baby. Those are puffer fish."

"Puffed or unpuffed?"

They both laughed.

"Eh, three-quarters full."

"I'll take that. Thanks, sis," Kaitlyn said.

Reo confirmed the rest of the orders and oiled down the grill.

Taylor whispered to Shelly, "Maybe you can get Reo to do that to you. He's very skilled."

Jenn said, "Let's stick to the agenda, shall we, ladies? Sis, I think you shouldn't worry about a man right now. Just do you."

"I do. All the time. I'm running out of batteries."

The girls all laughed.

"I'm only half-kidding," Kaitlyn said. *Or not at all.*

Jenn nodded to Shelly. "Do what she does. Amazon Subscribe & Save. Monthly deliveries."

"This is not about me," Shelly said. "Focus on your career. Your kids. Show that clown that you don't need him. You can handle that beverage team. It's time."

I do need him. Kaitlyn took a deep breath and exhaled. "I don't know."

A giant ball of flames burst forth toward them, nearly consuming all eyebrows within a six-foot radius, but the whole restaurant shrieked with pleasure as if eyebrows had no use.

Jenn grabbed Kaitlyn's hand. "You said it yourself. He's held you back. And I'd say he's belittled you. Undermined you. Taken advantage of you."

Kaitlyn's desire to eat vanished with her sister's words. "Thanks. I didn't think I could feel any worse."

"Unleash the beast, Kaitlyn!" Taylor yelled, thrusting her fist in the air.

"I think you'll rock it," Shelly said.

Could I? "I don't know if I can do beverages. Plus, run a whole team?"

"You whipped Carl into shape, right?" Shelly asked.

"I'm gonna whip Carl so good," Taylor said, nodding her head.

A laugh escaped Kaitlyn's mouth.

Jenn shook her head with a chuckle. "Don't you deserve more? After all you do for your kids? All the time you've put into the job?"

"Get it, girlie," Shelly said. "I know you can do it."

Kaitlyn nodded. Goosebumps ran up and down her arms as her whole body began to tingle.

Jenn smiled. "If you don't do it. I'm gonna show up and do it for you."

"That would be weird, so I'm gonna do it. Gonna. Friggin'. Do. It."

~

Kaitlyn stood outside of Josh's office, grateful that his assistant, Becky, was still out to lunch. She paced in a circle like a muscle head at the gym about to squat a billion pounds. Would she crumble under the weight? No, she was gonna crush it.

Kaitlyn smacked herself across the face and then stormed into Josh's office ready to ask, no demand, leadership of the new beverage team. She pushed the partially-open door with authority. It hit the wall and rattled. She stepped in, shoulders back, heart pounding.

"Holy—" Josh yelped. He took a deep breath and ran his hands across his bald head, as he sat behind his glass desk and oversized monitor. "You scared the life out of me."

"Sorry." Kaitlyn gave her sheesh face, adrenaline still pulsing through her veins, and then nearly puked up a scallop, maybe two. *Oh, God. No.*

Sasha, a senior account manager, stood in the corner of the room, leaning against the wall. Her long legs were exacerbated by the skin-tight short skirt she wore. She crossed her arms. Kaitlyn wondered how she was able to accomplish that with so much silicone in the way. And don't get her started on Sasha's seemingly permanent selfie lips. In all fairness, though, Sasha's life *was* like a walking Instagram story. They called her the sex bot. Behind her back, of course.

"Uh, we're in the middle of something," Sasha said, twirling and examining her straight black hair. Without looking up, she said, "Did someone get poisoned by one of your little taste tests?"

Kaitlyn's mouth went dry. "No."

"Then move along."

Josh held up his hand. "Hold on a sec. It's obviously important. What do you need, Kaitlyn?"

She took a deep breath. *You got this.* "I heard that you're looking for someone to lead the beverage team. That someone is me."

Sasha laughed. Josh glared at her and the laugh morphed into a cough.

Josh frowned. "Where did you hear that?"

Not the best response, but it wasn't a no. Kaitlyn shrugged. "It's going around."

"Not many people know about that. No matter." He shrugged. "We kept it quiet for a reason. We already have someone in mind. And, unfortunately, it's...not you."

Deep breath. Deep breath. Kaitlyn nearly sucked in all the air in the room and exhaled slowly. She refused to let Sasha see her cry. Within an hour, her new nickname would be Krylyn or something worse, and she would never live it down. With a shaky voice, she asked, "May I ask why?"

"A team leader has to take charge. Have the confidence to make difficult decisions. Tell the client when they're wrong. Like Sasha."

"I don't want to be like Sasha." Did she say that out loud? Judging by the look on Sasha's face, it was an emphatic yes.

Josh was doing a poor job of holding in his laughter. "Look, Kaitlyn. We love you here. You're great at what you do, but Monica is a better fit for the role."

Kaitlyn threw her hands up. "Monica? Monica has half the experience I do." Her hands started to shake. Kaitlyn clasped them behind her back and looked at the ceiling and then back at Josh.

Josh traced his salt and pepper goatee with his fingers. "Experience is important, and you have it, but there are other traits required, and you don't have those. Perhaps you could develop them in time. But for now, I'm sorry."

"Don't be." Kaitlyn turned on her heels and rushed out of the office, tears bursting from her eyes.

She hurried down the hallway, eyes glued to the floor. She turned the corner and thrust open the door to the stairway, nearly blasting it off its hinges. She ran down the four flights of stairs, leaving a trail of tears in her wake. The door to the lobby opened just as Kaitlyn jumped from the bottom step. She swerved around the door and then the entrant, Heidi from accounting.

"Whoa!" Heidi shrieked. "Kaitlyn?"

Kaitlyn spun around Heidi and through the door, knocking into Dimitri, the cardboard cutout. He looked at her like he always did, mysterious and longing for connection. But this time, he sickened her. She thrust her fist at his face. It connected with a crack, pushing the frame back across the floor into the wall, and creasing Dimitri's neck so that his head leaned back at an impossible angle. "You stupid mother frigger!" She followed the savage blow with a devastating crotch kick, lifting Dimitri off the floor. He wobbled on one foot before toppling over on his side.

Kaitlyn stared at the demoralized Dimitri, her chest heaving. Laughter erupted behind her. She turned to see a man in a suit, no tie, staring at her, a wide grin on his face.

She glared at him. "Why are you laughing at me?"

"Are you not aware of what you just did? I've never seen someone punch a cardboard cutout and yell, 'mother frigger.' I'm not sure which one is funnier, to be honest. The only thing funnier is when mascots fight. I love seeing those."

Kaitlyn wiped her eyes. A laugh somehow escaped. "I have kids. I don't curse. I'm sorry you had to see that. But you didn't hear what he said to me." She took a closer look at the man. Tall. Tan. Athletic. Intense blue eyes. *Hot.*

"Not sure anyone deserved that kind of T.K.O. Even dudes in 2D." The man smiled and ran his fingers through his black hair, making it stylishly messy, a foreign concept to Kaitlyn. The messy part, she had down pat, though.

Kaitlyn shifted from foot to foot. "I don't know boxing terminology. Does T.K.O. stand for a testicle knockout?"

The man burst into laughter, grabbing his side. Kaitlyn joined him. When they stopped, he asked, "I don't mean to pry, but you were obviously upset." He narrowed his eyes. "If you two were dating, remind me never to dump you."

"I thought you were actually gonna be serious there for a second."

"Never. I don't get serious."

Another player. Kaitlyn smirked. "Not dating. I'm sure, much to your surprise, I'm single. How could you possibly have guessed that, right?" Kaitlyn ran her hands up and down from head to toe as if she was the consolation prize on *The Price is Right*. "How could you possibly have guessed that all this is single? This hot, revolting mess." She wiped her nose, reinforcing her point.

"Stop it. What *did* happen? If you don't mind me asking."

Kaitlyn took a deep breath. "Work stuff. Not worth discussing. I didn't get a job I wanted."

"That's tough. I'm sorry to hear. There's always MMA. You could be world champ."

That would require winning at something. "Yeah," Kaitlyn said, with a sarcastic chuckle. "I gotta run. Thanks for cheering me up. I'm gonna get some fresh air and show my face back there."

"Not a problem. Good luck, slugger."

Kaitlyn smiled sheepishly and headed for the exit. The man covered his crotch as she walked by.

"Very funny."

4

The rest of the afternoon was uneventful and the car ride home with Shelly was quiet. There wasn't much to say. Kaitlyn gnawed on her nails, her knee bouncing up and down. Normally, she couldn't wait to get home and see and hug the kids. They were why she did all that she did. And then she could fill her comforter with tears as an added release. But Aaron would be there, too. And it was too soon to see him. Her stomach churned as Shelly stopped the car in front of the house.

"Take it one moment at a time, sweetie. You'll get through this." Shelly forced a smile. It oozed with pity. "If Aaron didn't fix the car, I'll drive you and the kids tomorrow."

"Okay. Thanks. I'll let you know." Kaitlyn got out of the car and headed toward the house.

She glared at the grounded car that sat in the driveway. The one that had started this whole mess, ironically, by not starting. "I loathe you and your dirty spark plugs. And all your hoses are small."

Kaitlyn entered the house, kicked off her shoes, and tossed her bag on the couch near the door.

"Mommy!" the kids yelled from the kitchen.

She smiled and headed into the kitchen. "Hi, guys!" she said with manufactured enthusiasm, and avoiding eye contact with Aaron. She narrowed her eyes. The three of them sat around the island, licking chocolate ice pops. She forced her eyes upon Aaron. "I thought we agreed on no sugar."

"I had to call an audible," Aaron said, flashing that smile.

"What?"

Ronny rolled his eyes. "It's a football term, Mom. You wouldn't understand."

She swallowed her annoyance, but like bad sushi, it came right back up. It was evident in her tone when she said, "What did you have for dinner?"

"Ice pops," Riley said, dryly.

Mother frigger. "You couldn't even give them a real dinner, first? I had one rule. One. And you broke it. I may not understand football terminology, but I understand that!"

Aaron responded, calmly, "We're both parents. I had to change the rules. You can understand that, can't you? The situation called for ice pops. Just calm down."

Fire replaced blood in her veins. Through gritted teeth, she said, "Tell me to calm down again. I dare you. I already kicked one jerk's butt today." He didn't have to know that Dimitri was paper thin. And totally not real. Except in her dreams.

"What?" Aaron asked, his head jolting back in shock.

She turned away from them. "Nothing." The mystery of it all was a lot more menacing than the real story. She took a deep breath. Maybe he had bailed on dinner because he fixed the car. "Did you have a chance to fix the car?" Kaitlyn asked, attempting a measured tone, but failing miserably.

Aaron grimaced. "Sorry, Lynnie. We got distracted."

A million words in the English language and none of them were applicable. Kaitlyn stomped toward her bedroom mumbling incoherently. She entered, slammed the door, and collapsed on the bed, her head pounding.

Kaitlyn lost track of time, staring at the ceiling with blurry eyes, no sense of time nor motivation to move.

What's wrong with him? What's wrong with me? How pathetic am I that I want him to comfort me?

A knock at the door. *Oh, God. Is it him?* But then Riley's voice slipped through the door, "Mommy, can I make you a sandwich or something?"

Kaitlyn hadn't eaten since the failed intervention at Seicho, but her stomach sensation gauge was closer to 'regurgitate' than 'hungry.'

"I'm not hungry, but thank you."

"Okay. Love you."

"Love you, too."

A faint ding rang out between nose blows. Kaitlyn searched for the phone, which was stuck in an unknown fold of the comforter. She found the phone and unlocked it. A text from Shelly was waiting.

Messages
Shelly
Details
How'd it go, girlie?
Need to add boogies to the fabric material list of my comforter. It's a solid 10% right now.
Well, that's good Aaron repellant. But forget about all that. We can still salvage this.
Or I could just accept that I will never be loved the way I want to.
Deserve to.
I don't deserve it. That's the thing.
Messages
Shelly
Details
Not true. You're amazing.
I suck in love. I suck at work.
If you'd suck at work, you might make it to the top.
That's so wrong.
Seriously- about work- you need to schmooze more. Come with me to the cocktail party Thursday night for the clients and prospects.
I don't schmooze.

Messages **Shelly** Details

You don't schmooze, you lose.

Nobody says that.

I'm insulted. 😠

I just run taste tests and product polling. Nobody wants me to schmooze them.

You have to go if you want a bigger role, but give up if you want to.

🤐 What time is the party?

5

Thursday night had arrived. A horn outside Kaitlyn's house beeped rapidly, but respectfully. Kaitlyn grabbed her purse from the kitchen island, kissed each kid on the head, and said, "Be good. I'll see you in the morning." She looked at Victoria, the kids' twenty-something babysitter, and smiled. "Thanks. You know the drill. Call or text if you need anything. Or if you get any attitude."

Victoria laughed. "Oh, they never give me any trouble."

Isn't that how it always works? Kaitlyn shook her head and hurried to the door.

"Bye, Mom!"

"Love you, sweeties."

Kaitlyn walked outside and locked the door behind her.

A car door slammed, followed by Shelly's voice calling out, "Oh, no. No. No. No."

Taylor was out of the car right behind her.

Kaitlyn stopped and looked around. "What's the problem?"

"All of it," Taylor said. "Do you know how many fashion gurus you've just offended with this outfit?"

Kaitlyn looked down at her flowered dress and tan platform sandals. "I thought this was cute."

Shelly said, "It is, sweetie. If you're hanging out at the pool. This is a power party. You have to control the room. Not serve ice pops, lemonade, and mac and cheese bites. Although I do hope they have those."

"But we're gonna be late."

Taylor said, "It's better to be fashionably late than unfashionable."

Shelly stared at Kaitlyn, tapping her lips.

"Why are you staring at my crotch?" Kaitlyn asked.

Shelly ignored her. "Do you still have that black sequin dress with the asymmetrical midi skirt?"

"Yes."

"And the red heels?"

Taylor sang operatic, "With the red berry lipstick!"

Shelly said, "Turn around."

Kaitlyn did as she was told and swirled around.

"I meant turn around. We're going back inside."

Kaitlyn rolled her eyes. "Thanks for dressing me, mommies. Want a bomb pop before we go?" *Or did the kids finish them all for dinner?*

KAITLYN STOOD WITH SHELLY, Taylor, and Carl underneath a huge crystal chandelier at the top of a large staircase. Plush red carpet led down to an open area. Clusters of people stood around, socializing.

Kaitlyn looked around. "Wow. The boss' country club spares no expense."

"This is what Josh's $100k membership gets him. Sweet Water is small, but there's money." Shelly looked at Kaitlyn. "Time to get you to the ball, Cinderella."

Kaitlyn took a deep breath. "How do I look? Presentable?"

"Presentable?" Shelly scoffed. "Have you no faith in us?"

"Showing some leg. Some cleave." Taylor leaned in for a peek. "I'd do you," Taylor said, pursing her lips out. "Gimme some of those red berry lips."

"No, seriously."

Shelly stepped in-between Kaitlyn and Taylor, and rubbed Kaitlyn's bare arms. "You look amazing. These beach wave curls are crashing beautifully on those shoulders."

"Stunning," Taylor sang.

"I should've worn a shawl, no?"

Shelly waved her concern away. "Nonsense. This is very *inviting*. The curls. The bare shoulders. The sequins. The bold lipstick and shoes. And you're actually wearing heels. That, in itself, is a miracle."

Kaitlyn said, "Carl, what do you think?"

Carl took a bite of a prawn. "This is the biggest shrimp I've ever eaten."

"She meant her outfit," Shelly said, rolling her eyes.

"Oh. You look great. Shiny, like a fish lure."

Taylor whispered, "Carl, I think you should play the strong, silent type. And I like that." She winked at him.

Carl swallowed hard. And he was out of prawns.

"No, that's good. Symbolic," Shelly said. "You're gonna reel in some fish with fabulous fashion and then eat 'em alive with interesting conversation."

Kaitlyn's stomach morphed into a butterfly conservatory. Did she have anything interesting to say? Yes, she was well versed in PB&Js, puke, Cub Scouts, and binge-worthy television, but that was not going to play well among advertising execs, who hated streaming services.

Taylor said, "Hey. We're just having fun. Have some wine. Have some apps. Talk to a few people about marketing and brands. And that's it. You don't need to get a promotion in one conversation."

Shelly added, "I'll introduce you to some nice people at good accounts. Somebody likes you, they ask for you on their project. It's simple. It's a relationship business."

Taylor did a double take, staring down the stairs. "I'd like to have relations with that guy. Who is that hottie?"

Everyone looked down to where two small groups had congregated on opposite sides of the staircase.

"Oh, my God." Kaitlyn nearly rubbed her eyes like she was in a cartoon. It was him. The guy from the lobby who had witnessed her assault on poor Dimitri.

"What?" Shelly asked.

Kaitlyn shook her head. She couldn't speak.

And then Sasha strutted across the floor, the slit in her red dress so high it could catch on the chandelier. Confidence oozed from her pores. Her shiny black hair bounced off her bare shoulders like in a shampoo commercial and her boobs bounced like she was on Baywatch. All 147 eyeballs in the room were glued to her. Steve Izzo's glass eye didn't count. Kaitlyn rolled her own eyes. Sasha stopped next to the hottie. He turned to her with a smile and handed her a glass of red wine. He held some sort of mixed drink, clinked glasses with Sasha, and took a sip.

Shelly looked over at Carl. "You might want to wipe that drool off your lip. Hello? Are you there, Carl?" She ran her hand in front of his face. He didn't even blink.

Carl's eyes glazed over and he spoke in a monotone voice. "I don't know why she's not wearing a bra."

Shelly looked up at the ceiling. "Oh, God. Why have they not evolved? You're all like boob-controlled, well, boobs. Keep the eyes up, Carl. Women don't like to be ogled. Look her in the eyes with confidence. Don't get lost in the headlights like a deer."

"We're all looking down the stairs," Carl said.

"But you're the only one looking down her dress," Shelly said.

"Speak for yourself," Taylor countered.

Kaitlyn's stomach grumbled like her tectonic plates were shifting. The rest of the crew stared down at Sasha and the hottie.

Taylor said, "She and the hottie are a true power couple, like Louie the sixteenth and Marie Antoinette."

Shelly frowned. "Didn't they lose their heads for treason?"

"I don't know. I didn't really pay attention in history. Either way, they look stunning together. Look at how they're looking at each other. She looks like she might tear the pants right off him. I might like to see that." Taylor looked at Carl. "How about you, Carl?"

"Huh? Oh, umm, yeah. Wouldn't be the first time she did that at one of these events. I'd just like to be in the guy's pants when it happens."

"That's...weird, Carl," Shelly said, laughing. She nudged Kaitlyn. "I know you hate her, but you gotta get in good with Sasha if you want to move up in the world at Sutton."

Kaitlyn did a double take. "What? Why? She's never helped anyone."

"But she can tear you down."

"Dun. Dun. Dun," Taylor said. "Way too dark a thought when there's *crab cakes,*" she sang. She raised a finger and her eyebrows at the woman carrying the appetizer tray. She grabbed one and stuffed it into her mouth and then another. "You want one?" she asked Kaitlyn. "They're spectacular."

"No. I can't eat right now. My small intestine is livid at me for coming here. And I don't know how you stay thin."

"My trainer. Reaaaar," Taylor said, with her cat claws. "Carlos is muy caliente. Never miss a session."

"If your brother only knew your true colors," Shelly said, laughing.

"What bro Joe don't know won't hurt him."

Shelly shook her head. "Poor guy is too nice to have a little sister like you." She looked at Kaitlyn. "Well, it's time. You lead the way. Chin up, boobs out. Nice and slow."

Kaitlyn nodded, exhaled deeply, and then started down the stairs with poise. Well, at least for the first two steps. Kaitlyn's left ankle buckled, her body following. She reached for the bannister on the right, but missed.

She rolled down the stairs like a shiny log. Every muscle in Kaitlyn's body tensed as she tumbled, except unfortunately for her sphincter, which seemingly felt compelled to announce her progress on each new step like a royal horn blower. As if she hadn't made her presence quite known already.

Kaitlyn stopped with a groan and lay on her stomach in a heap at the bottom of the stairs. Pain surged through her hips, shoulders, and arms. She blinked, the floor shifting right in front of her eyes. She was surrounded by her crew and those at the bottom of the steps with concern, some laughter, and others muttering in disbelief at the impromptu butt trumpet performance.

Once she regained her senses, dread overtook the physical pain. She would eventually have to stand up and look at these people. Her friends. Her colleagues. Sasha. The hottie. *Oh, God. The hottie.*

"Are you okay?" the hottie asked, holding out a hand.

She got to her hands and knees, then looked up. *Not him.* "The fall didn't kill me, so no. Not okay." Kaitlyn's face burned. The blotches ran up and down her face like she was a human lava lamp. Without the swanky vibe. She grabbed his hand, as Shelly and Taylor joined in.

The hottie helped her to her feet. The crowd stared for a moment, as Shelly and Taylor helped Kaitlyn fix her hair and dress, but then dispersed.

"Did you break a heel?" Taylor asked.

"No, just a rib. And what little pride I had."

Sasha smirked. "Way to make an entrance."

Kaitlyn glared at her.

The hottie moved in. "Don't be embarrassed. That was the most spectacular entrance I've ever seen. You even had your own theme music."

Kaitlyn wasn't sure what to think. Was he making fun of her or trying to console her? Or both?

He continued, "I've found that in moments like this, you can let it crush you or you can own it. I'd own it, because, let's be honest, no one is ever gonna forget that."

"I'm hoping that my emotional coping mechanism blocks it out of my memory." Kaitlyn looked at Shelly. "I'm about done for the evening. Thanks for the invite. It's been great." *I'm never doing this again. I will be a taste tester lifer.*

The hottie held out his hand again. "My name is Hunter, by the way. Hunter Dixon." He grabbed her hand, leaned in, and kissed it.

Despite the recent fart(s), her stomach still rumbled with angst. "The lost art of chivalry. Thank you. I didn't think I could be more embarrassed, but we've met before."

Hunter narrowed his eyes and then gasped. "Slugger?"

"No, Kaitlyn."

Hunter chuckled. "I know. I was joking."

"Oh, right." Cue the lava lamp. She should just set it on a timer.

"Slugger?" Taylor asked.

Hunter looked at Taylor and Shelly, and said, "She beat up a cardboard cutout."

"That was you?" Taylor asked. "Unforgivable. We should probably do another photo shoot with Dimitri, no? In tight boxer briefs this time?"

Hunter looked at Kaitlyn. "You're like a new woman from the first time I saw you. I mean, wow."

She shifted from foot to foot, thankfully not rolling any ankles. "Nope. Unfortunately, the same woman." The angst was reaching epic proportions. "I really need to, umm, go. It was nice meeting you. I'm just too embarrassed to stay." Kaitlyn turned to leave.

Hunter grabbed her arm. "Wait."

Shelly grabbed Taylor and pulled her over to Sasha.

Hunter continued, "I have to tell you a story."

Kaitlyn turned around and looked at the ground. "What?"

Hunter said, "I don't really talk about this often, but..." He leaned in as if about to tell a secret. "I once puked in the lap of the Emperor of Japan. True story."

She chuckled. "Yeah, sounds true. Also, sounds like President George Bush. Excuse me. I really have to go."

Kaitlyn broke away and headed for the exit, tears at the ready.

6

Kaitlyn burst through the door. It was like a dam exploding. She rushed over to a line of hedges, her chest heaving and face dripping with tears. Why did these things always happen to her?

"Kaitlyn?"

She turned around to see Josh putting his cigar out on an ashtray. He walked across the cobblestone patio toward her.

Oh, God. She turned away and wiped her eyes. What would she tell him? Her muscles tightened at the thought, defending against a second round of tears.

Josh stepped beside her. "What's wrong?"

Shelly and Taylor burst through the doors and rushed over to Kaitlyn before she could answer. Shelly put her hand on Kaitlyn's shoulder. "What happened?"

What the heck kind of question was that? "Umm, did you not see me fall down the stairs and serenade the audience with my colon?"

"Oh, boy," Josh said. "That was *not* what I was expecting."

Taylor whispered, "It was a one-in-a-million entrance. There are no words."

Kaitlyn glared at her. "Really helpful. Thank you."

Taylor gave her sheesh face. "Oops."

Kaitlyn avoided their eyes. "Please, just take me home. This was a mistake from the start. I don't belong here."

Josh shook his head. "You want their respect?" he asked, nodding toward the building. "You have to stay."

Kaitlyn huffed. "Can I at least hide in the bathroom as a moral victory?"

Josh chuckled. "You can hang out here for a little while. Compose yourself and then you should head back in. These are good people. Nobody's gonna care. Remember when Charlie puked on Donovan McNeilly's shoes?"

Shelly frowned. "Didn't you fire him the next week?"

Josh waved his hand. "That's not important."

Kaitlyn fidgeted with the zipper on her purse. "Are you sure running away won't work?" *It worked for Aaron.*

"It won't, but I know something that will. Wine. Wine always works. I'll go get some," Josh said, turning on his heels.

"I am whining." Kaitlyn turned to Shelly, "Are you sure we can't go?"

The door opened, revealing a waiter and a tray of food. Shelly's eyes widened, seemingly forgetting the gravity of the situation. She grabbed a pig in a blanket and dipped it in the mustard. She held it out for Kaitlyn and then grabbed one for herself. "Eat this. You need something in your stomach."

"Yeah, mystery meats ought to help calm my gastric system." Kaitlyn took the tooth-picked dog, but didn't eat it.

Taylor grabbed two for herself. "I haven't had two weenies since college." She took a bite. "Oh, but these are better than those were. That's the best honey mustard I've ever had."

Shelly said, "I don't even know how to respond to that. But the answer is no. We're not leaving." Shelly took a bite and smiled.

Kaitlyn scoffed. "No? I'll just take an Uber."

Shelly shook her head. "No."

"No?" Kaitlyn angry chuckled.

Shelly laughed. "You heard me, girlie."

Kaitlyn stared at Shelly. "Why not?" She chomped down on the pig in a blanket with anger, but then perked up. "Oooh. This honey mustard *is* spectacular."

The door creaked open again.

Shelly said, "You can't leave now because he's coming over."

Kaitlyn swallowed and shrugged. "I can't leave because Josh is getting wine?"

"Not Josh," Shelly said.

Kaitlyn turned to see Hunter heading their way. Her face morphed ghost white. "What? Oh, my God. My pits are swamps." She did a slow chicken dance with both arms, too slow to fly away to safety. "Breathe. Breathe."

Taylor asked, "Are you talking to your pits or yourself?"

"Both."

Shelly leaned down to her pit and inhaled. "They're decent."

"Don't sniff me," Kaitlyn whisper shouted.

Taylor was seemingly excited by the prospect. "Oooh, let me get a whiff." She grimaced. "D-plus."

"What?" Kaitlyn did a double take.

Shelly smiled. "We're just kidding. You smell terrific."

Taylor added, "And it just makes the sequins even

shinier in the moonlight. Reel in the fish, baby. Everything that's happened tonight comes down to this."

"Thanks for the pressure. 'Have a drink and some apps,' they said." Kaitlyn's stomach gurgled—half hunger, half nerves.

Hunter arrived with a raised eyebrow. "Am I interrupting some strange female ritual?"

Oh, God. He saw. "I'm not sure what you're talking about," Kaitlyn said.

"The pit sniffing. Both of them." He nodded at the guilty duo.

Kaitlyn laughed, nervously. "Umm, no. They both...have a disorder. It's really sad, actually."

Shelly nodded. "We should probably go take our meds. See you in a bit." She grabbed Taylor and pulled.

"I don't want to leave. He's hot," Taylor said, and then whispered loud enough for all to hear, "Should I sniff him to sell it?"

The deranged duo walked away, but at least Josh was heading over with her drink. Kaitlyn needed some liquid courage. And then Shelly grabbed Josh by the arm and turned him around, holding him off to the side.

*No...*Her mouth had nothing to say. And her butt had done enough talking for the night.

Hunter said, "I just wanted to make sure you were okay."

Kaitlyn forced a smile. "I'll survive. I have an unusually high tolerance for pain." She shrugged with a sheepish grin. "Marriage." *Why is he here? Talking to me?*

Hunter laughed. "I'm sorry for laughing. I mean, not now. That was funny. I'm talking about when you fell. Seriously..." He broke out into laughter again.

Kaitlyn pursed her lips. "Your wellness check has been

really therapeutic, Doctor. But I'm bailing on my co-pay. Thanks, and good night."

"Wait. I'm sorry. Seriously—"

"I thought you didn't get serious?" Kaitlyn glared at him.

Hunter stepped toward her. "I exaggerated, perhaps a little. I wanted to apologize. And tell you that you're not alone. You're not the first woman to face plant center stage. Lady Gaga. Beyoncé. I mean, you're in great company. Did you see the news story about the Queen of England and how she fell out of a boat?"

"Yeah, but did she toot?"

"Toot?" Hunter laughed.

Kaitlyn rolled her eyes. "Fart."

"Unconfirmed. There *was* suspicious bubble activity in the water around her persons."

Kaitlyn tried to hold in a laugh, but couldn't.

Hunter continued, "Seriously, it's a character builder. Lady Gaga didn't cancel her concert. She kept singing."

"Yeah, but that's Lady Gaga. And I'm not getting paid a million bucks."

"I once walked out of the high school locker room in my tighty whities by accident into the gym filled with cheerleaders. If you can survive what happened back there, you can survive anything."

"You did?" *I'd pay to see him in his underwear.*

Hunter seemingly tried to keep a straight face, but did a poor job of it. "As far as you know."

Kaitlyn shook her head, breaking out into a smile. "You've got a lot of stories that you conjure out of midair."

"This is the advertising industry. That's what we do." Hunter nodded to the half-eaten hot dog. "How are those? I've been eyeing your wiener since I came over here."

Kaitlyn popped the rest of it into her mouth and swallowed it down. "So good. The honey mustard is like an orgasm in your mouth."

Hunter choked, nearly doubling over.

"Oh, my God. Do you need the Heimlich?"

He put up his hand. "No, I'm okay." Hunter cleared his throat. "I've just never heard pigs in a blanket described that way."

"Sorry, I'm a blurter. I don't even know what I said. You make me so nervous."

"I'll say it back to you. Imagine it as a commercial... Mustard so good, it's like an orgasm in your mouth."

Kaitlyn looked up at the sky. "You must think I'm such an idiot."

"Not at all. I think you're funny." Hunter narrowed his eyes. "But why do I make you nervous?"

Kaitlyn deadpanned, "You were staring at my wiener. It's weird."

A waiter stopped beside them and held out a tray. "Swedish meatball?"

Kaitlyn's heart nearly imploded. "Oh, God, no!"

The waiter's eyes bulged.

Hunter patted him on the shoulder. "No offense, but your balls aren't wanted here."

The waiter shot Hunter a look and scurried away, seemingly in need of therapy.

Kaitlyn laughed, nerves bubbling up inside her. At least it was better than gas. "The poor kid is probably still in high school." She fidgeted with her hair. The urge to run was met equally by the urge to do, well, unspeakable things to Hunter in the bushes. Or maybe even the backseat of a car without booster seats. She nearly laughed. He would actually need to feel the same way. *He's probably gay, looking at my wiener and all.*

She realized that Hunter had been talking, but she hadn't been paying attention.

Hunter asked, "I think you need a drink. Care to accompany me to the bar?"

"I don't really want to go back in there."

"Nonsense. If anybody laughs, just pretend they're cardboard cutouts and do your thing. I've seen you do worse for less," Hunter said.

"Funny. I do remember you laughing at me. What am I supposed to do to you?"

Hunter's eyebrows hit his hairline. "Kaitlyn, we've just met."

Kaitlyn closed her eyes, hoping he would forget she was there.

"I'm just kidding. Come get a drink. I'll be with you every step of the way and there aren't any stairs," Hunter said, holding out his arm to guide her. "My lady."

"I *should* probably attempt to forget this night ever happened." She looped her arm in his and followed. She looked back at her friends after she passed them. Shelly smiled while Taylor made inappropriate hand gestures about male and female anatomy intermingling.

Hunter opened the door for Kaitlyn and asked, "What do you like to drink?"

"I don't really have a go-to. I think I need something hard." She hoped his mind wasn't as dirty as hers was seemingly becoming. *You need to chill on binge-watching Starz, girl.*

"Well, then we'll get you what I'm having."

She checked his glass, but it was nothing but half-melted ice. She didn't want to shoot whiskey. Bourbon? No, thank you. She could manage a little vodka with some juice or soda, but that was about it.

Hunter pulled up to the bar, threw up two fingers, and

said, "Bay breezes. And the lady likes hers stiff."

Kaitlyn's face matched the cranberry juice in the bartender's hand.

"No problem, sir."

It *was* a problem. Hunter was totally gay. That explained why he was with her and not Sasha.

"Why are you staring at me like that?" Hunter asked. "I like sweet drinks. I make no apologies."

"You probably should," Kaitlyn said, grabbing the drink from the bartender. "Thank you."

Hunter chuckled. "Cheers, Kaitlyn."

Kaitlyn took a sip. "This is actually really good," she said, with a laugh.

"I wouldn't steer you wrong. But let's change the subject anyway for my ego's sake. You pick the topic."

"Anything but my wiener."

Hunter shrugged. "Well, if that's off limits, let's talk about something real."

Why does he even care? Does he feel bad for me? Could he actually be interested in me as a person? Yeah, right. "I thought you don't do serious? You only seem to ridicule women at their lowest points."

Hunter shook his head. "No. Never. Well, I only ridicule you at your lowest points."

"Lucky me. But somehow, you're still nice. It's a strange conundrum."

"I think they call it charm." Hunter smiled extra-wide.

Kaitlyn frowned. "Nope. Not what I was thinking."

Hunter smiled sheepishly and then said, "Seriously, I want to know about you. Tell me something you're passionate about. What are your hopes and dreams? What adventures have you had or want to have? Have you ever fallen down the stairs and farted?"

As much as she knew he was joking, she had never met anyone like him. Kaitlyn feigned anger. Well, half of it was fake. "I'd throw this bay breeze in your face, but it's too refreshing for what you deserve." She took a breath and stared at Hunter's shoes. "Look, I appreciate you making sure I'm okay, but I don't need a pity hangout."

"I'm not here to pity you." Hunter leaned down to catch Kaitlyn's eye. "I think you're interesting."

Kaitlyn looked up at him. Her heart raced. "All you know about me is that I have a weak colon," she blurted. *Way to bring that up again.*

"That's not true. I mean, your colon *is* questionable, but I know more than that. And I want to know more."

Kaitlyn examined his eyes. Was he telling the truth? Those baby blues triggered goosebumps like a brush fire.

"There you are!" a female voice called out. Sasha bounced next to Hunter, slipping her arm into his.

Kaitlyn breath disappeared.

Sasha gazed at Hunter. "We never finished our conversation. Why don't the two of us grab a drink at the bar and do just that?" She tugged at his arm.

"You're right." Hunter held his ground and spoke to Kaitlyn, "We were talking business, specifically the Mrs. Potts brand."

Sasha said, "You know what, I—"

Hunter interrupted, "Kaitlyn, what do you think about Mrs. Potts?"

Sasha scoffed. "She's just a taste tester."

Kaitlyn ignored Sasha. Her pulse quickened. This was her chance. It had to be good. She needed to show Sasha and Hunter that she meant business. She had no idea who Hunter worked for, but he could be her ticket. *Reel him in.* "I think the brand's lost its way. I used to love their products."

Hunter frowned. "How so?"

"As a mother, I refuse to pump my children full of their chemicals. It used to be about wholesome meals that made my life easier, but then I couldn't even pronounce half of what was in the food. And don't get me started on Mrs. Potts' plunging neckline. Not sure if she's selling chicken soup or her, umm, dumplings. With all the changes they've made, they might as well take Mrs. Potts off the label. She's long dead and turning over in her grave, no doubt. Replace her with Frankenstein or a toxic warning sign." Kaitlyn shook her head. "I don't envy whoever does their advertising. They're not going to be in the busy very long, I'll tell you that much."

She searched their faces for approval. Hunter pulled at his collar. Sasha's eyes were wide, seemingly in surprise, as if watching a train wreck. Horror spread throughout most of Kaitlyn's organs. Her spleen was in knots and her gall bladder was on the verge of a full shutdown. On a positive note, her colon was chill.

Hunter whispered, "Well, ummm....that would be me. I, umm, I'm gonna...I need a little fresh air. Please excuse me." He headed for the door.

What had she done? "I'm sorry," Kaitlyn called after him.

"You should be," Sasha said, through gritted teeth. She chased after Hunter. "I told you, she just hands out food samples."

Kaitlyn closed her eyes, willing herself someplace else. Anywhere else. But her red shoes weren't made of rubies. She opened her eyes to find herself stubbornly in the same embarrassing place she had been prior to her wish. *When are you gonna learn to keep your mouth shut, Kraplyn?*

7

The next morning, Kaitlyn sat in the passenger seat next to Shelly, her head leaning against the window, staring at the passersby and wishing Shelly would throw the car in reverse.

They idled at a red light. Shelly broke the silence, "When are you getting the car fixed? Not that I don't love driving you to work."

Kaitlyn didn't bother looking over. "I'm not sure unemployment is gonna cover the repairs."

"Oh, stop. You're not going to lose your job. I'll fire Taylor and hire you. I mean, she doesn't really work, anyway, unless personal shopping online is in her job description." Shelly laughed. "I love her, but she's gotta figure out what she wants to do with her life. And grow up."

Kaitlyn said, "She's only twenty-six. I'm thirty-nine and I still need to figure it out, apparently. Our fabulous plan of fixing my work life failed miserably. So, now what? My love life and my career are both in the toilet, which makes for a nasty clog, and I hate plunging."

"You *could* use a plunging." Shelly face palmed herself. "God, I sound like Taylor."

"You should talk. You haven't had any tradesmen anywhere near your appliances in like forever." Kaitlyn laughed sarcastically. "And I'm talking as if my love life is fixable. Or now, my career."

Shelly said, "I *got you*, girlie. I'll be your wing man. Wing woman. Wing person? Whatever it is, I got you. The Sweet Water girls grow through what we go through. That's the whole reason The Circle started back in your bedroom. I still miss that poster of Justin Timberlake with the frosted tips, by the way."

"Yes! I need a wing woman. That's my whole problem." Kaitlyn raised and shook her fists in faux cheer. She watched a red Mercedes convertible turn the corner. "I should probably get myself a sugar daddy. I'm not that hideous that I can't land some old, rich dude, right?"

Shelly smacked her lips. "Is that really gonna fix your love problem?"

Kaitlyn shrugged. "Maybe money *can* buy love, but they signed a non-disclosure agreement and can't tell us it worked. I'll ask Jenn if she's ever worked on any love cases."

Shelly pulled into the parking lot and found an empty spot up front. They got out and headed toward the building.

Shelly said, "We need to shake things up, girlie. Say goodbye."

Kaitlyn jolted awake and took a step away from Shelly. "What're you gonna do? Kill me? I'm not happy, but I'm not ready to die just yet."

"Think of it more like a rebirth. Are you in?" Shelly asked, excitedly. "You're in. You're totally in."

Kaitlyn asked, "What are you even talking about?"

Shelly stopped, grabbed Kaitlyn by the shoulders, and

yelled, "Are you in?" Only half of the people in the parking lot looked over. "Say it with power."

"I'm in. For what, I don't know. And you need to stop going to so many motivational seminars."

"That was mediocre, but we'll work on it. We need to mark this momentous occasion with a ritual or a ceremony, like burn everything related to Aaron."

"Not my kids, though, right?"

Shelly scoffed. "No, those are the only two good things he's done. And I'm starting to think you don't have a very high opinion of me. Twice, you've questioned me a murderer. Seriously, this will be fun and therapeutic."

Kaitlyn stared off into the distance. "Oh, God. I'm so dreading this."

"I know Josh. He's a good boss. Address it first. Apologize and move on."

"I was talking about your therapy. But thanks for the reminder. I just ruined a huge opportunity. And you know Sasha is gonna be in his office, guns blazing. And don't get me started on what her boobs'll be doing."

"You ever see how they shake when she yells?" Shelly shook her head. "I have so many questions about her boobs. Before you get fired, can you ask a few?" Shelly nudged Kaitlyn.

"I so hate you...in a loving way."

As they hit the walkway in front of the entry doors, Taylor sidled up next to them. "Morning, bitches."

"It's a big morning," Shelly said. "We're shaking things up. Burning the boats and forging forward. We're taking Kaitlyn's love life to the next level."

"We should probably take it a few levels higher than that," Taylor said. She turned to Kaitlyn. "No offense."

"None taken."

Taylor smiled. "I think a coming out party is necessary."

"When did I agree to becoming gay?"

"I was thinking more re-entry into bachelorette-hood, but if you like the coming out idea, I'd meet you halfway." Taylor winked at Kaitlyn.

Kaitlyn laughed. "Yeah, that's not a thing."

Taylor cocked her head. "Are you sure?"

They passed through the lobby and stopped in front of the elevator. Kaitlyn avoided eye contact with Dimitri. Which was pretty easy since he had a cardboard flip-top head and was staring at the ceiling. Her fine handiwork.

Kaitlyn's heart pounded harder with each step closer to the office. By the time she had dropped her lunch in the kitchen and made her way to Josh's office, she was nearly in cardiac arrest.

She stood outside Josh's office, took a deep breath, and decided not to blast his door open and make any demands this time. Voices conversed inside. She knocked gently on the partially-open door and waited.

"Come in," Josh's voice called out.

Kaitlyn pushed open the door and walked in. Sasha was already there, grumpy face locked and loaded.

"Have a seat." Josh nodded to the chair opposite his desk.

Kaitlyn did as she was told.

"Sasha, sit."

"I'm not your lap dog."

Josh chuckled. "I know that. You're my attack dog. And you've been marking your territory all morning. I'm tired of the stink. Sit and relax."

Sasha scoffed. "Fine." She slid into the seat next to Kaitlyn without so much as a glance.

"So, how do you think it went last night?" Josh asked, calmly.

It was the question bosses asked after you really screwed up. A laugh somehow escaped Kaitlyn's mouth. "Phenomenal. I'm gunning for your job, Josh. My poise. My professionalism. Five stars." She gave a thumbs up for good measure, and then wanted to vomit. It was not how she wanted to approach this.

"I'm glad you can find some humor in all of this, because I can't."

Kaitlyn's stomach churned. "I'm sorry. I'm just as frustrated as you. More."

Sasha chimed in, "I doubt that."

Josh gave Sasha a shut-your-face look. He then leaned forward toward Kaitlyn and said, "There are some calling for your job."

Kaitlyn glanced at Sasha. "I wonder who *they* are. I do good—"

Josh held up his hand. "I don't agree with those calls. You're great at what you do. Nobody is getting fired."

Kaitlyn exhaled. Sasha groaned.

"Thank you, Josh." Kaitlyn mustered up some courage. "I'm sorry about what happened. I obviously didn't do it on purpose."

Sasha scoffed. "Insult the biggest opportunity this firm has ever had? Do you know how long I've been working on reeling him in? I got him to fly in from Austin for this. He was going to meet all our happy clients and sign on the dotted line. The party was the final step to show him how much fun we were to work with. You blew it. Big time."

Kaitlyn gripped the arm rests and attempted to squeeze the life out of them as a proxy for Sasha. "Yeah, he's really missing out, because you're *amazing* to work with. Maybe if you had given me a heads up about who he was or perhaps been professional and introduced me instead of laughing when I fell down the stairs, we wouldn't be in this position."

Sasha laughed, annoyed. "Oh, this is my fault? Shooting your mouth off like a—"

"Ladies!" Josh stood up and slammed two hands on the desk.

Kaitlyn jumped back and froze.

Josh stared at them back and forth, and then returned to his seat. "What's done is done. Let's move on. Kaitlyn, stick to what you're good at. We already talked about this on Tuesday. Stay in your lane. Stop trying to be more than you are."

Sasha added, "And stay away from Hunter. Not that he's ever coming back to Sutton. And we have *you* to thank for that."

Kaitlyn fought back tears. "I'm sorry again, Josh. I didn't mean for this to happen." She stood up. "Excuse me." She rushed out of the room and nearly knocked over Becky on her way to the hallway. She navigated a few co-workers and dodged a flying coffee before shoving open the glass doors to the Sutton suite. She slammed the elevator button and paced in a circle, stewing. *Friggin' Sasha. I want to pound her porcelain face in.*

The elevator dinged and the door opened. She rushed inside, nearly concussing herself on what seemed like a brick wall.

Pain spread throughout her face. Kaitlyn grabbed her nose. "What the..."

"Whoa!"

A pair of hands guided Kaitlyn back out of the elevator. She looked up to see Hunter staring back at her, but all she saw was red.

"What's wrong?" he asked.

"God, I frigggin' hate her! She tried to get me fired!"

"Who?"

She looked up, finally registering that it was Hunter. *Oh, God.* She took a deep breath. "Umm, nobody? What are you doing here?"

"Seems like more than nobody, but okay. If there *was* a somebody trying to get you fired, there's a cardboard cutout of some guy downstairs who probably doesn't deserve it, but you could take it out on him. Innocence hasn't stopped you before."

Kaitlyn took a deep breath and fixed her hair. *I am such an idiot.* "I'm sorry you had to witness that. Yet again. And I'm sorry about last night." She stared at the floor.

"Forget about it," he said with a smile.

She looked into his eyes, surprised. "Why are you here? To sling more insults at my colon?" She'd rather joke about that than Mrs. Potts.

"No, I'd hate for it to retaliate. Although your little fists of fury aren't to be messed with, either. I'm here because I have good news. Prince William tooted during a speech. I just wanted to personally deliver that to you. I'll see you later." He gave a wave, turned, and pressed the button for the elevator.

"Really?"

Hunter turned back, laughing. "Kaitlyn. Kaitlyn. When are you gonna learn?"

"You don't do serious..."

He stepped toward her. "There's two reasons I'm here, actually. *I* wanted to apologize. I'm sorry about walking out on you yesterday. There's one thing I do take seriously. That's my work. I overreacted. If this project goes well, I'll be seen as a serious contender for the chief marketing officer position at Bountiful when Jim Hanlon retires."

"Well, thank you, but you didn't need to apologize. What's the second reason?"

"I also wanted to tell Josh and Sasha, and you, that I informed Mrs. Pott's senior management that we would be hiring Sutton for Mrs. Potts new ad campaign."

"That's great news!"

Hunter's smile disappeared. "On one condition."

"What?" Kaitlyn asked.

"Only if you agree to work on the project with me."

Kaitlyn's shoulders slumped. "Aaahhh, doody."

"Did you say doody?" Hunter laughed. "I don't think I've ever heard anyone over six use that word. But more important, why?"

Kaitlyn gulped. "I'm sorry. I can't accept." *He'll ruin me.*

Hunter frowned, but didn't say anything. And then the doors opened. Sasha's boobs entered a good two seconds before any other part of her, heading toward them like submarines. Hunter did a double take.

Sasha groaned.

What was she pissed off about now? "What?" Kaitlyn said, rolling her eyes.

Sasha shook her head. "Haven't you done enough?"

Hunter answered, "No. She has a lot to do, actually."

Sasha smug look disappeared. "Huh?"

"I was just telling Kaitlyn here that upon further reflection, I appreciated her criticism. It was on target. Tough to hear, but on target. You guys are getting the account. If...you agree not to put Frankenstein on the label. And Kaitlyn works on the project with me."

Sasha stood there, hands on hips, mouth open, and seemingly in shock. Kaitlyn didn't try to hide her smile.

KAITLYN SAT beside Sasha in front of Josh yet again while Hunter grabbed a coffee, so they could have a team discussion. How was she going to get out of this? She didn't want to help sell Mrs. Potts' chemical chicken. Even more so, she did not want to be tormented by Hunter. She would fall for him. She was well on her way already. And even if he seemed interested now, which was still very curious, what would happen when the project was over? He'd go onto his next project and forget all about her. Her heart would shatter. It was already broken thanks to Aaron.

"Josh, I'm sorry. I don't believe in the product. Putting lipstick on a pig isn't in my job description." *Neither is soul-crushing heartbreak.*

Josh laughed, but it wasn't the good kind. "Tuesday, you wanted more responsibility. Today, you don't?"

Kaitlyn thought for a moment. "Well, if that's your rationale, you told me to stay in my lane an hour ago. Not a good fit to lead. Don't try to be more than you are. Did you not say all these things to me?"

"The situation has changed. You have a benefactor. You should be grateful. Either you want the opportunity, or you don't. You can't have it both ways. We have a good prospect who wants to work with you. Now, you're saying no out of principle? This is advertising. When I was starting my career, I had to sell cancer sticks to kids. Do you hear me complaining?"

Kaitlyn shrugged. "Yeah, kind of."

Josh looked at the stewing Sasha. "What do you think?"

Sasha glared at Kaitlyn. "I think she'll screw it up, but I don't see any other way." She scrunched up her face like she had just licked a stripper pole after midnight. And it wasn't glitter that she tasted.

"Well, you have Sasha's support," Josh said, chuckling.

Kaitlyn scoffed. "Yeah. I've never doubted it."

Josh said, "Here's the deal. Take the account or else the firm loses out. If you don't, I assure you that you will lose out, too. Do well on this and maybe you'll get your own team along with a raise and bump in bonus. I've wanted to hire Hunter for years. Despite the blemish of Mrs. Potts, his reputation in the industry is stellar. This is second best. And maybe even better if we can get access to other brands under Mrs. Potts' parent company, Bountiful." Josh folded his hands on top of his desk and leaned forward. "So, what's it gonna be?"

Kaitlyn crossed her arms and stared back for a moment. She had little choice. "I'll take the project." *This should end well.*

8

Kaitlyn walked out of Josh's office, not sure if she'd won or lost. Or would be destroyed. She slinked around the corner, her mind racing while heading to the bullpen. She passed Carl's cube, waved mindlessly, entered her cubicle, and stopped short.

Hunter stared up at her from her chair. "So, you couldn't resist working with me?"

"I didn't have much of a choice. It was either that or work at Dee's Burgers. And they put more chemicals in their food than Mrs. Potts."

"I'm just glad Dee chose burgers instead of nuts." Hunter grabbed a framed picture from Kaitlyn's desk—it was the four of them hiking. "Cute kids. And I'm not ashamed to say it. Your husband's a good-looking man."

"First the bay breezes. Then my wiener. Now this." Kaitlyn laughed. "Ex. He's the one who built up my pain tolerance." *Still not high enough, apparently.* "What, umm, can I do for you?"

"I have a scheduling matter to discuss."

"Okay?"

"When can we get together for a makeover of the slutty Mrs. Potts?" Hunter stood up. "How rude of me. Please sit."

They swapped spots. She remembered when Aaron used to ask her if she wanted to swap spit. She hated that. But it made her wonder what Hunter tasted like, and she liked the idea of that. "I've got a few things to finish up here today, but we can start first thing Monday morning, if that works for you. I have a few consumer panels and some taste tests to do for some other projects, but I have time."

"That should work. We should put together a plan. What's first?"

Kaitlyn shrugged. "An STD panel for Mrs. Potts?"

Hunter shook his head. "Another savage takedown. Remind me never to get on your bad side."

"Don't ever get on my bad side."

"Noted." Hunter sat down on Kaitlyn's desk. "So, what are your plans for the weekend?"

"I'm a single mom, so pizza, a kids' movie, and a soothing coma. I *do* have a girls' night out on Saturday, but it's complicated."

"Oh, really?" Hunter asked. "How can girls' night out be complicated? Sounds like fun. Throw down some bay breezes and let the night take you where it will."

"We'll see. You?"

"Well, you know me." She didn't, but... "Since we're hiring Sutton, I'm here until we get Mrs. Potts on the straight and narrow, and then we'll see what marketing fire I need to fight next. So, no friends or family within a few hundred miles."

Kaitlyn said, "I'd invite you out, but girls' night. Not really your thing, although with the bay breezes, you might just fit in. Actually, not sure you can hang with my girls. They don't go soft."

Hunter leaned in, a stern look on his face. "Do not forget, Mrs. Colby, that you work for me and I demand to be treated respectfully. And I never go soft."

Not again. "I'm, umm, so..."

Hunter bust out laughing. It was infectious. Like the rest of him.

Kaitlyn shook her head and joined in. "You got me."

"Too bad I'm not invited. I'm not against connecting with my feminine side."

"Clearly."

Sasha stopped outside the cubicle. She frowned and then said, "Sorry to interrupt...whatever this is." She looked at Hunter. "Can you meet in a little bit to finalize the agreement? We'll probably need a few hours plus lunch to finish everything."

Hunter nodded. "I'll be right there."

Sasha said, "Meet me in the main conference room behind reception. I'll be there in a minute."

"Will do."

Sasha disappeared. It was Kaitlyn's favorite thing she did.

Hunter smiled sheepishly. "I guess I gotta go. I'm looking forward to working on this with you."

"Thank you for trusting me with this project."

Hunter nodded. "If I don't see you later, enjoy girls' night out. Drink a bay breeze for me."

"And risk peer ridicule?"

"I thought I had you as a convert." He shrugged. And then he was gone.

Kaitlyn wheeled to the edge of her cubicle and peered out of it, straining to get just one more glimpse of him, hoping, maybe, just maybe, he would look back. The glimpse was quite fine. She leaned forward just a touch more, the back wheels of the chair coming off the floor. The chair toppled forward, propelling her face first into the hallway. Aaaand, he looked back. Kaitlyn scurried back into her cube, hoping he hadn't seen her. *I'm such a klutz.*

Kaitlyn picked up the chair and plopped back into it, and stared at the fluorescent lights above. What had just happened? It was barely 10 a.m. and she had gone from dreading the unemployment line to getting a shot at a big promotion and raise, all while putting her heart on the line. This could end fabulously or horrifically, and based on Kaitlyn's luck, she had a solid idea of which one it was gonna be.

Before she could get too excited or too scared, Sasha returned. "I see how you look at him. Don't let him get to you."

Kaitlyn frowned. "I could say the same about you." But she was right. "Thanks for your suggestion. I'll keep it in mind. What should I know about him? I know you want this to be successful. So do I."

"Just keep it professional. You're really good at that. Don't let yourself fall for him. He's a splash and dasher."

"What's that?"

Sasha looked outside the cube and then leaned in and whispered, "When Josh was talking about his stellar reputation, it was strictly from a creative perspective. He bounces around professionally, which means it happens personally. You don't want to get hurt in all that."

Kaitlyn narrowed her eyes. "He's good enough for you, but not for me?"

"I'm trying to help you, here. I just see him for what he is. When something is too hot, what happens? You get burned. You'll fall in love, he'll reject you, and then your life will be ruined. More than it already is..." Sasha pointed to the picture of Aaron, and then tapped the wall of the cubicle. "Have a great rest of the day," she said with faux enthusiasm.

Kaitlyn gave a thumbs up. "You as well." And then muttered, "Suck it, Sasha."

She called back, "I just might!"

Kaitlyn put her forehead down on the desk. "Thank God it's Friday."

By 4 p.m. on a Friday, Sutton was a ghost town. Josh usually left to play golf by 2 p.m., so the weekend parade kicked off at 2:01, beginning a leisurely exit for the next two hours or so. Kaitlyn looked up from her desk to see Shelly leaning into her cubicle.

"Ready to go?" Shelly asked.

Kaitlyn nodded and grabbed her pocketbook.

"It's Friday, bitches!" Taylor yelled, as she danced up behind Shelly and started twerk-bumping her.

"Ahhh!" Shelly jumped into the cube. "Do you realize no other boss on the planet would put up with you?"

Taylor stood up from her twerk. "I think what you're trying to say is that we're perfect for each other."

Kaitlyn laughed, stood up, and said, "Let's get out of here before somebody gets dry humped." She stepped out in front of Taylor, careful to keep her distance. She turned to see Laura Gaines, the worst director of H.R. in the history of corporate America. "H.R. alert," Kaitlyn whispered.

"Hey, Laura!" Taylor called out, laying it on thick.

Laura stopped next to them and leaned in. "Ladies, time to bring your A-game. We landed a new account. Real hottie. Might want to start wearing some makeup." She looked at Kaitlyn and Shelly. And then down at Shelly's chest. "Hey, your boobs look bigger. You get work done or are you pregnant?"

Shelly raised an eyebrow. "Umm, neither."

Laura shrugged. "Well, they look spectacular. Carry on and have a fabulous weekend." Laura disappeared down the hall.

Kaitlyn frowned. "She does work in H.R., right?"

Shelly laughed. "Apparently, not for long."

Taylor eyes widened. "More importantly, who's this hottie she speaks of?"

Kaitlyn said, "Hunter Dixon." She continued walking out of the suite as if she hadn't just dropped a bomb on them.

"From the event last night?" Taylor shrieked.

"Yep. One and the same."

"What?" Shelly yelled. "How could you not tell us?"

Kaitlyn led the ladies into the elevator and pressed the lobby button. "He hired us. Me, really. I start work Monday on the Mrs. Potts' project."

Taylor grabbed Kaitlyn by the shoulders. "This is insanity. He's muy caliente."

Kaitlyn sighed. "Taylor, you're young. You fail to see the downside of muy caliente. It just means the burns are more devastating."

"He's third degree all the way," Shelly added.

The elevator doors dinged and then opened into the building lobby. "Bad news for someone like me." Kaitlyn shrugged. "Not like I have a shot, anyway."

They stepped out of the elevator and Taylor gasped. "Oh, my God. There he is."

Hunter bowed. "Ahh, the pit sniffers. Always a pleasure, ladies."

For the first time in her life, Taylor's face flushed. "That's not really a thing."

Kaitlyn smiled. "I never know when I'm gonna need them. They just follow me around at the ready. Ever since we were kids, they called her Smelly Shelly."

Shelly scoffed. "They did not. Well, Ryan Fitzgibbons did, but he was a douche."

Kaitlyn looked at Hunter. "What are you still doing here?"

"I just grabbed a smoothie. I was doing some work. Better than sitting in my hotel room all afternoon. Have fun at your girls' night out." He raised his smoothie in their honor.

Taylor threw her hair back over her shoulder. "Do you wanna join us?"

Hunter shrugged, sheepishly. "Well, Mrs. Colby didn't invite me when we discussed it earlier."

Kaitlyn stepped forward. "I didn't mean to be...I just..."

Hunter smiled. "I'm just messing with you. I'm having dinner tomorrow night with Sasha, anyway."

Kaitlyn would rather he had kicked her in the stomach. "Oh, really. That's umm, wonderful."

Hunter laughed. "Sounds like anything but."

Kaitlyn shifted back and forth. "No, she's, ummm. She's... If you want to swing by tomorrow night, we'll be at Mi Cocina. It's basically one of five restaurants in the whole town. It's next to Cuts, that new swanky steak place."

Shelly said, "It's great for dates." She shrugged. "You know, if you have someone in mind and need an idea." She glanced at Kaitlyn. Repeatedly.

Hunter nodded. "Good to hear. That's where Sasha is taking me, actually."

Mother frigger.

After a somewhat awkward silence, Hunter shrugged.

"Well, ladies. Adiós. Disfruta de su noche." He looked at Kaitlyn. "See you Monday."

Shelly interjected, "Saturday. Mi Cocina."

Once Hunter was out of earshot, Taylor fanned herself with her hand. "He speaks Español."

"Do you even know what he said?" Shelly asked.

Taylor shrugged. "Something about nachos. I'm not eating carbs right now, but still, it was sexy."

Shelly looked at Kaitlyn and frowned. "What's wrong?"

Kaitlyn shook her head. "Nothing."

"I sensed a spark there," Shelly whispered.

"Yeah, maybe between him and Taylor."

"You think so?" Taylor broke out into the macarena.

Shelly shook her head. "Surprisingly, I prefer the twerking." She looked at Kaitlyn. "He didn't take his eyes off you."

"Just stop. There's nothing between us." *I can't allow it.*

9

Kaitlyn, Jenn, Shelly, and Taylor sat around a high-top wooden table at Mi Cocina. Both the restaurant and bar were packed.

"I love it when they have cheap beer specials." Taylor sang, "Sausage fest!"

"The perfect crowd for tonight's mission," Jenn said, smiling.

Kaitlyn did not reciprocate.

Shelly deepened her voice, "Tonight, you will be reborn. We will baptize you with margaritas and bay breezes."

Jenn frowned. "It seems we're all more excited than the woman of honor. What's wrong? Are you really sad to move on from Aaron?"

Kaitlyn shook her head. "It's not Aaron."

Shelly asked, "Is it Bay Breeze?"

Jenn asked, "Who's that?"

Taylor answered, "Hunky Hunter. He's the guy interested in Kaitlyn."

Kaitlyn laughed. "Is not."

Shelly said, "Is too."

"Is not—"

"Children, please," Jenn interrupted.

"Well, anybody is better than Aaron," Taylor said.

"He's the father of my children."

Jenn said, "He's your sperm donor."

Kaitlyn huffed. "He's a good father. He's always there for them. Usually with frozen pizza or snacks, but he's there. He was just not a great husband sometimes."

Shelly asked, "What do you even see in him?"

"*Did* see, not *do*," Jenn corrected.

Taylor said, "It's what she saw. He's eye candy."

Jenn looked at Kaitlyn and said, "You have more depth than that."

"And what has that gotten me?"

Jenn smiled. "Let's look forward. You're now free to find someone who matches your depth."

Taylor nodded enthusiastically. "You need someone who will *take* you deep."

Jenn rolled her eyes. "That's not what I was talking about." She laughed. "But sign me up."

Kaitlyn waved her hand at Jenn. "Oh, stop. You've never had problems...there with Russell."

Jenn stared into her water, focusing on whatever was floating in it. "There's nothing wrong when it happens. It just doesn't happen all that often." She looked at Kaitlyn and smiled. "I shall live vicariously through my big sister."

Kaitlyn laughed. "I know you better than anybody, sis. You don't have the patience for that."

Jenn shook her head. "I don't know why you're always selling yourself short. You're amazing." She looked around the room. "Look over there." She nodded to a table a few feet away, occupied by a twenty-something couple. "You're not the glass of water with stuff floating in it and the free chips." She slapped the table. "Damn it, you're the margarita with the top shelf tequila and the guacamole."

Shelly added, "Made table-side."

As always, Taylor took it too far. "You're table-side guacamole, bitch."

Jenn said, "I mean, look at him. He's basically licking it clean."

Taylor smiled. "Maybe he'll lick you clean."

Kaitlyn scoffed. "I don't need to be licked clean."

Taylor chuckled. "If ever there was a person who needed to be licked clean, it's you."

"Can we get a drink around here?" Shelly asked.

"Yes, *please!*" Kaitlyn closed her eyes and bowed her head to pray hands.

Taylor looked around and spotted a waiter halfway across the room. She snapped her fingers. "Excuse me, Mr. Tight Shirt? We need four tequila shots. Every fifteen minutes."

Jenn waved her off. "Just one round will do."

Mr. Tight Shirt nodded.

"So, Kait..." Jenn said.

"You never call me Kait."

Jenn shrugged. "That's probably because you dorked out in middle school and told everyone that your name was Kaitlyn and you wouldn't speak to anyone if they called you anything else. Remember that?"

Kaitlyn laughed. "Yes. I guess I didn't follow my own rule. Aaron's always calling me Lynnie. I hate that."

Shelly said, "You should change your name to Kait."

"I should."

"So, do it," Shelly said.

"I'm thirty-nine. I can't tell people to call me something different."

Jenn threw her hands up. "You can do whatever you want. Why do you always let life happen to you?"

"What else should I do?"

Jenn said, "Go after what you want. Don't make any apologies for how you live your life."

Mr. Tight Shirt arrived with a tray of tequila shots and handed them out. "Don't forget, ladies. It's Margarita Mania until midnight."

Shelly said, "On second thought, we're gonna need another round."

Jenn added, "And four pieces of paper and your pen."

"Umm, okay?" Mr. Tight Shirt tore off four pieces of paper from his order pad and pulled out a pen from his apron.

Taylor said, "Write your phone number on it."

Shelly laughed. "That's not what we're using it for."

Mr. Tight Shirt smiled nervously. "I'll be back with another round shortly."

"What are we doing with the paper?" Kaitlyn asked. "You're not giving my phone number out, are you?"

Jenn said, "Maybe later. Who do you trust more than anyone?"

Kaitlyn didn't hesitate. She looked at Jenn and Shelly. "You two."

Taylor threw up her hands. "What?"

"You too, T." She then mouthed, *I'm lying.*

"Knock it off," Taylor said, smacking Kaitlyn on the arm.

"We're going to play a little game. Ladies, do you swear that we have not discussed this game at all?"

"I swear," Shelly said.

Taylor put her hand on her heart. She then squeezed her own boob.

"I'll take that as a yes," Jenn said, shaking her head.

"We're all going to write down why Kaitlyn hasn't been as successful as she'd like in life and in love. And then we'll share them."

Kaitlyn took a deep breath. "Can't wait. I've been looking forward to this for as long as I can remember."

"Knock it off." Jenn scribbled on her piece of paper. "This'll be helpful. Good advice from your two most trusted advisors. You might want to ignore Taylor's, though." She handed the pen to Shelly.

Kaitlyn leaned over, attempting to look at Jenn's paper.

"No peeking," Jenn said, hiding the sheet.

Shelly handed the pen to Kaitlyn. She stared at the blank sheet before her. *I don't deserve it. I'm not worthy.* She thought for another moment and wrote, 'Need a supportive partner.' She covered it with her hands and passed the pen to Taylor.

Taylor spoke as she wrote, "Needs to be licked clean."

"Everybody satisfied with their answers?" Jenn asked. "Kaitlyn, why don't you share first?"

"Lovely." She looked at her paper and read, "Need a supportive partner."

"Interesting," Jenn said. "Let's get Taylor's out of the way. Unless 'needs to be licked clean' was your actual answer?"

"A close second, actually. My number one answer is that she needs to believe more in herself. In her power. In her beauty."

Kaitlyn bit her lip and nodded.

"Deep thoughts by the frat girl," Shelly said.

"I like it deep," Taylor said.

Jenn rolled her eyes. "Shelly?"

Shelly opened her folded paper and read, "Discounts her true worth."

Tears started to well up in Kaitlyn's eyes.

Jenn removed her hands from atop her paper and read, "Doesn't love herself like we love her. Unconditionally."

Tears ran down Kaitlyn's face. She wiped her eyes with her napkin.

Jenn rubbed Kaitlyn's shoulder. "You are so amazing. You deserve so much better than you are willing to allow yourself. The only thing holding you back is you." Jenn wiped her eyes. "You're gonna make me cry, too."

Kaitlyn said through sniffles, "I…just don't…believe I deserve it."

Shelly wiped her own eyes. "Deserve what?"

"Success. Love. Happiness."

Mr. Tight Shirt arrived with another round of tequila. He looked around the table at all the teary-eyed women, seemingly confused. "Should I leave these or no?"

Taylor said, "We'll be fine. Just leave the booze and back away. Don't make any sudden movements. And bring four margaritas."

Mr. Tight Shirt did as he was told and disappeared.

Jenn grabbed her shot glass and held it up. "Well, let tonight be the start of something new. A fresh start. We all deserve success, love, and happiness."

Thirty-nine years of self-doubt bubbled up, but Kaitlyn forced it back down. She nodded in agreement.

Shelly asked, "Kait, what do you think?"

"Okay. Fresh start. And with that fresh start, I'm changing my name. Or at least dropping the lyn. From now on, I'm just Kait."

Taylor said, "You're not *just* Kait. You're Kick Ass Kait."

"Can I put that on my business card?"

Shelly said, "I'm sure H.R. would allow it."

Jenn raised her shot glass higher. "To Kait 2.0!"

Kait tossed her shot back. The burn trickled down her

throat. And then Mr. Tight Shirt arrived with a tray of margaritas.

Jenn frowned. "There are eight. She ordered four."

Mr. Tight Shirt smiled. "Twofers. Margarita Mania. Enjoy." He placed two margaritas in front of each woman.

Kait grabbed a margarita and took a sip, a queasiness rising in her stomach. Was it the booze or the thought of a new beginning?

MARGARITA MANIA WAS in full swing. The chatter had grown a few decibels louder every new round of drinks. The ladies all held a shot glass in hand, about to drink. Eight margaritas sat empty in the center of the table.

"We're running out of things to toast to!" Jenn yelled, hoisting up her shot glass and spilling half of it.

"Arriba!" Kait yelled, and then took a sip without waiting for an actual toast.

"I got one," Taylor said. "Bottoms up, bitches and bachelorettes!"

They threw the shots back. Kait finished hers off and tossed the shot glass on the table. It fell on its side and spiraled out of control across the table, much like the night.

Kait stood up on her chair, surveyed the room, and yelled, "Everybody! I have an announcement!" The restaurant quieted down, most everyone staring at Kait. "It's my back-churlerette party! Whooh!"

The crowd cheered.

Taylor stood up on her chair and thrust her arms into the air. "Let's get tramp stamps!"

The crowd's response was not as positive.

"You gonna get yours on top of the one you already have?" Shelly laughed.

Taylor shrugged and sat down. "Maybe I'll get a tittie tat."

Jenn yelled across the table to Kait. "Time to mingle, girlie. Happy hour is in full swing. Let's see what's out there!" She walked around the table, grabbed Kait by the hand, and led her toward the bar.

Two men stood at the outskirts of the bar, leaning up against the wall. Kait stopped in front of one of them, waiting for a couple to pass by. She looked up at the man, his face on the verge of blur. "I like your mustache. It's sinisterrrr."

The man smiled. "Thanks. Do you wanna ride on it?"

"Ride on what?"

"My mustache."

"What do you me—ohhhhh." Kait's eyes widened. A normal woman probably would've smacked him, but after a decade of Aaron, she was used to it. "Umm, I'll get back to you. I have to talk to my friend at the bar about something... other than mustache rides." Kait pointed to some random dude at the bar. "I'll see you in a bit."

"Later."

Shelly ushered Kait toward the bar. Kait sidled up to the random dude. "Hey there! I've got a matter I've been meaning to discuss with you!" she yelled for effect.

Kait glanced over her shoulder to see Mr. Mustache walking away. She looked at her new friend. "Sorry. Needed to escape some guy." Kait did a double take. "Did anyone ever tell you that you look like Hugh Jackman?"

"No, but thank you."

Kait shrugged. He may look like Hugh, but his voice was a little higher pitched.

Hugh's possible twin asked, "What's your name, sweetheart?"

"Kaitlyn. Kait."

"I like that."

"What's yours?"

"Eileen."

Kait's face flushed.

"You okay?" Eileen asked.

Kait nodded. "Yep. Sometimes I get a little flushed when I drink. But I need one."

"What do you want? I'm buying."

"Thank you. Umm, a bay breeze, please."

"You got it," Eileen said. "Sweet. Like you."

Eileen hailed the bartender and ordered. He poured their drinks and disappeared.

"Thanks," Kait said, taking a big sip.

Kait felt a tap on her shoulder. She turned around to find an early twenty-something staring back at her, dancing. "Hey there. What's up? You wanna dance? I got the moves like Jagger!" The kid attempted to back up the statement, but failed miserably.

Kait narrowed her eyes. "Evan?"

The kid leaned in. "Mrs. Colby?"

"What are you doing?"

"I'm so drunk. I thought you were hot. What's wrong with me?"

It was like a kung-fu kick to the gut. Kait and Shelly watched as Evan disappeared into the crowd. Jenn and Taylor made their way over, half-walking, half-dancing.

Shelly nodded at Evan and asked, "Who the heck was that?"

Kait swallowed hard. "Works at the ice rink. Gives the kids lessons sometimes. He's so friggin' fired."

Shelly laughed. "Obviously. Maybe he can be a dance instructor."

Jenn leaned in and asked, "How's it going? This night is epic!"

"Just peachy. This is what's out there." Kait scanned the crowded bar. "I think Eileen is my best bet." She shook her head. "I think this night's backfired. Aaron's not looking so bad right now. If he'd have me."

"Nonsense," Jenn said. "He's in the past."

Shelly asked, "What about Mr. Bay Breeze?"

Kaitlyn ignored them. "Why can't life be like the movies?"

"You want the happy ending?" Jenn asked.

Taylor nodded to a group of guys, staring over at them. "I think that can be arranged."

"I'd settle for the awesome gay best friend. But I've gotta put up with you guys."

Jenn scoffed. "What are you talking about? First of all, I'm offended. I'm your sister and best friend."

Taylor said, "And I swing both ways. I'm always telling Shelly how nice her rack is."

Shelly laughed. "H.R. does that too, so don't think you're special."

Kait glanced toward the door and did a double take. "Oh. My. God." It was Hunter and he was heading toward the bar.

"What?" Shelly asked.

Kait fussed with her hair. "Holy hell! He came."

Taylor raised an eyebrow. "You talking about the guy I was grinding on the dance floor?"

Shelly stared in Hunter's direction. "Ewww. And no. She's talking about Hunky Hunter." Shelly searched the room. "And there's not even a dance floor here."

Kait opened her purse, rifled through it, and pulled out a compact mirror. She opened it and assessed. She grabbed the bottom of her shirt and rubbed the mirror. She assessed again. "Why is this thing so blurry?"

"It's not the mirror, girlie," Jenn said, laughing. "And don't worry! You look fab!"

Kait turned away. "No. No. No. I can't let him see me like this."

"Oh, God. He's with Sasha," Shelly said.

"What?" Kait shrieked and turned, which seemingly caught the attention of Hunter. Kait met his eyes and then looked away. "He was having dinner with her at Cuts. We invited him. We. Are. Dumb."

Hunter and Sasha scooted their way through the crowd up to the bar. Hunter looked over, but Kait avoided his eye. He yelled across the bar, "How is ladies' night out going? Kaitlyn!"

Eileen grabbed Kait's arm and tugged. "Somebody's talking to you."

"I'm avoiding him," Kait whispered.

"Why? I'm gay and I like looking at him. Besides, it doesn't look like you'll be able to avoid him for much longer. He's coming over."

"Oh, God. He's always coming!"

Jenn said, "Doesn't seem that's as much a problem as you believe it to be. Hunky is right."

Hunter arrived with Sasha, and then leaned over to Kait. "What are you having? We were just gonna have a drink and head out. The vibe next door is too stuffy."

"Yeah, this is much better," Sasha groaned, to no one in particular.

Shelly cut in. "I think we're done for the evening. We hit our monthly quota. For the entire year."

Kait used her deepest voice, "For-ever!" And then snort-laughed.

"All right. Water for you two." Hunter looked at Sasha. "You want a bay breeze?"

Sasha scoffed and said, "I'll have an old-fashioned."

Kait laughed and said a tad too loud, "Typical Don Draper wannabe."

Hunter ordered the round of drinks and paid.

Kait leaned into Shelly, hid her mouth as if to tell a secret, and then said for the entire bar to hear, "Why does he like her? Is it the boobs? I think it's the boobs." She grabbed Shelly around the waist. "Hey, Shell—now would be a good time to ask Sasha all the questions you have about her boobs, don't you think?"

Shelly looked at Hunter and Sasha and said, "I don't have any questions. We're gonna be going now. Have a wonderful rest of your evening."

"Not too wonderful. She's evil," Kait said with a nod to Sasha. Her attempt at subtlety failed miserably. She looked like she was trying to shake a gallon of water from her ear.

"Okay. Be safe ladies," Hunter said, laughing.

Shelly steered Kait away from Hunter and Sasha.

"You, too. Have fun! Just not with each other!" Kait called back.

Shelly said, "Let's find Jenn and get out of here."

"What about Taylor and Eileen?"

"Taylor met up with some friends her own age that can handle staying out past midnight. And who the heck is Eileen?"

"Apparently, nobody to you. She could be Hugh Jackman's stunt double. We could meet him!"

Shelly chuckled. "Let's go. I'll get the Uber."

Fifteen minutes later, Kait sat in between Jenn and Shelly on a bench outside Mi Cocina, a crowd growing.

Jenn put her arm around Kait and said, "I think your back-churlette party was a big hit. It may be the margaritas talking..."

"Or the tequila," Shelly added.

Jenn laughed. "But those tramp stamps are sounding pretty good to kick off the new you..."

"You first," Kait said. "I got a long...to-do list. Number one is hurl like a girl. You wanna watch?" She stood up. "Gots to find me some bushes." Kait wobbled back toward the front door, the parking lot spinning. The urge to hurl grew exponentially. And it wasn't just the booze. Sasha leaned against Hunter underneath the entrance's overhang, her arm around his back while she whispered into his ear.

Kait stumbled past the entrance, seemingly without being noticed, and found a hibiscus that she hoped would be forgiving for what was about to be done to it. She grabbed the light post that stood in the garden and leaned over, expunging a host of Mexican foods and beverages, much like an exploding piñata, but without the fun of the beloved party game.

Kait stared down at the ground, spitting. She muttered, "I don't wanna be *that* table-side guac."

Shelly's voice echoed in the background, "Kait, let's go! The Uber's here. Ooooohber. Is Sasha's Uber called, 'The Boober?' Oh, maybe I do have questions."

Kait turned to see Jenn and Shelly standing behind her, staring at the puke. "Think you can do better?"

Jenn grabbed Kait's arm. "Let's hold each other up."

Kait slipped and her hair fell into her face. She glanced at the dangling chunks. "Pretty. You like the flowers in my hair?"

Sasha said, "I think that's puke."

Kait used her hand like a finger wall to block her face from Hunter. "I'm invisible to Hunky."

Hunter asked, "Kaitlyn, are you okay? Was that you hurling in the bushes?"

"You've got the wrong girl." Kait laughed. *Wrong girl.* "My name's Kait." She laughed again and stumbled off the curb toward the waiting Uber. "Arriba!"

10

Kait awoke to what sounded like high-rise demolition in the living room. Her head pounded. The coffee was gonna need to be delivered intravenously and more than just a typical IV drip. Was there a fire hose setting, perhaps? And her mouth tasted like a butt. She hoped that was just a coincidence. She slid out of bed, even less graceful than when rolling out from the memory foam crater she and Aaron had left behind.

She slumped toward the bedroom door. Upon arrival, she reached out a hand for the knob, but missed. Her second attempt was successful. She pulled open the door. The light hit her full blast. She recoiled like a vampire, but forced herself down the hallway, shielding her eyes. She arrived in the den to see Ronny bouncing on the couch.

"Don't do that."

"But it's fun!" The squeaking of the couch made her want to vomit as she remembered her ill-fated college evening with Porky Pete. Or it could've just been the previous night's alcohol.

"Just stop. Please. I'll give you a dollar."

"Two," Ronny said, bouncing harder.

"Done. Just stop."

Thankfully, he did.

Riley frowned. "Mommy, you're wearing the same clothes as last night."

"Huh?" Kait looked down seeking the truth. "You're right. I, umm, was very tired. What time is it?" Kait looked at her phone. It was 9:15.

"Victoria left at nine. She gave us breakfast. She told us to let you sleep until 9:30." Riley asked, "Do you want breakfast? I could heat up a bagel or make some oatmeal."

How about filling a cereal bowl with aspirin? "Thank you, sweetie. Can you get the aspirin bottle and the bag of chocolate chips?"

Riley scoffed. "You said we can't eat snacks before lunch."

"Shhh. This is not a snack. This is mommy's medicine." She turned and headed into the kitchen. "When you're older, you'll understand." She turned on the Keurig and fumbled with the cabinets, desperate for a mug.

Kait's phone dinged with a text. She grabbed the mug, started the Keurig, and then checked her phone. It was Jenn. 'Knock knock.' She had no desire for visitors, but at least Jenn hadn't actually knocked or rung the doorbell.

Kait whispered to Ronny, "Go let Aunt Jenn in. She's at the front door."

"Okay, Mommy."

The Keurig spit out the final drop of coffee. She grabbed the mug and guzzled half of it while an angelic choir sang from the heavens.

Ronny returned with Jenn, Shelly, and his cousin,

Cooper. Jenn and Shelly wore the previous evening on their faces. Cooper plopped a paper bag onto the island.

"We brought bagels, Aunt Kaitlyn!" Cooper yelled excitedly. He was eight, like Ronny, and had the same ability to inflame a hangover.

The three women all responded in unison, "Shhhh."

"Good morning, sunshine," Jenn said.

"Is it really?" Kait asked. She looked at the three kids. "Grab a bagel. You can eat it on the patio and then play outside."

Shelly looked around. "Where's Mr. Tight Shirt? I need him to bring me a cup of coffee."

Kait laughed and then said, "Owww. He sure as heck didn't come home with me, but I'll make you a cup."

Jenn said, "Me, too. And I think Mr. Tight Shirt went home with Taylor."

Kait asked, "Should we now call him Mr. No Pants?" The Keurig spit out more life-saving liquid.

"I guess you're not the only one with the name change last night, Kait," Jenn said, laughing.

"Yeah, the new me," Kait said, less than enthused. She handed the ladies two mugs.

"God, I feel like ass," Jenn said, taking a swig of coffee.

"I didn't lick you last night, did I?" Kait asked. "Because my mouth tastes like one."

"What? No!"

Kait shook her head. "What a disaster."

Shelly chuckled. "You don't sound too excited about your rebirth."

Kait laid her head down on the table. "That's probably because I've been reborn on my death bed. Last night was a huge mistake."

Jenn threw her hands up. "What are you talking about?

It was epic. I mean, I'm disappointed you didn't go on the mustache ride, but still." She shook her head and frowned. "I haven't been on a mustache ride in God knows how long."

Shelly said, "Russ doesn't even have a mustache."

"It was metaphorical."

Kait muttered, "At least your closest companion isn't a mechanical wiener."

Jenn took another swig of coffee. "At least I would be somewhat satisfied if it was. Walk into my bedroom after 9 p.m. and you might see tumbleweed blowing across the room like the Old West."

Shelly grabbed a bagel and held it out to Kait. "You should eat something light."

"You still love him, right?" Kait said, tearing off a piece of bagel.

Jenn nodded. "Of course. The fire's gone, but I still love him."

Shelly took a sip of coffee. "This is so much better than tequila."

Kait's stomach nearly threw up last week's breakfast. "We drank tequila?"

Shelly threw her hands in the air and said, "Arriba!"

"Oh, God. Not so loud." Kait grabbed her stomach. "And it's more like arooohwulah. Not the fresh start I was hoping for. I should've probably started with not drinking so many margaritas. And tequila."

"Hindsight is twenty-twenty," Shelly said with a smile.

Jenn said, "No. I think she's right. But forget about all the craziness. How do you feel about the fresh start? Loving yourself. Success. Happiness."

"I really can't say I feel all that good about anything. But I will try."

Shelly said, "Everyone is worthy of love. But if you don't earn your self-respect, you'll not feel worthy."

"Like drinking too much?"

"Like sleeping with Aaron," Jenn said.

Shelly sipped her coffee and said, "You know what would be epic? The freshest of all fresh starts? Taking Hunter from Sasha."

"Yeah, right. Like that could happen." Kait laughed. "You guys are hysterical."

Shelly said, "Just ask him out for a drink after work. He doesn't even have to know it's a date."

Kait said, "I think drinks are a bad idea after last night. And it's hardly stealing if he doesn't know it's a date." She grabbed her hair and smelled it. "I shouldn't have done that."

Jenn asked, "What do you think about a new hairdo? Ride the rebirth train."

Kait shrugged a shoulder, thinking. "Aaron always liked my hair long, so I kept it that way. Even after he left. I'm not against cutting it."

Shelly said, "You should get a crew cut just to stick it to him."

Kait shook her head with a frown. "I think I'd be sticking it to myself more. I could do shoulder-length."

Shelly said, "Meet you at a pixie? We need to shake things up." Shelly grabbed Kait by the shoulders and shook.

"The only thing you're gonna shake up right now is the contents of my stomach."

"As if there's anything left after last night," Jenn said, patting Kait on the back.

The sliding glass door opened, and Ronny stuck his head in. "Mom, we have scouts today."

Mother frigger. "Please tell me we're working on your napping merit badge."

"We're tying knots."

"Okay, babes. Go play."

Ronny closed the door and disappeared.

"Sorry. Didn't want to remind you about that. But the knots could be useful with Hunter," Jenn said.

"I dreamt I saw Hunter last night after I puked in the bushes."

Jenn grimaced. "That was no dream."

"What? Oh, God. No." Kait laid her head down on the island. "I don't want to go to work tomorrow."

11

Mondays. Why did they exist? Kait couldn't find the reason. She parked her newly-fixed car outside Sutton's building. Even though she was still holding a grudge against the car, she closed the door softly, as a headache still floated beneath the surface. She walked toward the building, dread starting to percolate. What was she going to say to Hunter about Saturday night? She must've made such a fool of herself. One thing was certain, she would not be having any discussions with anyone without a second cup of coffee. She made her way into the building and stopped in front of the elevator. She didn't have the energy to take the stairs, nor did she want to see Dimitri.

As people started to gather outside the elevator, Sasha's voice surprised her from behind, "It was great seeing you on Saturday. Puke, that is."

Kait turned around and shrugged. "I'm sorry, but that's just how you make me feel."

Sasha scoffed. "Once again, your professionalism was off

the charts. You invite our newest, most important client to an outing where you are puke-worthy drunk."

Kait said, "I can see how you might think that, but it wasn't the alcohol. It was the thought that he was somehow interested in you."

Sasha laughed heartily. "Oh, you think he should be more interested in *you*? In what world do you think that would be possible?"

Kait bit her lip in an attempt to keep her anger from spewing everywhere, even though she knew it was true.

Sasha didn't wait for a response. "He'll never go for you."

Kait stared at Sasha. *It's on.* She didn't have the courage to say it out loud to Sasha, but still, it was on. While reborn was a strong term to use, she *was* a woman on a mission. The elevator doors opened. Kait turned and walked in.

Sasha laughed. "Your silence is deafening."

"God, I wish you would be silent for once."

Sasha leaned in, their shoulders touching, and said, "Just because you don't want to hear it, doesn't mean it isn't true." She laughed again.

We'll see.

It was one of the longest elevator rides of her life. The longest had been when she peed while pregnant with Ronny. And the elevator seemed to stop on every floor. Kait closed her eyes and inhaled deeply. Finally, the doors opened, revealing Sutton's suite. Kait nudged Sasha and beat her out the door.

Sasha said, "Have a great day, Kaitlyn. Thanks for brightening mine."

Kait gave Sasha the middle finger in her mind. With more thrusts than Aaron gave her.

Kait disappeared into the kitchen and tossed her lunch

bag into the fridge. She made it to her cube and stewed for the next hour, wondering if she pushed Sasha off the roof, whether or not anyone would believe it was Sasha's top-heaviness that pulled her over. She scrapped the idea after realizing that Sasha had so much upper-body cushion that she'd probably survive the multi-story fall. She needed a better plan. Particularly, one that wouldn't end up with her in prison.

But more important, what was she going to do about Hunter? Sasha couldn't take him out every night he was in town, right? She would just do what her friends told her to do. Ask him to dinner. All she had to say was, 'Do you wanna grab dinner this week?' It wasn't that difficult. In theory. But what if he asked if it was a date?

Hunter arrived at Kait's cube and leaned in. "Good morning. You ready to get it on?"

Kait looked up, eyes wide. "What?"

"You ready to get going? Josh gave me a conference room for the time being."

Kait exhaled. "Yes. Good morning." She smiled, grabbed her purse, coffee, and laptop bag, and followed. She noted the view from behind. It was as pleasing as the front. At least while fully clothed.

Kait entered Hunter's new office and sat down across the conference room table from him.

He looked up at her and said, "Come sit next to me."

She narrowed her eyes, but didn't say anything.

Hunter seemingly noticed her confusion and said, "It's too adversarial. I like to align with my team on one side of the table and attack the problem together."

"Okay," she said. "Makes sense." She had heard that before in management meetings. She grabbed her laptop and sat down next to him.

"Better, right?" Hunter smiled.

Much. She nodded. *Just get it over with and ask him.* Kait looked over and up into Hunter's eyes. *You got this.* "I want to ask you something."

"Anything. What is it?"

Kate tried to swallow the anxiety that spread from her gut, but it persisted. *Just say it, idiot.*

Hunter cocked his head. "You okay?"

Kait's mind fumbled for the words until Sasha's boobs turned the corner. The rest of her eventually followed into the room. Kait looked up to see the tail end of a wink, most certainly not directed toward her. She glanced over at Hunter to see him smiling back at her.

"Morning," he said, leaning back in his chair.

Sasha crossed her arms, her boobs transforming into a bottomless mountain crevasse. "Hey, there. I had a great time with you on Saturday."

"Me, too. Thanks again. That was a great restaurant."

Oh, God. Saturday night. Kait had never even apologized.

Sasha threw her hair back. "And great company. Let's do it again soon."

"Absolutely."

"See you later," Sasha said. She gave Kait a wry smile and walked away.

How could I be so stupid? How could I possibly compete with...that? How could Hunter possibly be interested in Kait when there was Sasha? Why would Hunter pursue Kait's model when there was an upgrade available with more abundant features? There had to be some sort of universal law that would prohibit it.

Kait counted to three. She figured out why the kids never actually calmed down after using it. The technique was trash. She took a deep breath.

"What's wrong?" Hunter put his hand on Kait's arm.

She stared at it for a moment and then said, "I'm fine. Just, umm, totally forgot what I wanted to say. It's too early on a Monday, I guess."

Hunter said, "You were going to ask me a question."

"Right." *Can't ask that one now.* "Umm, how was your weekend?" *Oh, God. Why?*

He shrugged. "Low key. Gym. Hiking. Biking. A few meals out. And the girls' night out?"

How should she answer that? "Not much to talk about. Barely remember it."

Hunter laughed. "Oh really? That could've been the bay breezes."

She forced a smile. "I wouldn't be caught dead drinking bay breezes."

"You forget that I saw you drinking said bay breeze."

Kait smiled sheepishly. "I didn't forget that, but I would like to."

Hunter chuckled. "That's so kind of you."

"I didn't mean that I didn't want to see you. I'm embarrassed." Face flush front and center. "I'm sorry. The girls wanted me to start a new life chapter and apparently that meant tequila and *one* bay breeze. One. A decision made after my defenses were considerably weakened, I might add."

Hunter chuckled and waved his hand. "No big deal. I wasn't gonna mention it. I knew you were just blowing off some steam. As you said, I barely remember it, Kaitlyn. But I'll never let you live down that bay breeze."

"You can call me Kait."

"Okay. I'm still gonna go by Hunter."

Kait laughed. He always seemed to make her forget about whatever dumb thing she did while Aaron always reminded her of them.

"Gimme the gritty details. What big life changes are we talking about?"

Kait laughed. "*We're* not talking about them. And I'm not referring to lady changes or anything like that, for the record."

Hunter laughed. "I wasn't thinking that."

"I do hope you realize that I'm not normally like that. I haven't been drunk like that since college."

Hunter said, "I told you, I once puked in the Emperor of Japan's lap. I don't even remember how much sake I had that night."

Kait smirked and ignored the comment. "I don't know what was worse. The hangover or having to see Sasha on the weekend."

Hunter laughed. "You two are so catty. I don't see why you can't get along."

"You can't see it because you're looking at something else, or two somethings," Kait said. *Oops.* Her pulse quickened.

"There *is* a lot to look at," he said, laughing. "She's aggressive at times, but that comes from being a strong, confident woman. Knows what she wants and goes after it."

"And destroys anything in her way," Kait added. "But you wouldn't know about that, because you're what she wants."

Hunter's face morphed blank. "That's none of your business, Mrs. Colby."

I said too much. "I'm sorry. I didn't mean to get personal. I shouldn't have talked about her like that."

Hunter laughed. "I was kidding."

Kait exhaled and said, "Right, well, enough chit chat. We've got a different slutty woman to deal with—Mrs. Potts."

Hunter's eyes widened. "That's cold, Mrs. Colby. You're

like all sweet and cute and then bam! Knife between the second and third ribs for the kill."

"What happened to Kait?"

"You didn't want to get personal."

Ugh, but I do. "You can call me Kait and still be professional."

Hunter nodded. "Fair enough. Alright. Let's get professional. The slutty Mrs. Potts."

"Before we get on Mrs. Potts, I have a question for you."

"Get on Mrs. Potts?" Hunter asked with a chuckle. "You're blushing, Mrs. Colby."

"I didn't mean that." She looked into his eyes. He held her gaze. A nervous excitement rushed through every cell in her body. She hadn't felt like that, well, ever. Every word he said pulled her in deeper. Every smile. Every laugh. Every inappropriate joke.

"You were saying?" Hunter said.

"What I was trying to say *professionally,* was that companies typically hire us, give us the product and the budget and a general sense of what they're thinking, then stay out of our hair. Why are you so hands on?"

Hunter kicked back and crossed his arms. "I'm very handsy."

Kait rolled her eyes, but a little smile percolated on her pinkening face.

Hunter continued, "We used to have a ton of marketing resources, but after budget cuts and corporate bureaucracy, we lost a lot of talent or had to get rid of it. I need something fresh and I think it'll be best coming from the outside, but I need to be part of the process. It's my ass on the line. Mrs. Potts has been struggling. I've been given pretty much free reign to fix things."

"Well, you've come to the right place. We'll start with a deep dive on where things are at and build from there."

Hunter nodded. "Yeah, I really need to get deep into Mrs. Potts. She needs to be turned around and filled with some fresh energy." He pumped his fist. "She needs a real powerful thrust."

Every cell in Kait's body quivered. *He's going to ruin my life.*

12

Kait stood in the kitchen, preparing dinner. The kids sat around the island, worksheets spread on top of permission slips, which hid school notices. Kait grabbed a pot, filled it with water, and put it on the stove. She turned the knob and the burner popped to life.

"I'm hungry," Ronny said. "What's for dinner?"

"Pasta with veggies. Sorry, we're running late. It was the only time the salon could fit me in for a haircut."

Kait looked at her new reflection in the glass of the microwave door. She hadn't gone pixie, but it was short, curving around her face. *Meh.* She looked at the kids. "What do you think of Mommy's haircut?" Kait forced a smile, hoping it was better than she thought.

Ronny said, "Riley said you were gonna look like a fairy."

"I'm sorry, but your father is the... already Santa Claus. You guys would get too spoiled."

"Do you like it?" Riley asked.

Kait shrugged. "It's okay. I thought it would feel different."

"You're still you," Riley said.

That's the problem.

Kait's butt buzzed. She grabbed her phone from her back pocket and answered, "Hello?" It was Hunter. Her heart raced.

"Hey, there."

"Hey. What's up?" Kait asked.

"How do you feel about dinner?"

Kait chuckled. "I feel pretty good about it. I'm a big fan. I like it so much, I eat it once a day." She looked at the empty water on the stove. "I like when someone else cooks it. But the much bigger question is, how do you feel about it?"

"We're on the same page. I should tell you that I'm on your front porch with dinner that someone else made."

Kait shrieked, "What?"

Hunter said nonchalantly, "I was in the neighborhood. Or maybe Josh told me where to find you."

Kait shut the stove, hurried to the front door, and opened it.

Hunter stood there, hunky as ever. Or even more so. He had a steaming bag of dinner hanging from his hand.

If the kids hadn't been there and he grabbed the vacuum, Kait was pretty certain she would jump his bones right there. She eyed the bag and then him, and said, "So, you were just roaming around with a butt-ton of Chinese food?"

"Yes. And they only sell it in butt-ton volume. It's an industrial nation."

Kait crossed her arms and raised an eyebrow.

Hunter shrugged. "That's not believable?"

"Not really."

"That's my story. Unless it's more believable if I said it was actually just in my trunk when I picked up the rental?

Don't know how long it's been there. Is MSG a preservative?"

"You really want to get me started on food chemicals?"

Hunter shook his head, laughing. "No. Not in the slightest."

"Do you want to come in? How rude of me." Kait stepped back and aside.

Hunter stepped forward. "Totally rude, but yes. I'm starving. So glad I found this butt-ton of food in the trunk."

Riley asked, "Mom? You're inviting the delivery guy in?" She looked at Ronny and said, "Mom's finally lost it. It's your fault."

Ronny's eyes bulged. "He's staying for dinner?"

"Yes. Why don't you two set the table for four," Kait said.

"Do you even know his name?" Riley asked.

Kait said, "We call him Hunky Hunter."

Hunter laughed.

Ronny said, "No way I'm calling him that."

Kait' face dropped. "What?"

Riley said, "Hunky Hunter."

Kait's pulse hit Ludicrous Speed on the dial. "Is that what I said?"

Hunter smiled. "Yes. And I will never let you live it down. Add it to the bay breezes."

Kait's lava lamp kicked on without a warm-up. Just straight to full blast. She avoided eye contact with Hunter. "Umm, just call him Mr...Hunter. Or Mr. Dixon?"

"Hunter is fine. Most of my friends call me the Hunk Master. Either works."

Kait looked at the kids. "Go play in the den until we set up dinner."

"Why is Mom acting so weird?" Ronny whispered to Riley as they left the room. "Is he really the delivery guy?"

Kait laughed. "No, honey. He works with mommy." She looked around. The place was a wreck. The kids' backpacks had basically puked across the room, papers everywhere.

"I like your hair," Hunter said.

She shrugged. "Thanks. It was time for a change. Doesn't really feel all that different, though. I thought it would be a bigger deal."

"A haircut you don't see. You don't really feel. Something like weight loss, you would feel the change."

Kait scoffed. "Are you saying I need to lose weight? Very forward of the food delivery guy, especially when you show up with fried food."

Hunter threw his hands up as if he were surrendering. "I would never say that. And I don't need to. You are the Mary Poppins of advertising. Practically perfect in every way."

Kait laughed. "Just don't look in the closets."

"Too many skeletons?"

"Funny." Kait said, "Seriously, don't look in the closets."

Hunter took a deep breath and exhaled.

Kait cocked her head. "You okay?"

"Yes." He smiled. "Sorry to bust in on you. The heat is on. I had a call with our CFO. The quarterly numbers were released after the stock market close. The stock was down fourteen percent in the aftermarket. Mrs. Potts was the worst performer in the product portfolio. We need to accelerate our turnaround or there will be more cuts. And my plans for the CMO role could plummet worse than the stock."

"I'm assuming you don't mean haircuts."

Hunter grimaced. "Unfortunately, no. But I really do love yours. The short hair highlights your face."

"I was thinking that was the problem."

"Nonsense." He looked down at her and smiled. "You're beautiful."

Kait stared at the floor. "Oh, stop. You're the perfect guy. Hot and sweet, with bad eyesight." She looked at him and then away, changing the subject, "How bad were the numbers?"

"Sales were down eleven percent trailing twelve months, EBITDA down sixteen percent, and EPS down nineteen percent."

Kait laughed. "What language was that?"

"It was the fabulous language of financial math."

"I only know fractions. Nine out of ten doctors that were paid handsomely agree that this product is awesome."

Hunter asked, "It's that easy? We should totally do that for Mrs. Potts. Or we could just pimp her out."

"What's a pimp?" Ronny asked Riley in the other room.

"Oops," Hunter said, grimacing.

Kait looked at Hunter and pursed her lips. "Thanks a lot." She called out to Ronny and said, "It's not a word. He said, 'blimp.'" She returned her eyes to Hunter. "What else did HQ have to say? Come in. Let's get dinner set up."

Kait led Hunter into the empty kitchen, watching him as she walked.

Hunter shrugged. "There's talk about some changes to the team overseas a level up from me."

"Would that impact you?"

"Not sure. I don't work for any one region, but changes can have a ripple effect even if it's not a direct issue. Either way, the pressure's on. Heads are gonna roll if we don't right this ship."

"Great. Glad we had this talk. It's just the most important project of my career. The one that will decide if I will forever be a taste tester or be able to run my own team."

Hunter leaned closer to Kait. "The good news is that they like our ideas."

Kait's eyes widened and whispered, "You told them we were canning Mrs. Potts' cleavage?"

"No, haven't gone that far. And don't get me started on the European packaging. Have you seen that?"

"No. It's not the same?"

Hunter shook his head. "No. Mrs. Potts is actually topless—you know the Europeans. Even that hasn't helped. Sales are sagging worse than her boobs."

"Did they use those exact words on the conference call?"

Riley called in from the den. "Mom, what are you guys talking about? Some old lady's boobs?"

"It's business, honey. I swear."

"I wanna get into the boob business," Ronny said.

Kait rolled her eyes at Hunter. "Become a plastic surgeon." She whispered, "Maybe that'll motivate him to become a doctor."

Ronny yelled, "I'm getting a boob job!"

Kait and Hunter cracked up. Hunter whispered, "Or he could own a jiggle joint."

"What the heck is a jiggle joint?" Kait asked.

Hunter did a samba shoulder shake. Despite the rock-solid pecs, it was clear what he meant.

"Oh, a boobie barn," she said.

"Nobody calls them that."

"They do. You're just not that well-versed in them, I guess."

"Would you rather I be?"

Kait shrugged. "Makes no difference to me. Plus, why buy the cow when you get the milk for free?"

"What's that supposed to mean?"

"Sasha's the reigning champ of the county fair's biggest boob contest. She's won it so many times, they're thinking of retiring her bra."

Hunter smiled. "When's the next contest? I'm definitely free." He laughed. "I joke, but it's not like that."

"Sure," Kait, said, leading Hunter into the kitchen.

"Mom, there's no way you talk about boobs that much at work!" Riley yelled.

Kait's face morphed red. "Next topic, please."

Hunter put the bag on the island and started unpacking. He whispered, "But that's my favorite topic."

Kait shot him a look.

Hunter's shoulders slumped. "Okay, Mom."

The two of them set up dinner and then took their seats around the table for four.

"Get it while it's hot," Kait said, dishing out sesame chicken.

The kids ran in. The rest of the food was passed around and everyone dug in without hesitation.

After a few bites, Hunter put down his fork, clapped his hands and then rubbed them together. "So, kids. Let's get down to it. Tell me something embarrassing about your mom."

Kait shook her head. "You will do nothing of the sort. PlayStation gone. Ice skating gone."

"It was worth a try."

"The cocktail party wasn't enough, or Saturday, for that matter?" Kait asked, regretting it immediately.

Hunter smiled, evilly. "You really wanna go there?"

"Ummm, not on your life," Kait said.

"What happened Saturday, Mommy?" Riley asked.

"Adulting happened."

"That's not a thing," Riley said. "Mom, I'll be ten on Saturday. You can tell me."

Kait and Hunter laughed.

Kait said, "It was nothing, babe."

Hunter took a bite of sesame chicken and said, "This is good for finding it in my trunk."

Riley spit out her food. "Seriously?" She grabbed Ronny's fork before it made it to his mouth.

"What?" Ronny asked. "I don't care. I'm hungry."

Kait shrugged. "Boys."

Hunter took a bite of his food. "It doesn't get any better."

"Don't I know it," Kait said, and then smirked.

After dinner was finished, the kids headed off to their devices, leaving Kait and Hunter alone.

"Wine?" Kait asked.

"Absolutely. Unless you're hiding the bay breeze ingredients in the closet?"

"Not a chance."

Kait opened a bottle of wine and then they set up a workstation in the living room, both of them on a long, dark leather couch. Hunter's papers and his laptop were spread out across the coffee table.

Hunter looked over at Kait. "This was nice." He smiled. "I like you, Kait. You're funny. You're a real person."

Kait pinched her forearm. "Check." She shrugged. "Thought I may have been a hologram."

Hunter laughed. It was hearty and a little high-pitched. She liked it. "We should do this without the kids."

Energy surged through her body. Kait paused for a second and then narrowed her eyes. "Pinch ourselves? Not sure how long we could do that without getting bored or needing medical attention." *I could stare at the wall with you and not be bored.*

Hunter inched closer to Kait on the couch. "Have dinner together. Spend time together."

She wasn't ready for this, but at the same time, wanted to ravish him. "We do. We work together." She inched away, calling upon every ounce of self-control she had. The kids were only a room away.

"That's not the same thing."

Kait shifted in her seat and avoided Hunter's stare. "I don't know if that's such a good idea, mixing work and pleasure."

Hunter shrugged. "It happens all the time. It's not a bad cocktail."

"It *is* better than a bay breeze."

Hunter shook his head. "Why won't you just admit your true feelings?"

What the frig was he talking about? Did he want her to tell him how she felt about him? It was impossible. There was no way she could get the words out.

He shifted closer to her. Their legs were almost touching.

She gulped.

Hunter said, "Just admit it. You love...bay breezes."

Kait laughed. She forced herself to look into his eyes and said, "I'm totally in love...with bay breezes."

Hunter pumped his fist. "I knew it! Convert number sixty-four."

What? "How many women have you been with?"

Hunter laughed. "I was just messing around. I don't keep count of the converts. And they include men as well. But none who will admit to it on record." He leaned into her. "You're definitely on my list."

She pushed him away, playfully, but he came right back. When she looked at him, she could feel his breath on her.

How many women is it really? Sasha had warned her that he was a splash and dasher. Spreadsheet or not, she didn't want to be another number.

Hunter closed his eyes and leaned in toward her.

Kait's spidey senses tingled off the charts. She popped up off the couch like she had hit the eject button. The friction from her legs and the leather couch produced a sound that was only a few short notes away from her "Stairway to Hell" ensemble that she'd tooted at the cocktail party. "Well, this has been lovely. We have an early morning."

Hunter smirked at her with raised eyebrows.

Kait held up a finger. "That was not my weak colon, for the record."

"Noted. With an asssterisk. And put your finger down. I don't want to have to pull it." Hunter stuck out his hand for a shake. "How about this instead?"

"Funny, but stick to your day job—sexualizing elderly women while poisoning children."

Hunter stood up, but kept his distance. "How did you know that's what I have on my resume? Word for word. Well, except for one. It's wo*man*. Not wo*men*. And we're gonna fix it. But, it should be noted, we dominate the males seventy-five and over category."

"Great. So, our customer life cycle is three years. With so many chemicals already in there, might as well just mix the erectile dysfunction meds in as a two-for-one."

"Boner Broth. Oh, I like it. We might have to change her name to Mrs. Pop."

Kait shrugged. "Maybe we should go the other way and slap a chastity belt on her."

"Elderly or not, a woman has needs."

Kait raised an eyebrow. "How do you know the needs of elderly women?"

"I used to do strip teases in nursing homes, but the money sucked. And so did the women."

Kait laughed. "Really? What didn't you like about the old women?"

"No. I didn't say I didn't like them. I said, 'they sucked.' They took their teeth out..."

"Gross...Hwullah!"

Kait looked up at Hunter and frowned. He had a piece of lo mein on his cheek.

"What's wrong?"

She reached up to grab it and said, "I just noticed...you have a noodle."

Hunter laughed. "What?"

Kait laughed nervously. "I didn't mean..." She grabbed the noodle and showed it to him. "You have lo mein on your face."

He shrugged, grabbed it from her, and popped it into his mouth. "Boys. We never outgrow it. Hey, I umm, didn't mean—"

Kait said, "Right. Well, this was a lot of fun. But in all seriousness, now that I think about it, I think we should push for a full product redesign. Not just a catchy jingle."

"Or jiggle." Hunter nodded, considering her proposal. "That's a big deal. Logos and ads are one thing. Changing the ingredients, taste profile, and cost structure is totally different."

Kait said, "Let's run the panels and see what they say. You want to save the old bag or not?"

"I do."

Oh, God.

13

Riley's tenth birthday party was in full swing. Jenn's backyard was packed with family, friends, and at least a dozen kids in the pool. Of course, Aaron was late with the kids, the birthday girl included. Kait stood off to the side of the pool bar, checking her phone. Russ stood behind the fully-stocked bar, rubbing suntan lotion on his bald head, his hairy belly jiggling.

Jenn sidled up next to Kait. "He's just oozing with sex appeal, isn't he?"

"Stop it," Kait said, laughing. "Thank you both for hosting this for Riley. She was dying for a pool party. Now, if only Aaron would allow for her to participate in it."

Jenn shook her head. "No problem at all. The heating bill is in the mail."

"I'm sure you can write this off as a charitable donation to your poor sister and niece?"

"I'll talk to my accountant. There he is now." She nodded to Russ. "Let's grab a drink. I'm sure they'll be here soon."

Kait followed Jenn to the bar and asked, "Are you charging for the booze?"

Jenn laughed. "Nope. On the house. Whatever you want."

Kait looked at Russ. "Do you know how to make a bay breeze?"

"No, but it should be in my recipe book here," he said, patting a thick hardback book.

"Can you look it up? I love those things."

Shelly and Taylor joined the sisters at the bar. Russ put the finishing touches on Kait's bay breeze and pushed it in front of her.

"What are you drinking?" Shelly asked, examining Kait's drink.

Kait said, "A tasty bay breeze."

"Interesting."

Kait scoffed. "What? They're good. I can't drink them because Hunter does?"

Shelly shrugged. "No. I think you're drinking them because he does."

"I'm my own woman, thank you very much." She took a sip and stared down at the bar's countertop. "But to be honest, I haven't been able to stop thinking about him. He stopped by the other night after work. Brought dinner over."

Taylor shrieked, "You invited him for dinner?"

Kait shook her head. "No. He just showed up."

Shelly said, "He just showed up with dinner out of the blue and you think he's not into you?"

Kait scoffed. "He would never go for someone like me." *Someone who would be with Aaron.* "He's too sophisticated. If he's into strong, confident Sasha, why would he be into me? Plus, you know what Sasha said. He's a splash and dasher. He travels around the world fixing brands. Even if he's into me today, he'll be gone tomorrow."

"So, just let him get *into* you today. And don't worry about tomorrow," Taylor said.

"Funny. I don't want to be a conquest. I'm not a number."

Taylor shrugged. "Would it be so wrong to let him pillage your village?"

Kait said, "I'm not against a little fun, but I can't have just fun with him."

"Why do you think that's all he wants?" Shelly asked. "And why do you think he would never go for you? By all accounts, he is."

Kait shrugged. *Emily Page. Second best.* "I don't know. I just do."

Jenn said, "You know that we all think you discount yourself. You are amazing right now even if you don't see it. But if you think that you're not enough for him and you want him, then be the woman he would go for."

Kait said, "What would that do? The last thing I need is to fall for some guy way out of my league who is gonna leave me in a month and never look back."

Shelly said, "Sasha wouldn't think anyone was out of her league."

"She has the rack to support her claim."

Taylor asked, "The question should be—how does she support that rack?"

"I can't figure it out," Shelly said, scratching her head. "I'm going back to school to get my PhD in physics. Sasha's boobs will be my dissertation."

"Ladies, can we be serious for once?" Jenn took a deep breath and exhaled. "Confidence based on external things, particularly looks, are fleeting. It's an inside job."

Kait was interrupted by a tap on her shoulder. She turned around to see Joe standing before her. "Joe Joe!" she yelled, and threw her arms around him.

Joe hugged and kissed all the ladies.

Taylor said, "What's up, big bro?"

"Livin' the dream," he said, with a shrug. Joe stood about six feet tall with straight black hair. His jade green eyes stared at Jenn like she was the only one there.

"What's going on with you? Haven't seen you in a while," Jenn said.

"Well, been lying low. I'm sure you heard, but Nancy and I just finalized our divorce."

Jenn frowned. "I did. I was sorry to hear."

He shrugged. "It was in the making for a while. We tried to force it to work. But when it came down to it..." He took a deep breath. "I married the wrong woman."

Jenn fidgeted. *She* was the right woman. At least according to Joe. He and Jenn had dated in high school for a while before heading their separate ways in college. Jenn had dumped him after their first semester.

Jenn forced a smile. "Well, I'm glad you're here. I need to check on a few things inside. Grab a drink and have some fun." She turned and headed toward the house.

The gate opened, revealing Aaron, Ronny, and Riley. The kids ran toward Kait. She engulfed them in a three-way hug. "Happy birthday, Riley! I missed you guys so much."

Aaron threw a wave her way and headed toward Russ. Kait's arms still wrapped around the kids, she tapped her wrist with a smirk, and thrust a one-finger salute at him in her mind.

Kait looked at Riley and said, "How does it feel to be ten?"

She shrugged. "Not much different. Can we go in the pool?"

Kait smiled. "Yes, go have fun." She hoped that when she

turned forty in less than a month, she'd have the same feeling.

The kids ran off. Kait went in the opposite direction of the bar, where Aaron had made himself comfortable.

Kait was able to avoid Aaron for most of the afternoon, until she walked inside to refill the ice. As she bent over into the freezer, scooping cubes from the ice maker, the door to the patio squeaked open.

"Not a bad view," Aaron's voice said, from behind her.

She stood up, turned around, and placed the ice bin on the kitchen island. "Would you like it if someone spoke to your daughter that way?"

Aaron laughed and threw up his hands. "She's ten, Lynnie."

"Don't call me that. I've told you a thousand times. You can call me Kait like everybody else."

Aaron said, "Okay, Kait." He took a step forward. "I like you when you're angry."

Kait smirked. "Oh, is that why you've been a douche all these years? If only I would've known that was by design."

"That's harsh."

Kait crossed her arms and laughed. "You deny it?"

"Yes," Aaron said, sharply. He continued to walk toward her. "I'm sorry I upset you. I didn't realize you would be offended by it." He laughed. "I've said a lot worse in the past."

"That doesn't make it right."

"You're right." As if he flipped a switch, smooth Aaron stood before her, his eyes looking at her as if he wanted to devour her. "I never knew these things upset you. Can you forgive me?" He nodded toward the hallway. "Let me make it up to you. Let's hit the spare bedroom. Cake's not for another hour, right?"

Kait leaned in toward him. She grabbed his shirt, pulled him closer, and whispered, "An hour? You only need two minutes."

Aaron whispered into her ear, "Come on, baby. You're turning me on right now. And I know you want it."

Anger bubbled up inside her. She pushed him back with two hands. "You're such an idiot."

"What's the matter, Lynnie?"

Again. "You don't seem to realize that I'm not the woman you married. Or divorced. I'm better than this." Kait picked up her drink from the island and thrust the remainder of it into Aaron's face. He stumbled backward, the splash hitting his face and shirt, and turning into a persistent drip.

"What the—"

Kait stared at Aaron for a moment, not as surprised as he was, but pretty close. Her heart pounded. How would he react? She didn't care. She grabbed the ice and said, "And I'm better than you deserve. I'm not your plaything to use when you're bored. Your smooth words mean nothing to me. Your actions define you. And they define you poorly." Kait stormed outside to the party, slamming the door.

She rushed across the patio toward the bar and slid the ice bucket onto it. She leaned against the bar, nearly hyperventilating.

Russ looked at her with a raised eyebrow.

Jenn asked, "What's wrong?" She looked over at the door. Aaron walked down the stairs, his shirt soaking wet from the neck down. "Oh, well, I think I got the gist of it."

Aaron saw Kait and made a hard right toward the pool, avoiding any eye contact.

"Is he leaving?" Jenn asked.

Kait glared at Aaron. "He'll just sulk in the corner. He won't walk out on his kids."

Jenn raised an eyebrow.

Kait added, "For this, anyway."

"What did you do?"

Kait said, "I threw my drink in his face after he wanted a quickie."

Jenn's voice rose an octave, "He wanted a quickie in my kitchen?"

"Guest room."

"He's cut off," Russ said. "Not on my watch."

Jenn said, "Mr. Quickie. That's all he seems to want."

Kait countered, "Well, that's all he can give. He's a two-pump chump."

Russ nearly choked.

Kait's stomach roiled with anxiety. She shrugged. "I think maybe I should take kick boxing. I have a lot of pent-up frustration." *I know carboard Dimitri would appreciate me directing it elsewhere.*

Jenn said, "Why don't you just take it out on Hunky Hunter?"

Russ pushed a drink in front of Kait. "Hunky Hunter?"

Jenn rubbed Kait's shoulder. "Why are you so upset?"

"I don't know."

Jenn said, "You just earned your self-respect. You deserve better and didn't sink to his level."

Kait nodded, but chose to take a sip of her bay breeze rather than respond. Had she really just rejected Aaron? She let it all sink in. "Did I really just do that?"

"I didn't see it, but all signs point to yes."

Riley walked up to the cooler next to the bar and grabbed a bottle of water.

"Hey, sweets," Kait said. "How's the party going?"

"Good. But what's wrong with Daddy?"

"We just had a little disagreement, that's all."

Riley's face dropped. "You couldn't get along just this once? It's my birthday."

"Who says it's my fault?" Kait asked, throwing her hands in the air.

"It always is." Riley grunted and stormed off.

Kait watched her go, stewing in the unfairness of it all. "I just can't do anything right."

"You did everything right. She's just a kid. She'll get over it," Jenn said.

"My life is just such a mess."

"What are you talking about? For the first time in ten years, you didn't seek validation from Aaron. You didn't give in to him. You saw your worth as better than the table scraps he offered." She leaned in and whispered, "I think it's time to feast on Hunky Hunter."

Kait didn't say anything for a moment. She thought about the prospect of being with Hunter. Slowly, her anxiety shifted to excitement. "I'll ask him to dinner."

"Are you serious?" Jenn shrieked and threw her arms around Kait.

"I'm as serious as a bay breeze to the face."

14

Kait and Hunter stood at the front of the conference room as people filed in for the 9 a.m. Mrs. Potts meeting.

Hunter asked, "How was the birthday party?"

"Riley had fun."

"And you?"

Kait said, "A little. It was nerve-racking, too. I had a lot of work to do." *And other reasons.* "I felt like Cinderella cleaning up around my sister's place."

Sasha entered the room and waved like she was greeting a baby. "Hey, Hunter."

Kait had the urge to vomit, but steeled her mind against it. She had good coffee that needed to stay where it was. It was Monday morning, after all.

Hunter smiled at Sasha, and then turned to Kait. "I like that. I'm gonna call you Cindy."

"Please don't. It only fits from the cleaning aspect. There has to actually be a Prince Charming somewhere," she blurted, and then searched his face for a reaction.

Hunter feigned contemplation, hand on chin. "That's an interesting conundrum—"

Kait interrupted, "Alright. Let's get started. Thanks for joining us this morning." She had to be sure she was ready to go there. There was no going back, unless she wanted a whole bunch of heartbreak and unemployment checks.

Sasha groaned. "Nothing like a Monday morning meeting."

Kait ignored her and sat down at the head of the table with Hunter to her left. The rest of the team—Sasha, Carl, Amy Walker, and Dwayne Jenkins—sat around the U of the far side of the table, staring back at them.

Kait folded her hands on the table and looked at everyone, but Sasha. "This is our first project status meeting for the Mrs. Potts' project. We're excited to have Hunter Dixon and the Mrs. Potts team on board. You all should've received the documentation. This should be a quickie, er, quick as we are really just sharing the phase one schedule and discussing conflicts and any additions to the process, although I think you'll find it quite thorough."

She glanced over at Hunter to see him writing on a piece of paper. Was he taking notes?

Kait continued, "Carl, why don't you take the reins and get everybody up to speed with what we've lined up so far."

Carl nodded and started going down the list.

Hunter pushed a folded note in front of her. She raised an eyebrow at him, but he didn't return her gaze. She looked around. Nobody had appeared to notice.

As everyone's attention sat with Carl, she popped open her laptop and unfolded the paper on her keyboard. Amusement and anxiety grappled with each other inside of her.

The note read,

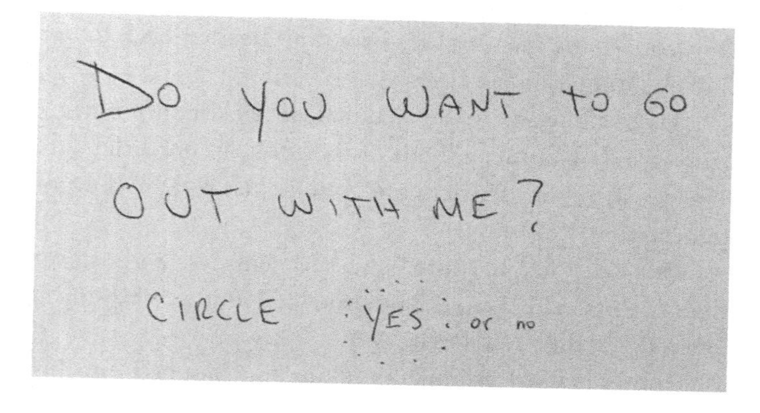

Her mind raced. It was funny and cute, but as she stared at the note, it became suddenly clear to her that rejecting Aaron was not at all the same as riding off into the sunset with Hunter. She cursed herself.

She was interrupted by Carl saying, "Kait? Anything else you want me to cover?"

She had no idea what he had actually covered. She looked at Hunter who shook his head, no. That was good enough for her.

Kait looked back at the group and said, "Nope. Those are the high points of the schedule. Any comments or concerns?" She held her breath, hoping Sasha wasn't about to unload any ammo.

She didn't say a word. And then Dwayne saved the day by asking a question about the exciting topic of canned soup-eating socioeconomics.

Kait didn't respond to Hunter's note during the meeting. She really hadn't had the opportunity to, but she didn't want to either.

~

As soon as the meeting was over, Kait headed back to her cubicle, Hunter on her heels.

"Hey, you want to do a quick debrief in my office?" Hunter asked. "I mean, both of us will keep our briefs on. There will be no debriefing of briefs. Just a debriefing of information."

Kait didn't laugh. "Sure," she said, with less enthusiasm than she normally would have. She led Hunter to his office, entered, but didn't sit down.

Hunter walked around the table and plopped into his chair. He touched his index fingers together at his lips and looked Kait up and down. "Good first meeting." Hunter looked Kait in her eyes and said, "An open question or two, but I thought it went well."

Kait nodded and smiled. There was definitely one open question. A less-than-civil war raged in her mind. *Just say yes, idiot. He'll break my heart. Am I stupid? I want him. But I couldn't keep Aaron happy. And I already know he's a flight risk. Don't I deserve this? Don't I deserve some happiness?*

Hunter smiled. "No rush, but just out of curiosity, did you have a chance to read my note? There's no expiration date, but I am eagerly anticipating a reply."

Kait took out the note. Could he see her hands shaking? She stared at it. Without looking up, she said, "That was a little risky, by the way. I wish you would've waited for a better time."

"There's no time like the present, as they say. You didn't like it?"

"I'm more of a historical romance woman than middle school tween."

Hunter scratched his head. "That'll have to do for now. I'm fresh out of parchment and my royal herald just went out for a coffee break."

Kait laughed, but her smile disappeared as Sasha entered Hunter's office. She hid the note behind her back.

Sasha said, "Tennis and brunch were great yesterday. When's our next dinner?"

Kait's hand squeezed the note, crumpling it.

Hunter looked up at the sound and then back at Sasha. "I have to get back to you on that. Unfortunately, we've got a lot of work to do. I can't commit to anything right now."

Sasha bit her lip and then flashed a seemingly-fake smile. "Okay. Too bad." She disappeared without another word.

Kait wanted to revel in Sasha's rejection, but didn't. Why had such a mighty occasion for celebration fallen so flat? She thought for a moment. *Can't commit to anything...* Yes, she was taking it out of context, and the words weren't even said to her, but she just didn't like hearing him say that.

"You okay?" Hunter asked.

"What's going on between you two?" Kait asked.

"Nothing."

"Nothing?"

"That's what I said. We've been friends for years. She's obviously been looking to land our account for a while—"

Kait interrupted, "And you."

Hunter shrugged. "It's not like that."

Kait ignored his response. "I don't understand how you don't see it. But what I really don't understand is this. If you like her, how could you like me?"

Hunter shrugged and thought for a moment. "There are things I like about her and there are things I don't. I don't have to like the same things about her that I like about you. I just don't know why you're making such a big deal about her. I told you, it's not like that. At least not for me, it isn't. Forget about her."

Kait laughed, but she wasn't amused. "Tennis, brunch, dinner, drinks. Not easy to forget." She grabbed her bag. "I've got to finish up a report for the Quest account. Josh will have my head if I don't get it done today."

Hunter frowned, but said, "Okay. We'll catch up later."

Kait turned and left without another word.

15

Shelly would know what to do. Kait headed down the hall toward her office. The uncivil war continued inside Kait's mind, but it was a little lopsided as the 'Are you stupid?' camp got reinforcements.

And then Sasha emerged from an office down the hall and headed toward her. She approached with a scoff. "Could you be more unprofessional? Passing notes like grade school? Batting your eyelashes instead of paying attention to the project that could make or break your career?"

"I didn't pass anything." Kait hoped Sasha wouldn't bring up her butt ensemble from the cocktail party. "I'm taking this seriously."

"Seems anything but. Josh will hear about it," Sasha said, with a wide grin.

"Whatever," Kait said, leaving Sasha behind. "It's shocking you don't have any friends here."

Sasha chuckled. Kait wished there was a cardboard cutout of Sasha downstairs that she could smash. Perhaps she should get a voodoo doll instead? She could pop her fake boobs with glee.

Kait thundered toward Shelly's office. She rounded the corner and stopped in front of Taylor's desk. Taylor looked up and smiled, nail file in her hand. A plastic bin of at least a dozen nail polish bottles sat on her desk.

"Hey, girlie!" Taylor said. She nodded to the polish. "I'm thinking denim blue. Thoughts?"

Kait grunted. "Where's Shelly?"

Taylor frowned. "She's in a meeting. What's wrong?"

"Do you know when she'll be done?"

Taylor checked her Outlook calendar. "An hour or so. What do you need?"

"Advice. Hunter asked me out."

Taylor shrieked with joy. "What? What possible advice could you need?"

"He sent me a note. I didn't respond."

Taylor threw her arms up. "I don't understand the problem. A hot, nice, funny guy that you like and are seriously attracted to wants to take you out. Am I getting this right?"

Kait nodded.

"So, go!"

Kait took a deep breath and exhaled. "I like him. I more than like him. I just don't want to get hurt again. And I don't want it to get in the way of my job. I can't survive on what Aaron gives us each month. I don't know what to do."

Taylor threw the nail file on the desk. "Have you tried not being a dumbass? You don't need Shelly. This is a job for Taylor."

Kait frowned and looked around. "Is there another Taylor around?"

Taylor mocked Kait with a fake laugh. "Funny. This is

my specialty. You need bold action. This is what you do. You go in there and push him up against the wall and kiss him like he's never been kissed before. He'll love it."

Kait could feel the excitement beginning to percolate. The prospect was certainly inviting, but not without risk. All of it. "How do you know?"

"Umm, do you know anything about guys? Not to mention, you always talk about how he must love Sasha because she's so confident—"

Kait interrupted, "I said liked. Love is a strong word for Sasha. Lust maybe."

Taylor shrugged. "I don't blame him. It's the knockers."

Kait shook her head. "You were saying that this was a job for Taylor? Do you want to do at least one of your supposed jobs?"

"Simmer down, Snippy Snippertons. If I don't look good, I don't feel good. If I don't feel good, I don't work good."

"Well," Kait corrected.

"Well, what?"

Kait shook her head. "What if it all goes wrong?"

"You never know what's gonna happen. You have to take a risk if you want something. So, go in there and take charge. Isn't that what a confident woman would do?"

Kait scrunched up her nose. "Sexually assault a colleague in the office?"

"Yes! Well, I wouldn't use those terms, exactly. He's tried to kiss you before, right?"

Kait nodded. "Yes. Maybe. It was a close encounter. Intentions remain unclear."

"So, they negate each other. Plus, have you seen our H.R. department? Laura leads the league in offensive behavior. Look it up online." Taylor stood up and grabbed Kait by the shoulders. "If you really wanna shake things up, give him a handy."

Kait scoffed and backed away. "I'm not giving him a handy!" She looked around, making sure nobody had heard her.

"If you don't give Hunter a handy, I'm giving Carl one before we leave today. Do you think he's a one-hander or a two-hander?"

"I don't even know how to respond." Kait shook her head with a smile, and then took a deep breath. "I'll go with plan A if you stay away from Carl. You'll ruin the poor kid."

"Deal. It's gotta be a forceful push, though. Nothing sweet. Rough him up."

"Okay," Kait said.

"And if the handy happens, it happens. There's no shame in that."

KAIT PACED around the empty break room, steeling her mind. Should she do it in his office? There were too many people around. But the focus group rooms would be perfect. The rooms had frosted glass and interruptions were off-limits.

So, she knew what she wanted to do and where to do it. She just had to build up the courage to actually get him there. Taylor may have gone a little too far on the handy, but there was some intelligence in what she had said. Maybe Shelly was rubbing off on Taylor. In a non-sexual way. *A confident woman would take charge. You have to take a risk if you want something. And I want that something badly.*

She exited the break room and nearly sprinted down the

hall to Hunter's office, unsure of how long she would have the nerve to implement her plan. As she stopped in front of Hunter's door, her stomach churn returned with a vengeance.

Kait took a deep breath and put on her best smile. She stuck her head into the small conference room.

Hunter looked up and said, "Hey."

Nerves rattled through every cell in her body. "I need to see you," she said, firmly.

"Okay. Here I am. What's up?"

"I need you to come with me."

Hunter stood up. "All right. Where are we going?"

Kait led Hunter through the halls. "The focus group room."

"Did we have a group set up? I thought they're starting later in the week."

Kait didn't answer. She walked with purpose, using her long strides allowing her to pass Dwayne Jenkins and One-Eyed Izzo on the left of the hallway.

Hunter said, "Sorry, guys. She's on a mission."

Kait opened a door that led to another hallway filled with glass meeting rooms, and kept walking. A few more strides and then she stopped in front of the closed glass door that read 'Focus Group 2' and opened it. She stepped into the dark room, waited for Hunter to enter, and then closed the door behind him. With the flip of a switch, the clear glass morphed into frost, the hallway and its lights disappearing.

Kait turned to Hunter, looked up at him, and then thrust him into the glass wall with both hands on his broad shoulders. Hunter's head snapped back and hit the glass with a thud. The glass vibrated.

"Oww!"

Kait pulled him closer. "Oh, my God! Are you okay?"

"I'm fine. I think," Hunter said, rubbing the back of his head.

"I'm sorry. I didn't mean to do that. I can never do anything right."

Hunter looked down at Kait, lifted her chin, and looked into her eyes. All of her anxiety vanished. Hunter whispered, "Are you trying to steal my lunch money?"

Kait shook her head, no. She wrapped her arms around his neck, leaned in, and pulled his head toward her. She kissed him deep and full. She pushed her body against his. Hunter's hands touched all of the right spots, as if he were playing some sort of sexual Simon game, and playing it well. Her body flushed with energy. She grabbed his butt and pulled him closer. He groaned. And then the door creaked open and the lights kicked on.

Kait's eyes opened wide to see Carl, staring at them, mouth wide open. She pushed Hunter away. Again, he collided with the glass, but seemingly avoided a concussion. Kait backed away and adjusted her blouse. Carl just stood there, gawking at them.

"What the frig do you want, Carl? Speak!" Kait yelled.

Carl stared at the ground. "Umm, the focus groups confirmations are in. As you know, we've got single moms and two-parent groups coming in Thursday and Friday for testing."

"Great. Anything else?"

Carl muttered, "I was, umm, going to set up the room."

Kait said, "Well, Carl, you can see it's occupied."

"There was nothing on the calendar. I'm sorry, Mrs. Colby." Carl backed out the door and closed it.

Kait's heart and mind raced.

Hunter stepped forward and touched Kait's face. "Don't worry about it. He's not going to say anything."

"How do you know?"

"We'll kill him after we're done, just to be sure."

Kait laughed. "Confirm you're joking and then we may continue."

"Confirmed."

Kait stepped toward Hunter and said, "Let's continue."

"It's not on the calendar, Mrs. Colby."

"Will you shut up and kiss me?"

"Yes, Mrs. Colby." Hunter pounced on Kait, the force of which drove them both to the table behind Kait. He held his weight from her as she lay on the table, and kissed her.

In between kisses, Hunter said, "You should fire him."

"I don't know who you're talking about, but consider it done." Kait grabbed the back of Hunter's neck and pulled him in again. Her body tingled from head to toe.

KAIT STOOD outside Carl's cubicle and checked her blouse to make sure all the buttons were done. Carl looked up at her and then back down at his desk. Kait smiled and said, "Hi."

Carl muttered, "Hey."

"Can you join us in Hunter's office?"

Carl's eyes widened.

The poor kid probably thinks I want a three-way.

"Sure."

Kait led the way into Hunter's office. She waited for Carl to enter and then closed the door. Carl stood facing Hunter with his hands clasped behind his back while staring above

Hunter's head, seemingly refusing to look directly at either of them.

Before Kait could find the words to say anything, Hunter said firmly, "What you saw was classified, soldier. Above your security clearance. We briefly discussed killing you for the good of the unit, but Corporal Kait talked me out of it."

Carl gulped and then asked a high-pitched, "What?"

Kait shook her head and said, "Carl, he's kidding."

Carl exhaled and perhaps questioned whether or not he needed a change of underwear.

Kait said, "Look at me. You don't have to be embarrassed. I'm sorry we put you in that position."

Hunter chuckled and then turned it into a cough.

Kait rolled her eyes and said, "This is very new and obviously sensitive around the office. We'd appreciate keeping this between us."

Carl nodded, glancing back and forth between Kait and Hunter. "Yes, definitely. You can count on me."

Hunter smiled. "At ease, soldier."

Carl forced a smile, but didn't seem anywhere near at ease.

Kait said, "While you're here, we need to schedule some time with Hunter and me to go over possible logo options. The design team is working on a few and should have them back in a few days."

Carl frowned, "What's wrong with the logo?"

Kait pointed to a pile of papers on Hunter's desk. Hunter rifled through the stack and pulled out the current logo of Mrs. Potts.

"Take a look," Kait said.

Carl shrugged. "I don't see any issues."

Kait smirked while Hunter smiled. Kait said, "Okay, let me ask you this way. What do you like about it?"

Carl considered the logo once again. "She has a nice smile."

Kait looked at the logo alongside Carl. "Anything else?"

"Umm, she's busty?"

Hunter looked at Kait with a smile and said, "See? Carl would motorboat Mrs. Potts, wouldn't you Carl?"

Carl's eyes darted from Kait to Hunter. "I...don't want to answer that."

Hunter smiled and gave a thumbs up. "I'm thinking that's a yes."

"It's okay, Carl." Kait patted him on the shoulder and laughed. "You're the only millennial who would ever use the word busty."

Hunter said, "I think that's why you two work so well together." He turned to Kait. "Remember when you said 'doody?'"

Kait smirked and said to Carl, "Speaking of doody, we need to run ingredient lists for the soup and pre-made meal products and compare them to the top natural and organic players."

Hunter chimed in, "And Carl, order me some blinds for this room, unless frosting is in the budget? I have a new need for privacy in here."

"Don't do that, Carl." Kait opened the door. "Thank you."

Carl, keeping with the military theme, nearly did a dive roll into the hallway to escape.

Kait shook her head with a smile.

Hunter said, "So, you never actually answered my question."

Kait put her hand on her chin and feigned contemplation. "Well, I was waiting for the royal herald to return, but since you ask. Yes. I will go out with you." Kait's couldn't stop herself from smiling even if she wanted to. "As long as you promise to kiss better than that."

Hunter's eyes widened. "What?"

Kait broke out into laughter. "I really got you there."

Hunter joined in. "You did. And I'm gonna get you, Mrs. Colby."

16

It was date night. Kait parked the car in front of Aaron's house. She thought about texting him the particulars about the kids' weekend, but decided to just get it over with. Seeing Aaron for the first time after she'd rejected him was going to be one step below meeting with the Grim Reaper. She prepared herself for some snark. The size of Aaron's ego all but ensured it.

The kids got out of the car first, slung their bags on their shoulders, and headed off to the front door. Kait exited the car slowly. Each step was like walking through quicksand. *I thought he was a douche before.* She shook it off and continued up the stairs.

Kait's heart pounded. Aaron opened the screen door for her and held it out. He stepped to the side. "Do you want to come in?"

She grabbed the door and said, "No." She barely looked at him. *Just get it over with.* "It's a light weekend of activities. No birthday parties. No team practices. You have to take Ronny to Lucas' house at two tomorrow. And I'll get the kids from you on Sunday afternoon at Riley's softball game.

Warm-ups are at three. You'll get a game reminder on the app in case you forget."

Aaron saluted her with a smile. "Got it, boss. Why so dressed up? Work event?"

"I have a date."

Aaron laughed.

Kait bit her lip and took a deep breath. "No, really."

Aaron stopped laughing and frowned. "Seriously?"

Kait shook her head. "You never cease to amaze me with the ways you find to insult me."

"I'm sorry. I just...I didn't...think you were ready for that." Aaron looked away. "And I'm sorry...about the party."

Kait waved him off. "I let you take advantage of me before. Why wouldn't you try again?"

Aaron crossed his arms. "Take advantage is a strong term."

"Okay, you used me."

Aaron countered, "We used each other."

Kait shrugged. "Regardless, it won't be happening again. So, unless you want whatever I'm drinking thrown in your face again, you won't pull that crap with me."

"I'm not sure I'll be able to stop myself."

"Not funny."

Aaron threw up his hands. "Because of how sweet that drink tasted. What was that?"

Kait smirked. "A bay breeze. It's not for you."

"Maybe. Maybe not. Well, I am sorry. If you don't want it to happen again, it won't."

"I don't. Ever."

Aaron threw his hands up again. "Okay. I get it. I get it. Geez. What's gotten into you?" He leaned closer and raised an eyebrow. "Has *he* gotten into you?"

"None of your business."

Aaron nodded. "No, you're right. Umm, where are you going?"

"A Taste of India."

"The one next to Twisted?"

"It's the only Indian restaurant around for miles."

Ronny yelled from inside, "Daddy, can you take us to Twisted? I want ice cream."

Aaron called back, "We'll see."

"Watch the sugar, please."

Riley and Ronny whined, "Please!"

"Fine." Kait yelled into the house, "Ice cream, but a real dinner, a significant portion of which must be made up by protein and vegetables."

Aaron shrugged. "Okay, kids. We'll just have broccoli ice cream."

Riley said, "Gross, Dad."

Kait said, "That'll be the day. See you Sunday. Love you guys!" *Not you, Aaron.* She turned and smiled wide.

KAIT PACED around the heavily-decorated lobby of A Taste of India, while couples and families filed in and were seated by the host. Tightness spread throughout her stomach. Was it hunger or nerves? Or both? The door opened, pulling Kait's eyes like a magnet. It was as if they hadn't seen each other since the war ended. Hunter nearly ran into the restaurant and wrapped a waiting Kait in his arms and pulled her toward him.

"I missed you," he said, and then kissed her.

She was grateful he was holding her tight. Otherwise, she would've been in a heap on the floor. Hunter's hands rubbed her back up and down as they made out like high schoolers under the bleachers. Kait forgot all about where they were.

A man's sing-song voice said, "Excuse me? Perhaps you would like to sit? Or move to the coat closet?"

Their lips parted. Hunter backed away and looked at the short, bearded host. "My apologies. I mean, look at her, though. How could I not kiss her like that?"

The host nodded. "She is very attractive woman. But that's not the kind of spice we prefer you taste here at A Taste of India. This is family establishment."

Kait's face flushed. "Noted. We're sorry about that, Ishaan."

"Just for reference, where is the coat closet?" Hunter asked, looking around.

Kait smacked his arm. "Knock it off. Ishaan is a nice man. Stop messing with him."

Ishaan grabbed two menus and said, "Follow me, please."

They did as they were told and were led to a table for two behind a giant elephant statue with a large, erect trunk. Ishaan pulled out Kait's chair and handed them the menus. He leaned in and said, "Enjoy your meal."

They both said, "Thank you."

Kait glanced at the menu and then at Hunter. He stared at the elephant's trunk. "Elephant envy?" she asked with a chuckle.

Hunter shook his head. "No, I pity the poor the thing."

Kait laughed. "Great first date conversation."

A twenty-something Indian girl stopped at their table. "Welcome. My name is Akira. I'd be happy to take your drink order." She looked at Kait. "What would you like, ma'am?"

Kait said, "I'll have what he's having."

Hunter smiled excitedly and said, "Two bay breezes please." Akira began writing on her pad, but Hunter interrupted, "Wait! We should get mango lassis!" He looked up at Akira. "Can you put booze in those? I want to get her drunk."

Akira stammered, "I...ummm."

Kait shook her head and said, "He's kidding."

Hunter said, "As far as you know. Let's go with virgin mango lassis and two bay breezes."

"Yes, sir." Akira disappeared quickly.

"I like what you did there. Got yourself a bay breeze without having to order one." Hunter said, "Oh, I have flowers for you in the car. I didn't know where you would put them in here, so I left them there."

Kait raised an eyebrow. "Seems like a way to lure me into your backseat."

"Of course not. It's filled with Chinese food, so there's no room for us. I just leave the car running with the A/C on to keep it fresh."

Kait shrugged. "Pity. Oh, and thank you. That's very sweet of you."

Hunter offered an exaggerated smile. "I'm a sweet guy. I think it's the sweetness of the bay breezes. And maybe a little bit from my mother."

Kait stared at him for a moment. She had so many questions. *Has he ever been serious? Can he be? What are his intentions?* It was a little forward to ask on a first date, but so was making out in the restaurant lobby. "It must be hard doing what you do."

"How so?"

"Never staying in one place for too long. Being away from family. Not being able to start a family." Had she gone too far?

"It is. I don't see my parents or my sister all that often. I've never had much of anything serious. Moved around a lot. Focused on my career. I've always been very driven. Once I had what turned into a long-distance thing, but she didn't like my job."

Kait groaned, but then feigned surprise. "Women don't like it when you're pimping out the elderly?"

Hunter shook his head, sheepishly. "Not really. Who knew?"

Kait said, "Did you ever want to have kids, or do you?"

Just then, Akira returned with a tray of the four drinks and placed them on the table. She took their order and disappeared.

Kait studied him, hoping to glean his answer before he responded.

Hunter stared at his bay breeze and then looked at her. "I love kids. My sister has kids. I love spending time with them. I don't believe in doing things half-assed. Do it right or don't do it at all. My dad always says that. I didn't want to be the kind of dad who was only there on weekends, or less. And then time slipped away. Now, I'm thirty-eight. I don't not want kids, but they haven't been a priority, I guess."

Kait asked, "Why didn't you just find a different job with less travel?"

Hunter shrugged. "Everything was going so well. I was moving up the ranks. Getting more responsibility. It was hard to get off the train while it was moving so fast. What about you?"

Kait chuckled. "That's a loaded question."

"I'm sorry."

"No, it's fine. I met Aaron when we were in college. He was...hot. Funny. Outgoing. I liked him immediately. He was smooth. Turns out, maybe too smooth." Kait took a sip of her bay breeze. She was sharing things she had not ever verbalized before, let alone took the time to think about for herself. "I didn't know what he saw in me. So, I was always just thankful he was with me. That led to him taking me for granted and advantage of me. I never stood up to him." *Until I met you.* "I realize that he was never as confident as he led on to be and I became weak to make him feel stronger." Kait swirled her drink, avoiding eye contact.

"You live and you learn. You were young." Hunter paused, seemingly waiting for Kait to look at him. She looked into his eyes, and he continued, "Just know that strong men aren't intimidated by strong women. Only the weak ones are."

Kait nodded and took a deep breath. "Enough of my sob story. I have to ask you about a trade secret."

"I'm not sure I can spill my secrets, but shoot."

She leaned in and whispered, "Is there a Mr. Potts?"

Hunter thrust his chair back. "Whoa, that's like asking for the Coca Cola formula." He looked around at the crowded restaurant, and then whispered. "But I kinda like you, so I'll tell you."

"Kinda?"

Hunter shrugged. "It's more like a toleration, really."

"You tolerated me real good in the lobby. And the focus group room," Kait said, and then blushed.

"You nearly concussed me. You're lucky I didn't take legal action."

Kait smiled and said, "You're lucky to have just gotten the action."

"Touché." Hunter fidgeted with his fork. "Is it weird that I feel like I've known you forever?"

Kait smiled. "No. We get it on well." Her stomach nearly

imploded. "I mean...get on well." She smacked her forehead and stifled a nervous laugh.

Hunter laughed. "We do. And can't wait to find out."

Kait looked up to avoid Hunter's eyes and the subject, but the elephant trunk didn't help much.

Hunter said, "I'm not sure why I'm gonna tell you this, but there *was* a Mr. Potts."

"Really? What happened to him?"

"He died of chemical exposure. But with the cleavage Mrs. Potts is showing, she has reeled in a few boy toys."

"With the stock down fourteen percent, she might have to cut back on the spending a little. Can she still afford them?"

"Mrs. Potts sold to Bountiful a few years ago in an all-cash deal. Three billion smackers."

"What?" Kait shrieked. "That's more than Billionaire Ben has."

"Who's Billionaire Ben?"

"Benjamin Bach. He grew up here. We went to the same high school. He was a year in-between me and Jenn. Shelly, too. Jenn does some of his personal legal work."

"You know him? I love that guy. He's a beast."

"Knew him. He's a workaholic. Lives in Silicon Valley now. He comes back every now and again." She shrugged. "So, what are we doing after this?"

Hunter rubbed his hands together, excitedly. "Well, I know you like the outdoors."

Kait raised an eyebrow. "So, you're gonna take me outside? So romantic."

"We're going axe throwing."

"What?"

"I found a place like twenty minutes from here that just opened up. I thought it would be cool. Have you ever been?"

Kait said, "No. But it's a skill that could come in handy."

Hunter nodded. "Yeah, you could keep one in your top drawer at work. If Josh messes with you, just take it out and start sharpening it. See what happens."

"I won't ever get it sharper than Sasha's claws, though."

Hunter rolled his eyes. "What do you have against Sasha? I still don't get it."

"I don't want to talk about Sasha on our date."

"Me, neither. I just wanna get to know you better." Hunter stared into her eyes.

Kait felt heat rushing through her body and she hadn't even had a bite to eat yet.

After dinner, Hunter grabbed Kait's hand as they exited the restaurant. Her stomach fluttered like she was in middle school. Maybe he knew her better than she knew herself.

Hunter said, "Since we're working together, I'm not sure you need your own vehicle for an escape. Why don't you ride with me and I'll bring you back here after? We can frolic in the lo mein in the back seat." He led her to the passenger side of a red Infiniti SUV and opened the door.

"I have no interest in frolicking with more than one noodle at a time. I'm not that kinda girl." Kait smiled playfully.

"Okay, we can throw the heat on and see if we can make a won ton hot tub in the trunk."

"You know how to treat a woman."

Kait slipped past Hunter, about to enter the SUV when Hunter grabbed her and turned her around. Surprised, she let out a squeak before meeting his lips again. She pulled away and smiled. "We just had Indian food. I probably taste like cumin."

"You taste spectacular. But if you don't want to be self-conscious, we'll stop and get gum, because I'm not stopping. Can't stop."

Kait gave him a peck and slipped into the car. Hunter closed the door behind her and smiled at her as he walked around the front of the SUV. He hopped in, hit the ignition button, and took off.

Hunter held her hand on the console while he steered with his left. Their hands eventually ended up mid-thigh on Kait's leg and inching higher.

They pulled into the parking lot for Get Axed, fitting for what the night could do to her career. Kait popped three pieces of gum into her mouth and got out of the car before Hunter could make his way around to her door. He stuck out his bottom lip. "I still want credit for my chivalry."

Kait shook her head. "Sorry. Too late."

Hunter said, "Well, if I see a puddle and dive across it, I want extra credit."

"I would pay to see that. If we don't get inside soon, I'm gonna make my own puddle. Too many mango lassis."

Hunter said, "Well, Chris. The date was going well. She was a leading candidate for a hometown visit, until she peed in her pants."

"Oh, I didn't realize I was on an episode of *The Bachelor*. Where's the rest of my competition?" *Sasha?* "Do I get to keep all the roses you gave me or just one?"

Hunter smiled. "Just one, but pick the one you like best."

Kait stared at him with hands on hips. "I know you're joking, but you should know better than to make me angry. You wanna head in and get me a shiny axe?"

Hunter interlocked his fingers and held his hands under his chin. "Please, it was just a joke. Don't hurt me."

Kait grabbed his hand and led him into Get Axed.

They checked in, completed training, and then were led

to an empty throwing station that had two axes lodged into a wooden stump.

"You wanna go first?" Kait asked.

"Ladies first."

"I think Mr. Chivalry is scared."

"Nonsense," Hunter said, laughing. "I'll go if you want me to." He didn't move.

Kait raised her hand. "No. No. I can show you how it's done. I see you're a little tentative."

Kait grabbed an axe and held it at her side and stared at a target about fifteen feet away. Thwacks, laughter, and groans echoed throughout the open area.

"He said start with two hands," Hunter said.

Kait stared at the floor, setting her feet. She took a deep breath.

"Let me help," Hunter said, sliding up behind her. He put his left hand on her waist and guided the axe above her head with his right.

Kait chuckled. "This is so cliché."

Hunter let go. "What?"

She turned and smirked at him. "First date getting behind me to teach me how to hit a baseball or golf ball. It's like in every date movie."

"Well, there's one thing you don't know."

"What's that?"

"I have no idea how to throw an axe. I just wanted to get close to you."

Kait admired the shine of the axe. "Careful, I have an axe."

Hunter threw his hands up. "I didn't say it was a good plan. Well, I thought axe throwing was the opposite of cliché, but if you know what you're doing, have at it. Show me who's boss."

Kait lined her right foot a step ahead of her left nearly touching the half-wall guard. She held the axe in front of her with both hands, staring at the target. She leaned forward, rocked back with the axe behind her head, and then thrust her arms and the axe forward. The axe tomahawked handle over blade twice before sinking into the bull's eye of the target with a 'thwap.'

She raised both hands in the air and looked at Hunter. He scratched his head with a frown. "How am I supposed to follow that? I should've taken you to sumo wrestling instead. That way I could body slam you."

"I'd whip your tight little butt."

"I do not have a little butt. It's muscular and full. I do tons of squats."

Kait raised an eyebrow. "Turn around and let me see."

He did as he was told.

"Now, back it up."

He bounced back, thankfully never approaching a twerk, and rubbed his butt on her. He turned around, both of them laughing.

"I should give you twenty bucks."

"I told you, I used to be a pro. The amount of cash I made from those old bags at the home. Maybe I should've used it for butt implants." He looked at the axe that stuck in the target. "Are you sure you've never done this before? I really don't want to throw now."

"I'm the mom of a Cub Scout and I watch a lot of historical fiction."

"Do they teach axe throwing in the scouts?" Hunter asked, surprised.

"No. I think it's just osmosis from being in the outdoors."

"Oh, yeah. That makes total sense. That's cool that you like the outdoors. A lot of moms don't like camping. My mom only glamps. It's like more expensive than going to a resort. I don't get it, but whatever. It's a compromise with my father, I guess. He and I always went camping growing up."

"That's nice. I love camping, hiking, fishing. Anything outdoors in nature. Being a working, single mom is not exactly peaceful. Even when I take the kids, it's more peaceful in nature. Plus, there's s'mores. I would run through a gauntlet for chocolate and marshmallows."

"Good to know." He pointed to the line of other axe-throwing participants. "We could gather up all the axes, put some s'mores over there, and see if you could make it through alive."

Kait put her hands on her hips and glared at him. "Yeah, Chris, the bachelor gave me a rose and our first date was going great until he suggested I run through a barrage of axes for s'mores."

"It was your idea!" Hunter feigned anger. He shook his head and grabbed his axe.

"What about you?" Kait asked.

"Don't distract me." Hunter lined up his feet and took a deep breath. He licked his index finger and held it up in the air. "The wind is coming from the southwest. I'd say eight miles an hour."

"Indoors?" Kait asked.

"That HVAC system is top of the line." Hunter focused on his target, did an exaggerated lunge, and let his axe fly. It sunk into the target, but a foot left of center. He turned around, shoulders slumped, feigning humiliation.

Kait walked up to him, wrapped her arms around his waist, and kissed him. "Strong men are not intimidated by strong women."

He buried his head in her shoulder. "That's just something people say when they're not getting whipped by a strong woman. I'd take you camping, but I'm afraid you'll embarrass me with your knot-tying skills."

Kait smiled. "Isn't a first date a little early to be talking about tying each other up? Although, I have been practicing."

Hunter's eyes widened, but not as wide as his smile. "You're naughty, Mrs. Colby. I like it. I like out-of-the-office Kait. And in the office, as well."

"I wouldn't embarrass you if we went camping. I promise."

He pulled her in close, rubbing up against her.

Kait said, "It's nice to unzip like this. I mean, ummm, unplug."

Hunter laughed. "I don't normally unzip in public. But I *have* skinny-dipped in a fresh-water lake or two when no one was looking."

"Aren't you afraid something will—" Kait used her hand to imitate a heavily-toothed beast chomping down on something. "You know, bite your might?"

Hunter laughed nervously. "Now, I am. But in reality, how many beasts would attack a wild anaconda?"

"Oh, well. You are setting expectations mighty high for a first date."

He shrugged. "I gotta lay it all out there. It was so hard to get you to agree to a first date, I'm not sure I'm gonna get a shot at a second."

Kait nodded. "Fair point. Just don't lay it all out, you know, right here. Especially with the axes around. Somebody might attack the anaconda."

"Thanks for the warning. I was just about to do just that." Hunter looked at Kait and said, "I could laugh with you forever."

Kait smiled and fidgeted with her hands. *Forever.*

After axe throwing, they walked down Main Street, in and out of the shops, and then ended up in a small park. They strolled through, the walkway lighting the path ahead of them.

"So, you like historical fiction?"

Kait said, "I do. The romantic stuff. Not the war stuff."

"So, no knights in shining armor?"

"Well, within reason. They don't always wear armor. Sometimes, they wear a kilt."

Hunter asked, "I go commando sometimes. Is that the same thing?"

Kait stopped and stared at him. "You're thirty-eight and sometimes you don't wear underwear?"

"I'm on the road a lot. So, wait. If I'm wearing shorts and no underwear, you have a problem, but if I'm wearing a skirt and no underwear, you're all good?"

"Only if you if use a Scottish accent and call me Sassanach."

Hunter uses a Scottish accent and said, "We'll swing by the Scottish specialty store and get me a man skirt."

"Thank you. You just ruined *Outlander* for me."

"Sorry."

"I'm lying. You could never ruin that show for me. And I know what I'm getting you for your birthday. If you work on that accent."

Hunter thrust his fists in the air. "Thank you, God! I've always wanted a man skirt." He looked at Kait and said, "Please, just don't get me the bagpipes."

After the date was over, Hunter drove Kait back to the restaurant where she had left her car. Hunter pulled into the empty spot next to Kait's Honda.

Hunter said, "Now for the best part of the night..."

More kissing. Kait inched closer.

Hunter continued, "Won ton hot tub!"

Kait laughed, but stopped abruptly as Hunter touched her face, leaned over, and kissed her. Good. It was high school all over again. Awkward angles. Hands flying everywhere. Jabbing gear shifters. Kait tried to gain control of her thoughts, but excitement kept shorting out her neural synapses. *Should I invite...oooh. What was I...yesssss.... Invite him back? The kids are with...my God! Certainly not with God. With Aaron. No. I can't. Ooooh, I so can. No, not yet.*

Hunter backed away. "You okay?"

Kait smiled. "Yes. This was wonderful. But I should get going."

"I had an amazing time, especially this last part."

Kait said, "This was the best first date I've ever had."

"Not the best date?"

Kait laughed and thought for a moment. "Top two or three best. I mean, I have been proposed to."

"Challenge accepted." Hunter's eyes widened. "On the best date. Just wanted to clarify that."

Kait's stomach roiled. *He doesn't do serious.*

17

Kait floated through the rest of the weekend on a high she had never experienced before. She worked around the kitchen, cleaning up dinner Sunday night, while humming and reimagining each moment of her date with Hunter.

Riley walked in and asked, "Can we have dessert?"

Kait didn't hesitate. "Sure. Anything you want." She threw the used paper plates into the garbage and continued humming.

Ronny entered and asked, "Mom, can I have a hundred bucks?"

Kait didn't look up. "Yes. Wait. What?" She stared at them.

Riley shoved Ronny and shook her head. "You took it too far." Riley looked at Kait and asked, "What's going on with you? You seem different."

Kait shrugged. She was happy.

At about eleven, Kait fell asleep thinking about Hunter, and woke up Monday morning, the high still present—shocking, since Mondays had been known throughout history to squash even the most-annoyingly optimistic and bubbly attitudes. Kait sat in Shelly's office, alongside Taylor, door closed.

Kait nearly lost her breath listing all of Hunter's attributes. "He's so amazing. So funny. We have such a great time. He soooo friggin' sexy." She closed her eyes. "And he kisses..."

"Do you want us to leave?" Shelly asked.

Kait opened her eyes and rolled them.

Shelly smiled and said, "We're so happy for you."

Kait said, "Jenn wants to meet him."

"Dun, dun, dun," Taylor said, with a deep voice.

Shelly said, "She's tough, but fair. And he's perfect anyway."

Kait glared at Shelly. "Stay away from him. I know how to throw an axe."

"Are you nervous?" Shelly asked.

"No. My sister will love him. What's not to love?"

Taylor's eyes widened. "You love him?"

Kait hesitated. "I love being with him."

"If your sister gets to meet him, so should we," Taylor said.

"You already have," Kait said, laughing.

"We need quality time," Taylor whined.

Kait smiled. "Me, too. I was thinking a backyard BBQ this weekend. Nothing crazy. I have the kids on Saturday and Sunday. Just our crew."

"I'm in," Taylor said.

Shelly added, "Same."

Kait stood up. "He's probably here by now. I'm gonna ask him before I lose my nerve. Or I wake up from this dream."

"Good luck," Shelly said.

Taylor laughed. "She doesn't need luck. Just flash him a boob after you ask. One hundred percent acceptance rate."

Kait nodded. "Should I do one or both?"

Taylor's eyes lit up. "Both! And why am I not going to watch?"

Kait laughed and left the office. She strode down the hallway, a woman with a purpose. After the night they had together, it would be easy. But then again, was she getting too serious bringing family into the mix? She took a deep breath, rounded the corner a few steps from Hunter's office, and stopped. Sasha's fake giggle escaped from Hunter's office like a punch that could pop even the strongest of spleens. Kait groaned, waiting outside his office. She wasn't eavesdropping, but she wasn't going to stick her fingers in her ears and hum like her kids did when they didn't want to listen to her rules, either.

Sasha said, "I just had a great idea. There's a new winery, Sweet Water Cellar. Do you want to take a tour and do a tasting this weekend? You would love it. The grounds are supposed to be spectacular."

"That sounds lovely," Hunter said.

Kait's heart dropped.

Hunter continued, "But, I'm afraid I have plans."

Sasha said, "Oh...Too bad. Another time then. Let me know a date that works."

A date.

Hunter said, "Will do."

"Well, I guess I'll see you around." Sasha exited Hunter's office and blew past Kait without a word, which was fine by Kait.

Kait entered the office and said, "Hey, there."

"Good morning," Hunter said through a wide smile, and then whispered, "I missed you."

Kait smiled and said, "I had something to ask you, but I overheard that you already had plans."

"What is it?"

"I wanted to know if you would like to go to a BBQ Saturday afternoon?"

Hunter said, "It depends."

"On what?" Kait asked.

"Whether or not you're going to be there."

Kait chuckled. "I was planning on it. Yes. Hosting actually."

"What's the occasion?"

Kait scoffed. "Do you need an occasion to cook meat?"

Hunter loosened his collar. "You are so hot right now."

"Shhhh!" Kait said, and then laughed.

"But seriously, what's the occasion?"

She didn't want to give the reason. "Just family and friends. A soon-to-be summer gathering."

"So, I will be meeting your family?" Hunter said, monotone.

"Umm, well, just my sister."

Hunter laughed. "Of course, I'll go. I'd love to meet your family."

"Don't get too excited." Kait was excited enough for the both of them. She turned and broke out into a huge smile.

18

Kait stood at the kitchen island mixing a salad in an oversized bowl. Hunter stood across from her, shaping hamburgers. He wore a flowery kitchen apron three sizes too small. It bulged in all the right places. Kait glanced up at him, stealing peeks between mixes.

Hunter smacked a burger patty with his hand. Kait looked up.

"Jealous?" Hunter asked.

"The kids," Kait said, with raised eyebrows. "And you look totally ridiculous." *But amazing.*

"What? I'm not afraid of getting in touch with my feminine side."

"Aren't the bay breezes enough?"

"So funny, Mrs. Colby. It's probably poor timing, but the brownies will be ready in five."

Kait walked around the island, leaned against his body, looked up at him, and kissed him. "Making me chocolate is the manliest, sexiest thing you could possibly do."

Hunter smiled and kissed her back.

"I want to hug you, but keep your meaty hands off me." Kait wrapped her arms around Hunter's waist and they kissed again.

The doorbell rang, followed by the creaking of the door.

Hunter held up his meaty hands. "Let me wash up. I'll be right there."

Kait hurried toward the door. Already standing inside were Jenn, Russ, and Cooper.

"Hey, guys! You're early. Did somebody die?" Kait asked.

Cooper's face dropped. "Somebody's dead?"

"No, honey. Aunt Kait's just kidding," Jenn said, rustling his brown hair. "Go find your cousins and have fun."

"The kids aren't here yet. Aaron's dropping them shortly." Kait hugged Cooper. "Why don't you play in the basement for a bit? There are some cars and dinos down there."

"Okay!" Cooper disappeared.

Kait kissed Jenn and Russ.

Jenn looked around. "The place looks great and smells terrific. It doesn't smell like Chinese takeout."

"I may be a single mom, but we rarely have Chinese takeout. You might be mistaking my kitchen with your own."

Jenn scoffed. "I am a domestic goddess."

Russ laughed. "Who are you kidding? Did you really say that with a straight face?"

"Oh, shut it, Russell."

Hunter entered the room with a smile, but no apron. "And don't let her kid you," he said, pointing to Kait. "She's dating the Chinese delivery guy."

Everyone laughed.

Russ said, "We heard that story. Kids are funny."

Kait made the official introductions.

Jenn said, "I *am* shocked. Fresh vacuum marks. The chocolate brownie aroma. It's unreal."

Kait pointed to Hunter. "I take no credit. It's all Hunter."

Jenn nodded. "That makes sense." She paused and then continued, "I'm not gonna lie. I think I just got a little moist down there." She nudged Russ. "Even a little dust busting would be a turn-on."

"That's why I want to get a dog," Russ said.

"You want the dog to turn me on?" Jenn asked, seemingly about to puke.

"No, I want a dog so I don't have to dust bust all my crumbs."

Kait interrupted, "Well, so glad that you have arrived. Let me escort you to the backyard."

Hunter said to Kait, "I love them already."

Jenn asked, "Anybody else here?"

Kait said, "Nope. Shelly and Taylor should be here soon."

"No Carl?" Hunter asked. "You didn't invite him?"

Kait shrugged, leading them into the kitchen. "He had other plans."

"What's better than this?" Hunter asked.

"I think he's busy motor-boating Mrs. Potts," Kait said, straight-faced.

"It's fun for the first hour, but after that it gets a little boring...and a lot sloppy," Hunter said.

Kait bumped Hunter with her shoulder. "Zip it, you."

Within twenty minutes, the barbecue was in full swing. Even Aaron had arrived reasonably on time, the kids in tow. Kait knelt down to hug Ronny.

"I missed you," she said, and then kissed him.

"Gross," he said, wiping the kiss from his face. He slithered out of her hug and ran off to Cooper, who swung Superman-style on the swings.

Riley hugged Kait. "Are Grandma and Grandpa coming?" she asked.

"Oh, no, sweetie. They couldn't make it."

Riley shrugged and ran over to Ronny and Cooper.

Kait looked at Shelly. "They couldn't make it because they weren't invited."

"I love your parents."

Kait nodded. "I know, but I'm not ready. I don't need my father's floozy catching Hunter's eye."

Hunter snuck up behind Kait and asked, "What's a floozy?"

Shelly laughed and said, "Yeah. What he said."

"Mrs. Potts and Sasha are good examples of a floozy."

Hunter frowned. "And you think I just chase after shiny new objects? Like a cat to a laser pointer?"

Kait shrugged. "Don't know. And I'm fresh out of laser pointers." She looked at the grass, uncertainty rising up. "But I worry about it." She looked at Hunter and smiled. "I *was* wearing sequins and sweating profusely when we met at the country club."

"And making loud noises," Hunter said.

Aaron walked over and said, "I'm gonna get going. The kids' bags are inside."

Hunter said, "Why don't you stay for a drink? We're all just kicking back, a little friends and family time."

Aaron looked at Kait.

"Yeah, stay for a drink," she said.

Hunter stuck out his hand for a shake. "Hunter, by the way."

Aaron shook his hand. "Aaron."

"You want a beer?" Hunter asked.

"Sure."

Hunter looked over to Russ who stood in front of the cooler. "Yo, Russ, my brotha! Hit me with two of those citrus brews!"

"Oh, great. The white zinfandel of beer," Aaron said, less than enthused.

Russ nodded and rifled over a beer. Hunter snatched it out of the air with one hand and held it out for Aaron. Another beer soared through the air. Hunter grabbed it, popped it open, and took a swig.

"So, good."

"No bay breeze?" Kait asked. "I've got the ingredients in the closet."

"I'm multidimensional. I have a menu of fruity drinks I like to select from." Hunter slid his arm around Kait. She leaned into him.

Hunter held out his beer to cheers with Aaron, who did so half-heartedly.

"So, umm, how did you guys meet?" Aaron asked.

Kait said, "Work."

Hunter scoffed. "It's a little more interesting than that. I guess you want me to tell the story, honey?"

Aaron said, "Honey?" His eyes bulged and he then seemingly guzzled half his beer.

"I'm not sure he really wants to know," Kait said.

"He asked, didn't he?" Hunter didn't wait for a response. "So, there I was—"

Kait interrupted, "I fell down the stairs and farted."

Hunter's shoulders slumped. "That just doesn't do it justice."

"That's about as much justice as it deserves," Kait said, and then smirked.

"That sounds like my Lynnie," Aaron said.

Kait rolled her eyes and huffed.

Hunter pulled Kait in even tighter. "Now, she's my Kait."

Jenn peeked her head out from inside the kitchen door. "Kait! Need you for a sec."

Kait's eyes bulged. She looked from Aaron to Hunter. Should she leave them alone?

It was as if Hunter had read her mind. "We'll be fine, honey. Let me know if you need help."

"Okay," Kait said, with a smile.

Shelly interrupted, calling across the backyard, "I'll go."

"Thanks, Shell."

Aaron said, "So...how was your date?"

Kait changed her mind. She wished she had gone.

Hunter asked, "She told you about that?"

Aaron sipped his beer, his eyes never leaving Hunter. "I watched the kids. And I watched you."

Kait snapped, "You were spying on us?"

Aaron chuckled. "No. I'm not pathetic. I was taking the kids for ice cream." Aaron looked at Hunter. "I guess when you got to the parking lot, you realized Kaitlyn had some chicken korma stuck in her wisdom tooth?"

Hunter smiled wide. "You should be more worried about my kebab."

Kait elbowed Hunter in the ribs.

Aaron laughed. "More like chicken sag. But I don't care about that. Just don't do it in front of my kids."

"You seem like a real world traveler. Lover of all cultures, but you should know that it's saag, not sag."

"That's not what she said," Aaron shot back.

Kait forced herself from Hunter's grip and said, "Thank you for the high school flashback, both of you, but enough." She stepped toward Aaron. "It's been great having you here, but I'm sure you have better things to do during your free weekend."

"No, I'm good," Aaron said, smiling.

Kait put her fists on her hips. "Well, you weren't invited, so I'm *not* good. Say goodbye to the kids. They'll call you tomorrow before bed."

"Wow. Okay," Aaron said, shaking his head.

Kait spoke to Aaron he walked toward the kids. "You shouldn't be surprised." And then she glared at Hunter.

Hunter grabbed Kait's hand. "I'm sorry. That was...bad. I shouldn't have instigated. But he deserved it."

Kait nodded. "He did. Let's just forget it and have some fun. I want you to spend some time with my sister."

"Let's do it."

Riley walked over to Kait, a frown on her face.

Kait said, "What's wrong, sweetheart?"

"Dad left. He barely said goodbye."

It's not the first time.

Kait said, "He was upset."

"Why?" Riley asked.

Because he's a jealous jackass, darling. "Not for you to worry about."

"Why?"

"Because it's not a big deal. But know that your father didn't mean to make you feel bad." *Just me.*

19

Another beautiful Monday. Kait sat at her desk in her cubicle at Sutton, reading through a focus group report on Mrs. Potts' taste test, but she kept stopping to remember how well the BBQ had gone, at least after Aaron had left. The intercom button on her phone lit up, interrupting her thoughts.

"Kait?" Nancy asked.

"Hey, Nance. What's up?"

"Delivery for you."

Kait wracked her brain. "Hmm. I'm not expecting anything."

Nancy whispered, "It's some dude with flowers. You gotta sign."

"Be right there." Kait stood up and walked to the lobby. *Hunter couldn't have hand delivered them?*

Kait walked to the lobby. As she pushed the glass door open, a pimply high schooler stepped forward, holding a bouquet of pink roses. "Mrs. Colby?"

She stopped in front of him and whispered, "Yes. Are these from Hunter?"

The kid shrugged. "I don't know, lady. There's a card." He held out a tablet, which she signed. "Have a good day." He handed Kait the flowers.

"Thank you." Kait plucked the stapled card from the wrapping and placed the flowers on the counter in front of Nancy.

"Who are they from?" Nancy asked, excitedly.

"Can't tell you. I have a secret lover," Kait said, smiling.

"I'll just ask Taylor," Nancy said with a chuckle. "I'm surprised I don't know already."

Kait rolled her eyes. "Of course." She read the card. "They're from my ex," she said.

"Ooh, that's juicy," Nancy said.

Kait shot Nancy a look, picked up the flowers, and walked back to her cubicle in disbelief.

He said he was sorry. That's kinda sweet. She plopped into her seat and took out her phone. She texted Aaron.

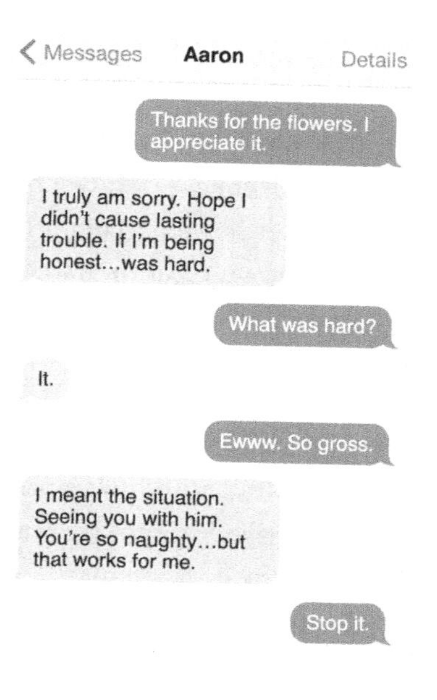

Shelly popped into Kait's cubicle and said, "I was looking for you."

Kait held up the flowers. "Got a delivery."

Shelly leaned in and whispered, "Hunter?"

Kait shook her head. "Aaron."

"That's nice. Wait. What?" Shelly asked, her voice shrieking. "What for?"

"I guess because they almost whipped out their wieners at the barbecue to see whose was bigger," Kait said, handing Shelly the card.

"Too bad. I'd like to see that. Who would win?"

"Ummm, don't know."

Shelly added, "Yet. Always think positive."

Kait laughed.

Shelly handed Kait the card back. "When was the last time he bought you flowers?"

Kait shrugged. "Probably our first date, if he even did that."

Shelly said, "I don't know if I know about your first date."

Kait laughed. "Campus Heroes. We were broke college kids. He got a ham and cheese sandwich, but instead of bread, he had them put it between cucumbers for the sake of his abs. I should've known right then and there. I did like the abs, though."

"What about his cucumber?"

Kait rolled her eyes. "You've been hanging out with Taylor too long."

Shelly said, "I know. It started innocently enough. I gave her a shot because Joe asked me to. He was worried about his little sister, but then she grew on me."

"Maybe you should let Joe grow on you. He's single again," Kait said, eyebrows raised.

Shelly said, “He only has eyes for Jenn.”

“So, step in front of her when he’s looking at her and see what happens.”

Before Shelly could respond, Hunter approached. “Morning, ladies.” He looked at Kait. “Can I have a moment of your time?”

“Sure,” Kait said, standing up. She looked at Shelly. “Think about it. Life is all about growth.”

Shelly laughed as they went their separate ways.

Kait followed Hunter into his office. “What’s up?”

Hunter turned and said, “Can you pull up your calendar on your phone? I need you to block off thirty-six hours of your time.”

“Okay?” Kait took out her phone. “For what?”

“We’re going camping.”

“We are?”

“If you want to.”

“I love camping. I take Ronny with the Cub Scouts. We tried it with the whole family when the kids were young, but Aaron only likes the outdoors if he can work his tan.”

“Well, great. I found an awesome hiking trail and camping spot by Lake Bourne.”

“It’s nice up there. We did some trails with the Cub Scouts around there, but never made it up to the lake. It’s a long hike for kids. Aaron can take the kids this weekend. Or Jenn if he has plans.”

“Done. Do you have gear?”

Kait scoffed. “I’m a den mother. I’ll crush you in gear.”

“It doesn’t have to be a competition,” Hunter said, laughing. “You said you wouldn’t embarrass me. I just wanted to see if we needed to get you anything. I’ve seen your axe skills. I want to be on the same team.”

“I guess that’s okay,” Kait said, shrugging.

"The journey begins Saturday morning. I'll pick you up at ten." Hunter turned to leave, but noticed the flowers. "Who are they from?"

Kait stared at the flowers, eyes wide. Should she tell him? "Umm, they're from Aaron. He felt bad about how things went."

"Return to sender." He smiled and then said, straight-faced, "When should I expect mine?"

"You weren't much better, mister."

Hunter smiled wide. "How can you say that? You haven't had me yet." He winked and turned, disappearing down the hallway.

Kait's lady parts quivered.

LATER IN THE DAY, Kait swung by Shelly's office to catch up. She sat next to Taylor across from Shelly at her desk. It turned into Circle time. Jenn joined the conversation from speaker phone on Shelly's desk.

"Camping? Are you sure?" Shelly asked. "What if he's an axe murderer?"

Taylor shook her head. "That's why you're single. You can't go through life thinking every guy you meet is an axe murderer."

Kait laughed. "He did take me to a place called Get Axed, but I've seen his axe-throwing skills. It's not likely. But I am a little nervous about the trip for other reasons. Am I making the right decision?"

Jenn's voice boomed through the speaker, "You're going hiking and camping. In a tent. Without a car to carry your stuff. It's the wrong decision. Ask him to take you to a spa. Get a couples' massage."

"That's not the problem," Kait said.

"What are you nervous about?" Shelly asked.

"Am I moving too fast? Will he lose interest? What happens to us when the project is over?" *This is so going to implode.*

"Are you gonna..." Taylor used her hands to illustrate the intermingling of male and female sex parts.

"Can't you just speak like an adult?" Kait asked.

Taylor frowned. "I'm pretty certain this is the official American Sign Language symbol for intercourse."

"Umm, no."

Taylor shrugged. "Agree to disagree."

Thankfully, Jenn interrupted, "I have a serious question. It could be a relationship killer."

"What?" Kait asked, her eyes wide.

"Are you sure you're gonna be able to part with Buzz for the day?"

Kait chuckled. "Don't be a Circle jerk. I think I can go one night without him...If I get some in the morning. And it's thirty-six hours, by the way, which is a long time."

Jenn scoffed. "I'm sure you can handle the separation anxiety."

Kait leaned forward toward the speaker. "Easy for you to judge. You're married."

Jenn laughed. "Oh, yeah. I'll trade you Russell for Buzz any day."

"Umm, no thanks on the trade. I'll just buy you a fresh one." Kait frowned and thought for a moment. "I don't know why you're so hard on Russ."

Taylor laughed. "She said, 'hard on.'"

Jenn ignored her. "That's a tale for another time. You'll miss your camping trip if I start now."

Taylor said, "Yeah, I'd rather hear the story about this tail, gettin' some." She reached over and pinched Kait's butt.

"It's so surprising that you're single," Kait said.

Taylor feigned hurt. "Oh, that pains me. They all try to tame me, but it can't be done."

Kait smirked. "This has been really helpful. Thanks for the advice."

Jenn said, "Ride the wave. You've got a great guy who wants to be with you. What's to be concerned about, outside of the accommodations?"

"It ending," Kait said.

20

Kait followed Hunter through a heavily-wooded area on a winding dirt path. Her pack weighed on her shoulders, but it was offset by her freedom and the excitement of the trip. Kait looked up into the trees, listened to the birds chirp, and stole glances of Hunter's butt, which was unfortunately partially obstructed by a rolled-up sleeping bag. One she hoped to be in that evening. Hunter turned, his backpack clanking. The sun broke through the trees and hit Hunter from behind. He looked like an angel. With a tight red dry-fit t-shirt that illuminated his pecs. She liked Rustic Hunter. He was perhaps even hunkier than normal.

"You okay?' he asked, wiping his brow. "It's hot."

It most certainly is. "Fabulous. So, how far are we going? I've never been here."

Hunter shook his head. "I can't believe you've never been here. You're missing out on the awesomeness right in front of you."

Kait smiled. "That is something I shall have to remedy. Are you free at sundown?"

"I'm free right now." Hunter stepped toward her and kissed her.

Kait broke free and scanned for witnesses. "Stop it."

"There's so many people around," Hunter said, with a smirk. "But, okay. I'll just be lonely up here," Hunter said, turning around.

"Hey, where are you going? Get back here," Kait said. She tugged on his pack, pulling him back into a kiss. She lifted her heel up like in the movies, but with muddy hiking boots.

"You are such a conundrum. I can't figure you out," Hunter said.

Join the club. "I like to keep you on your toes."

Hunter smiled, waved her forward, and started walking. "Let's go. I hiked this path when I first got here. It's three miles to the falls with some beautiful views on the way. Do you want to lead?"

Kait followed. "No. I can check out your butt when your sleeping bag bounces. That's the only beautiful view I need."

"Good to know. I may throw out a few deep lunges. For your pleasure..."

Kait laughed. "What's after the falls?"

"We'll have an afternoon snack there. We can do a little cliff jump. Maybe go for a swim."

Ummm, no. Kait stopped and put her hands on her hips. "You didn't tell me to bring a bathing suit. Or say anything about cliff jumping."

Hunter turned around and walked toward Kait. "Oops."

"You sound really broken up about it." Kait's heart pounded.

"It pains me to my core."

Kait ran her hands up Hunter's abs outside his shirt. "I like your core."

Hunter grabbed Kait by the waist and pulled her in.

Kait pulled back with a smile. "We do have a destination we need to get to tonight, right? Then we can kiss all we want."

Hunter smiled, turned, and took off sprinting down the path.

"Let's not get carried away!" Kait yelled, running after him.

Hunter stopped and turned back toward her. He rested his hands on his knees, breathing heavy. Kait caught up to him.

Hunter stood up and leaned down toward Kait. "I needed a break. And some energy." He kissed her again. "Okay. Good. Let's go." He grabbed her by the hand and pulled her down the trail. After three steps, he stopped again and pulled her in. "Okay. Break time." He landed one kiss, but she pushed him back, playfully.

"Stay back, you beast." And then she grabbed his backpack straps with both hands and pulled him in with a jolt. "On second thought, come get me, you animal."

"Roar."

Kait backed away from a kiss, *Matrix*-style. "That's just weird." She let go of Hunter and started walking, smiling back at him and then winked.

"You're like Jekyll and Hyde."

"I can't resist you, but it's getting late. We gotta get camp set up, make dinner before sundown."

Hunter said, "Maybe if you hadn't taken so many breaks on the way."

"Oh, yeah. It was me. My apologies."

Hunter said, "Mock me if you must, but I make no apologies for taking care of my lip health...and lower body circulation."

They hiked the trail for half an hour or so. Well, most of it was hiking, anyway. Hunter stopped at the opening of a small, less-worn path, and turned to Kait. Water splashed in the distance.

Hunter his best movie-trailer voice, "This is it. The moment you've been waiting for." He cut up the smaller path. Kait followed until she found herself next to him, staring at a beautiful waterfall. White water poured from a narrow gap between a mossy cliff face. The water splashed down twenty feet or so in a rippling blue pool of water.

Kait grabbed Hunter's arm as she looked down at the water below. Her heart raced. She hated heights. She had never had a bad experience that she could remember, but she'd never had a good one, either.

"I wanna swim in that." Hunter nodded to the pool below. "I skipped it last time."

"How do you get down there?" Kait asked.

"Umm, you jump." Hunter backed up and took his pack off.

Kait stared down at the water. "What if you don't want to do that? Then what?"

"I do want to do it, but if you don't, there are rock steps that you can climb down over to the left there." Hunter pointed toward the steps. "But that's no fun. Let's jump together. It's symbolic. The start of our journey together."

Before Kait knew it, Hunter's shirt and shorts were piled atop his shoes and he was at the edge of the cliff, standing in his red boxers. If they were leopard patterned, he could've been a dead ringer for a sexy Tarzan. She stared at his six-pack. He asked, "Do you wanna take the plunge with me?"

"I...I don't know." Kait's knees wobbled and her mouth went dry, as she looked back at the water.

"I saw five people do it last time. Two kids. It's a leap of faith, but it's safe and fun. Four of them survived. Eighty percent is pretty good."

Kait backed away from the edge. "I'm sorry. I can't do it."

Hunter laughed. "I'm just kidding. It's safe. I promise. I've done these plenty of times."

"I just...I can't. I'm sorry." She hated herself for disappointing him, but she just couldn't do it.

"It's okay. Maybe next time. Are you okay if I do it? You can leave your pack here and join me down below?"

"Sure," Kait said, the desire to hurl disappearing.

Kait tossed her pack down and turned to Hunter. He blew her a kiss, took a step toward the ledge, and jumped off into a cannonball. Kait's eyes bulged as she glanced over the ledge. Hunter straightened his legs before impact and then disappeared into the water with a smack. She held her breath, searching for Hunter beneath the surface. He burst out of the water and screamed excitedly. Kait exhaled.

Hunter bobbed in the water. "That was amazing! You sure you don't want to join me? I'll be right here for you."

"I think I'll walk down. Be right there."

Hunter waved and then treaded water in a circle, looking around.

Kait found the make-shift stairs made out of giant, flat rocks. When she got to the bottom, Hunter stood knee-deep in the water, waiting for her. She tried not to look at the boxers that clung to Hunter's legs and all that they revealed, but she failed. Miserably. Her eyes bulged at his bulge, as air was sucked from her lungs like a vacuum. She whispered with the last of her air, "Hohohohoholy Christmas."

"Oh, my. That is refreshing," Hunter said, slicking his hair back, his abs flexing.

"It sure is," Kait said.

"What? You're not even in yet."

"Yet?"

"Get in here. Swim with me. You will not regret it." He adjusted his boxer shorts and smiled.

Kait leaned over the edge of the lake and attempted to assess the frizz level of her hair in the water's reflection. The meter was at 'Son of a...' level. "I would love to join you..."

"So, do it." Hunter splashed some water at Kait. It landed at her feet. "Next time, I won't miss."

"I didn't wear..." *Super-tight, shlong-hugging* "...boxers. I have a, umm, hiking thong."

"Oh, did Ms. Cub Scout den mother fail to prepare?" He shrugged. "Not my problem."

She took a deep breath, scanned his body from head to knees, paying particular attention to the middle. *Frig it.* "I can't believe I'm doing this. Cover your eyes."

Hunter covered his eyes, but peeked through a ginormous gap between his fingers. "Okay, you can strip now."

"Turn around," Kait said, with a chuckle. He did as he was told.

She undressed as quickly as possible, not wanting him to cheat or some random person to arrive to see her in her bra and hiking thong. She lay her clothes on top of her hiking boots and ran out into the water with a shriek. She ran past Hunter and dove into the water.

"I totally saw your hiking thong!" Hunter dove under the water and swam after her.

Kait resurfaced to find Hunter on top of her, kissing her face.

She swam back, away from him, laughing. "I can't take

you serious when you're doggy paddling and trying to kiss me."

"It's treading water, thank you very much," Hunter said. "I swam in college."

Kait looked up at the waterfall and then floated on her back, staring up at the blue sky. "This is incredible."

"The kisses or the locale?" Hunter asked with a raised eyebrow.

"Both."

"Which is better?"

"The locale."

"I think it's time to go," Hunter said, monotone.

"Oh, stop." Kait swam toward the falls. "Can we swim under the falls and umm, you know?"

"If you want a concussion. That's if we don't drown."

"So, is that a maybe or a no? I could stay here all day."

"I can't doggy paddle that long. We should probably get a move on so we can get to camp." Hunter swam back across the lake, toward the water's edge and stood up in thigh-high water. He looked back with a grin and then took off sprinting through the water. "Race you!"

Kait took off after him. "No fair!"

Hunter stood up near the edge and turned to Kait, his smile wide. "Now, what are you gonna do?"

"Wait until you turn around."

"Oh, really?" Hunter said, deflated.

"I'll let you see all this after the sun goes down."

"But I have terrible eyesight."

Kait smirked. "That answers a lot of questions."

Hunter closed his eyes and held his hands out boob high, squeezing air as he walked toward her. "Where are you, babe?"

Kait dodged him with a laugh, ran out of the water,

grabbed her clothes, and disappeared behind a tree. As she got dressed, she called out, "The good thing about a hiking thong is that you don't need a towel."

"I wouldn't towel off even if I could. Need to keep my boys cool for the rest of the ride."

Kait emerged shaking her head. "I guess I have to let you go back to get your clothes."

"There's also the tent and our food."

She looked him up and down. "I'm not sure it's worth it if it means you put your shorts back on."

Hunter walked toward her and kissed her. "I'll let you see all this after the sun goes down."

"Let's get the frig out of here," Kait said, laughing.

The rest of the hike was peaceful. The temperature dropped and the refreshment from the falls helped keep Kait cool, despite Hunter's body working against those cooling factors. They hiked for at least another two miles, maybe more. Kait kept pace with Hunter's long strides. His pack was heavier as he carried the tent, cooking gear, and food, but it didn't seem to slow him down.

Hunter stopped at the bottom of a large hill that wasn't overly steep, but was high enough that the top couldn't be seen from their position.

Kait rested her foot on a rock. "How far are we going?"

"We're going deep into the bush tonight."

Kait gulped.

"We're almost there. Just gotta climb this hill here and then we'll be in the promised land." He waved her forward and started climbing.

Kait followed Hunter up the hill. She huffed her way up, her pack weighing her down. When they got to the top, it was all worth it. The trees opened up to a grassy field that offered a view that had few rivals. Hunter tossed his pack to the ground, tore his sleeping bag from the pack, and held out his hand. Kait dropped her pack and took his hand. She wanted a better look at the view. Hunter led her toward a rocky edge, spread out the sleeping bag and sat down on it. Kait lay on her side, curled up, her head on Hunter's lap.

"Perfect timing," Hunter said. "Glad we took all those breaks."

Kait looked out at the horizon. Lake Bourne spread out below them while the pink sun lit the skyline. Beyond that, there was nothing but forest for miles. She inhaled the fresh air as Hunter caressed her face and hair. She could stay like this forever.

Hunter broke the long silence, "As much as I don't want to, if we don't get camp set up and cook dinner before dark, we'll regret it."

Kait stood up and arched her back. Hunter stared at her boobs and arched his eyebrows. Kait rolled her eyes and headed toward their packs.

"Ewww. There's a snake skin there." Kait pointed to a three-foot transparent skin. "That's gross." Her nerves jolted alive. "Are there snakes around?"

Hunter shook his head. "That's old. The snake is long gone. You *should* be aware that there's a trouser snake that wants to make your acquaintance, though."

"Swipe left," Kait said, laughing. "On serious matters, tent and firewood then dinner?" Kait asked.

Hunter said, "Yep. And then tent and wood and dessert."

Kait laughed. "You are incorrigible."

"I'm sorry. You shouldn't have mauled me so many times today. You got me all worked up."

"I mauled you?"

Hunter nodded. "That's what I recall."

"Was it something like this?" Kait jumped onto Hunter

and wrapped her legs around him. He stumbled back and they fell to the ground in a crash of intermingled limbs and tongues. Hunter grunted as they hit the dirt, but didn't seem to stop his lips or his hands.

Kait pulled back and sat up, still on top of Hunter. "Was it like that?"

"I don't know. I need another sample."

Kait stood up. "No more samples. You're like a child. Can't have dessert before dinner."

"You are going to be the death of me, woman," Hunter said, lying on his back. He sat up and stared at his crotch. "I pitched the wrong tent."

Kait stared at Hunter's pants tent. "So dramatic. But, intriguing." Kait stood up and walked to the tree line. She picked up a few sticks and brought them back.

Hunter unfolded the tent and glared at the sticks in her hands. "I'm so jealous."

Kait just shook her head and continued to set up camp. She added to the wood pile and glanced over at Hunter. "That is a mighty small tent."

"You said you had your own gear. I thought it would just be me."

Kait cocked her head and smirked.

Hunter added, "As far as you know."

"Mmm, hmmm."

"Well, I guess we'll have to share mine. It only fits one sleeping bag."

"Oh, really?"

"And I sleep nude. I prefer to be one with nature."

Images of naked Hunter, one with not nature, but her, flooded her mind. Her body tingled with excitement. Did she really even need to eat food when Hunter was there to devour?

"Will you stop talking and work?" Kait said, faking annoyance.

In less than an hour, the real tent had been assembled, a bonfire lit, and the remnants of filet mignon, roasted potatoes, and tin-foil veggies had been set aside. The fire danced in the darkness and warmed Kait and Hunter as they lay atop his sleeping bag next to the fire.

"I need to check you for ticks," Hunter said.

"It's dark out. How are you going to see anything?"

"We'll have to do a hand check."

"Mmm, hmmm," Kait said, and then laughed. "If you must."

Hunter cupped his ear. "Listen. Did you hear that?"

"What?"

"Owls."

Kait said, "I didn't hear anything. Are you trying to trick me?"

"No. I've just got a keen ear for hooters."

Kait shrugged. "As long as you don't have a keen eye for them."

Hunter's eyes widened. "Even yours?"

"I will allow some eyeing, but within reason."

"I can't see anything right now. What about handling?" Hunter reached for her, playfully.

She smacked his hand. "Get out of here."

"Okay," Hunter said, nuzzling into her neck and kissing her. He pulled back. "I can feel your pulse with my lips."

"I'm excited. And a little bit nervous." *Or a lot bit.*

Hunter smiled, sat up, and looked down at her. "It's okay, sweetheart. We don't have to do anything you don't want to do."

Kait kissed him. "I want to."

Hunter exhaled. "Thank God!"

"Stop it." Kait rolled on top of Hunter and kissed him. Clothes flew in every direction, Kait's hiking thong fueling the fire for at least three seconds.

Dessert was served. In fact, they devoured every item on the menu and even had seconds on some of their favorites. Kait lost track of time. And maybe consciousness. She didn't normally have a stopwatch handy for her sexual encounters, but one thing was for certain, the pleasure certainly lasted longer than two minutes and seventeen seconds. It was probably closer to two hours and seventeen minutes.

When the fire burned out, they made their way into the tent, their own fire still burning another two logs before petering out. Kait was not a typical after-sex crier, unless it was really bad, but she lay snuggled with Hunter inside his sleeping bag, and held back tears. Hunter was everything she had ever wanted and more. She fell asleep wondering how she was so lucky for Hunter to have happened to her.

The next morning, the light from the sun illuminated the tent. Kait could feel its warmth on her face. She opened her eyes and nearly did a double take as she saw Hunter lying next to her. She unzipped the sleeping bag to let in the cool, fresh air. She lay her head on his chest as he breathed deeply. The satisfaction from the night before remained with her, but it was more smiles than tears. Hunter stirred, but didn't wake. She missed him. As she lay on his chest, she looked down at his stomach and began to trace the depths of Hunter's six-pack. It was so absurd, she couldn't help herself and cracked up, snorts so loud they nearly rattled the tent.

Hunter woke up and said, "What the—" He looked down at Kait's hands on his stomach. "Lower."

Kait smiled and continued tracing his abs. "I could get

lost in these things. How do you keep these with all those bay breezes?"

"We hiked like six miles. Don't you think we burned a half a glass of cranberry and pineapple juice and a shot of vodka? Not to mention the calories we burned after midnight."

"I distinctly remember you having abs before then. How many after-midnight calories do you normally burn?"

"Sex burns four calories a minute, so..."

Kait's eyes widened. "Really? Let's do it again."

"Yes, for our weight management." Hunter grabbed her and pulled her in.

Down a dress size, Kait lay on her back, huffing. A strange buzzing rattled the floor. Kait raised an eyebrow and looked toward the packs. Had she packed Buzz by mistake? A physical Freudian slip? Her stomach churned.

Hunter said, "I think it's my phone. Can you grab it?"

Kait reached for Hunter's pack, found the vibrating pocket, and pulled out the phone. She looked at the caller ID and then handed him the phone. It was Sasha. Damn satellites.

Hunter answered it, "Hey, what's up?"

Kait leaned in to listen, but could only hear Hunter's side of the conversation.

"Tennis?"

Kait shook her head no.

Hunter mouthed, "No?" And then smiled. "Sorry, I thought I told you I was camping. Yeah, I'll probably be too tired when I get back. Didn't really sleep much." He blew a kiss to Kait. "I'm sorry. I'll see you in the office Monday. Yeah. Bye." He hung up the phone. He looked at Kait, laughed, and then said, "No?'

Kait nodded. "No. I don't want you to get a concussion

watching her boobs bounce all around." She sat up and stared at him. "Plus, you're mine. I'm not sharing you with her."

"It's just tennis. Do you wanna play?"

"Those aren't the type of balls I want to hit right now. Did she know we were together?" Kait asked, pointedly.

"Chill. Now I know how Dimitri felt. No balls need to be hit right this second. Yes. I told her we were going camping."

"Why?"

"I don't know. I wasn't thinking. I didn't see what the big deal was."

"It is a big deal. I thought we were trying to have some discretion. Carl knowing is one thing. For Sasha, this is ammunition," Kait said. She took a deep breath and exhaled. *Back to reality.*

21

The hike home did not match the euphoria of the rest of the trip. Kait stewed for most of it, despite Hunter's attempts to shake her out of it. How could she shrug off her anger when she'd done exactly what she hadn't wanted to do? She'd fallen for him, hard. And it was all going to unravel. And Sasha was pulling at the thread with two hands.

Kait entered the building the next morning and headed toward the stairs, navigating through the Monday morning hustle. Someone had given Dimitri a head splint made out of coffee stirrers and tape that removed Kait's guilt and reopened her preferred route to the Sutton suite. Though she barely noticed Dimitri that morning, her mind firmly locked on Hunter. She'd had a once-in-a-lifetime experience with him that weekend, in multiple ways, and her mind struggled to reconcile it all. It had been the best night of her life, but how would it work between them? They had a month left, at best, before their project was done. Plus, the whole Sasha thing had bent her out of shape, so the magic had certainly been missing on the way back home.

Kait entered the Sutton suite and nearly walked right by Nancy without seeing her.

Nancy looked up and said, "Good morning, Kaitlyn. Josh was looking for you."

Kait frowned and swallowed hard. "Okay. I'll swing by now."

"Good luck."

Kait made her way to Josh's office. She usually knew why he wanted to see her. It was never good. She hoped that since there was nothing obvious that it was something good this time. When she arrived outside his office, she looked at Becky and asked, "Is he there?"

"Yep. Go right in."

"Is it bad?" Kait asked, an eyebrow raised.

"Don't know."

Kait peeked her head into the office. Josh waved her in.

"Have a seat, Kaitlyn."

She did as she was told. She fidgeted with her hands in her lap as she waited for Josh to say something.

Josh cocked his head and looked at Kait. "So, how's everything going?"

"Good. How are you?"

Josh pursed his lips. "Fine. I'd be a lot better, though, if I hadn't gotten a report that alleges you're having a relationship with Hunter." Josh eyed her, seemingly with suspicion.

Ahhhh, doody. "Who reported that?"

"That's none of your concern."

"Oh, no? It's Sasha. I know it is," Kait said, rolling her eyes.

Josh threw his hands up. "You know I can't disclose that."

"You don't have to."

"Well, are you?" Josh asked, seemingly studying her.

Kait frowned. Her pulse rocketed higher. "No. No more

than dinner together. Same as Sasha." She conveniently left out the make-out sessions at the office and in the car, the near-naked lake swimming, and the very naked sleeping-bag sex, hoping to God that those occurrences were actually different than what Sasha had done with Hunter. A lot different.

Josh weighed her answer without saying anything.

Kait added, "And Sutton's had like fifty affairs in the office. It's worse than *Mad Men* here."

"That's why H.R. is enforcing the relationship policy."

Kait nearly laughed. Had he seen his crap H.R. staff in action? "You know how important my career is to me. I'm a single mom. I need this job. I wouldn't do anything to jeopardize it. Sasha's just jealous."

"I never said it was Sasha."

"You didn't have to."

Josh smiled. "I want you to be happy, but you know you can't see him, or anyone else at the firm, for that matter."

Kait nodded, her stomach in knots. "Understood."

KAIT TRUDGED to the office kitchen, her conversation with Josh complicating her thoughts that much more. She tossed her lunch into the fridge, not caring how it landed. Some lunch Nazi would probably leave her a passive-aggressive Post-it note about it, but she didn't care. She shut the door and grabbed a coffee cup. Should she just commandeer the Keurig for her cubicle? The pull was strong, but she decided against it and just poured herself a cup. She headed to her cubicle and made it with only one coffee-swig stop. She was about to sit down when she saw Hunter's head bobbing down the hallway.

"Hey, there," Hunter's voice called out.

Kait stepped out of her cube and smiled at him, as he walked toward her. It wasn't lung-collapsing, bulging Lake Hunter, but still, he wore his signature hunkiness as he approached with two coffee cups.

"I got coffee, baby! And some sugar." He leaned in and kissed her.

"You can't do that," Kait said, her eyes bulging. She pushed him away, gently. Certainly not enough to concuss him. She looked around, scanning for Sutton employees. She didn't see any, at least none that seemed to notice.

Hunter scoffed. "What's better than coffee and my kisses?"

Kait stared at him, hands on hips. "Umm, a paycheck," she whispered.

"That hurts." He waved her off. "But I'll be your sugar daddy."

Carl walked by, eyes wide.

"Hey, Carl!" Hunter said, raising a coffee cup in his honor.

Kait shook her head. "The poor kid is doomed in this place. Or maybe it's just you." She leaned in and whispered, "But seriously, Josh warned me about having personal relationships with people at work."

Hunter's eyes bulged. "How many people are you having relationships with at work?'

"I'm being serious. After this project, you're gone. If Josh finds out about us, I might be, too."

"You're dumping me after the project?" Hunter asked, nearly spilling the coffee cups.

Kait said, "You'll be leaving to work on another project. I won't have you, and possibly my job, if we keep this up."

"Is that what you think? How did he even know?"

Kait felt her anger rising. "*Someone* reported it. No names or bra sizes given."

Hunter stepped back, a confused look on his face. "Do people normally have to give bra sizes when reporting work incidents?"

"It's optional. I wouldn't be surprised if H.R. was working on making it mandatory, though."

"What about wiener size?"

Kait smirked. "As if it would be accurately reported."

Hunter nodded in agreement and then said, "This place is awesome. I mean, you're totally gonna get sued by someone and probably go out of business, but it'll be awesome while it lasts."

Kait reached out for a coffee cup and said, "I already grabbed coffee, but I suddenly need to chug this. Does it have a rum floater?"

"Forgot." Hunter took a deep breath and checked his watch. "We should have a serious conversation, but not here. And not now. Can we put a pin in this for now? We have a conference call with HQ."

"We?" Kait asked.

Hunter said, "Yes. They want an update on our plans for the slut."

"Why do they care about Sasha?" Kait asked.

"Wow. Stone Cold Colby, comin' atcha."

"Okay," Kait said. "I must've missed that on the calendar. I'm not really in the mood. Why don't you just tell them what's going on?" Kait asked.

"I want you on. To show you off. The team has done a great job."

Kait nodded, but she couldn't put a pin in it. Her mind raced. They made their way to the boardroom without discussing their relationship or much of anything else. Kait's mind juggled conflicting thoughts. She was falling for him. Or had already fallen. Hard. Was he going to leave? Would she lose her job? She would rather lose in love than hurt her children. But she would lose so much. Could she find another job? They were easier to come by than Hunter.

Kait followed Hunter straight into the boardroom. Sasha, Carl, Amy, and Dwayne had already assembled.

"Morning, everyone," Hunter said, placing his coffee down on the table next to the conference call pod. "Let's get Freddy boy on the phone." He dialed the number from memory.

Kait sat down and opened her laptop. She overheard Sasha whisper to Amy, "She must be glad it's not a video conference with that hair she's sporting today."

Kait took a deep breath, willing herself to abstain from thrusting the pen sitting a few feet from her into one of Sasha's fake boobs. It was bound to be an H.R. complaint, even at Sutton. And would she have to report the victim's bra size? It would get complicated. There would be one D and one deflated.

A gruff voice on the other end of the conference call said, "Hello?"

"Fred, it's Hunter and the team at Sutton here in Sweet Water."

"Ahhh, yes. Good morning to you all. I had the chance to look at the files you uploaded to Teams. It looks great. I just have a few questions."

"Fire away," Hunter said.

Fred fired away. The meeting was pretty boring as far as meetings went. For Kait, the biggest fireworks exploded at the conclusion of the call.

Fred said, "Great job. I'm really impressed with what you, Sasha, and Kait have come up with."

Kait didn't recall Sasha doing anything on the actual project. She was in sales and relationship management. Mismanagement was more like it. And seemingly very good at the relations part.

Kait's ears perked up when Fred continued, "Hunter, I think you've got a real shot at that European job. I already put in a good word for you."

Kait's stomach nearly imploded. She could survive farting down the stairs or puking in the bushes in front of a co-worker on her personal time. But puking across the conference room table was an entirely different matter.

"Thanks, Fred. Your support is always appreciated. I'm not sure what I'm doing there, but umm, thank you. Will catch up with you soon." Hunter hung up the call. He looked at Kait and the rest of the team and said, "That went well. He likes to be kept in the loop and I wanted him to know how well it was going."

Kait just nodded.

Sasha asked, excitedly, "Are you really throwing your hat in the ring for Europe? That would be amazing for you."

"Well, you heard Fred. I guess he already threw it in. It *would* be the opportunity of a lifetime."

"So it seems," Sasha said. She looked at Kait and said, "I hope you get it. Not that I'd be happy you'd be across the *entire* Atlantic Ocean. That's probably a nine-hour flight from here."

Kait eyed the pen again, but stood up instead of grabbing and stabbing, and walked out of the boardroom without a word.

Hunter tracked her down. "I was thinking we should have lunch today."

"Your going-away party?" Kait asked, annoyed. "I brought my lunch. Let's just go to your office and do it now."

Hunter raised an eyebrow. "Do *it* now?"

Kait shot him a look. "Not the time."

"I see that now." Hunter led her to his office without another word and closed the door behind her.

She looked up at him. *Stay strong. At least don't fart.* She clenched her cheeks just to be safe.

Hunter stepped toward her and said, "I understand your concern. And I don't know the answer. I didn't *get* the European job. There's a lot of politics involved. Honestly, I didn't even apply for it. I hadn't made a decision. Let's not worry about the future. I just know that I don't want this to end."

Kait exhaled some of her anxiety. "I don't either, but my biggest fear is that it will. Well, my biggest fear is that my kids get eaten by an alligator, but this is a close second."

"That's fair. Alligators are so freaky, right?" Hunter rubbed her arm. "It's gonna be okay."

Kait's anxiety spiked again. "Is it? How can you be so cavalier? It's my life that will be upended. Not yours." She huffed. "I need some fresh air."

"Let's grab lunch outside."

Kait said, "I need some time to think on my own."

"Okay," Hunter said, scratching his head. "I'll be here to talk whenever you're ready."

KAIT GRABBED a smoothie in the lobby and just started walking. She left the building and followed the sidewalk out of the complex. The bright sun warmed her face, but did nothing to brighten her thoughts. *This is all too good to be true. He can say what he wants about not wanting it to end, but how can it not when he goes back to Austin...or Europe? When*

he's not working with me, but some other woman who falls for him? I can't get hurt again. Maybe Sasha was right. What happens when something is too hot? You get burned. I'm gonna get scorched.

Kait thought about swinging by Hunter's office when she got back to Sutton, but didn't. Instead, she stopped at her cubicle and plopped into her seat. She didn't know what to say, nor did she have the energy to discuss the issue more with Hunter. Even if she did, Sutton was the last place she wanted to have that conversation. But she knew she'd have to face him eventually.

That eventuality occurred two minutes later. Hunter stepped into Kait's cubicle. She looked up at him, but didn't know what to say.

He smiled and said, softly, "I know you don't want to talk about personal matters right now, but we do have some work we need to get done. Carl has all the panel results. He'll organize them by tomorrow afternoon, but we need to analyze them. Can you work late tomorrow?"

Kait nodded. "I'll check with Victoria. I'm sure it'll be fine."

He smiled and headed down the hall.

Kait took a deep breath and gathered her thoughts.

Shelly stopped at Kait's cubicle and popped her head in. "Coffee run?"

"I just went on a smoothie walk, but a coffee run sounds good," Kait said, standing up.

"What's wrong, girlie?"

Kait shrugged. "Oh, not much. Josh just warned me about seeing Hunter. Hunter and I talked about breaking up."

"What? Why?" Shelly said, as they headed into the Sutton lobby.

"Well, Sasha reported our camping trip. And what's the point of continuing on with Hunter when he's just going to leave and move on to his next project? And love interest."

"You don't know that."

"I don't, but I fear it with every fiber of my being. I am soooo crazy about him. I love everything about him. He's not going to quit his job for me. And I can't lose my job for him."

Shelly frowned. "Why not? What if he stays?"

The elevator opened. Kait said, softly, "Then I could lose my job."

"They don't appreciate you anyway," Shelly said.

"But I appreciate the paycheck. And there aren't too many places around that do what I do. This isn't New York City. I don't want to start a different career. I'm in a no-win situation."

22

After an afternoon of avoiding Hunter, Kait pulled into her driveway, fear coursing through her veins. Aaron's car sat parked out front. Had something happened to the kids? Victoria? She grabbed her bags and hurried into the house. A smoky haze hovered above her. She dropped her bags and rushed into the kitchen. Her heart pounded. "Hello? Is everything all right?"

She turned the corner and stopped abruptly. Aaron stood at the island, spatula in hand. "Hey, there. Sorry for the smoke."

Kait fanned the smoke from her face. "What the heck happened? Where are the kids?"

Aaron nodded to the backyard. "Playing. And getting oxygen."

Kait peeked through the blinds and exhaled. Ronny hung from the monkey bars while Riley kicked on the swings. She turned to Aaron and said, "You didn't tell me what happened."

Aaron grinned sheepishly. "It was supposed to be steak, but I burned those, so it's eggs. I blame the stove."

Kait nodded, but then raised an eyebrow. "So, the rules of physics don't apply for steaks, but they do for eggs?"

"I know, it's crazy. It's just one of life's great mysteries."

Kait shrugged. "It's fine. I burn stuff with that pan all the time. And I like a good breakfast for dinner. It's a single-mom staple. Thank you, by the way. It's the thought that counts. As long as the fire department doesn't show up."

"They left five minutes before you got here."

"Funny," Kait said. "Where's Victoria? What are you even doing here? There's a fan above the stove, by the way."

Aaron searched for it and flipped it on. "Guess I should've known that."

"Well, you have to actually help out in the kitchen to know such mysteries."

Aaron nodded and cracked an egg into the pan. "I gave Victoria the night off."

Kait frowned. "That's nice of you, but she works for me."

"I know. I paid her for the night," Aaron said, focusing on the pan.

"What services did you pay her for?" Kait asked.

Aaron turned and smirked at her.

Kait raised an eyebrow. "She and I are gonna have a little chat. You never answered my question."

Aaron shrugged. "Does a guy have to have a reason to see his family?"

"No, but in the past year, I can count the number of times you stopped by unannounced."

Aaron looked over at her. "So, you're punishing me for it?"

Kait shook her head. "No, I'm sorry. But it *is* my house."

Aaron said, "You're right. I didn't think about that. Do you want the key back?"

"Would you want me alone in your living room when you came home?"

Aaron smiled. "I'll take you alone in any room."

Kait rolled her eyes. "Yeah, right. I don't want the key back, but you can only use it for emergencies or with advanced notice."

"Deal."

"Glad you approve," Kait said.

"Sorry again about this mess," Aaron said, holding up the steak-charred pan.

Kait said, "It's disastrous, but it's the thought that counts. Oh, and I should show you where the Brillo pads are because I'm quite certain you don't know where any of the cleaning supplies are."

"You got me again," Aaron said, with a chuckle.

Kait opened a cabinet and pulled out a bottle of Malbec. "Wine?"

"No. The kids have given me enough whine." Aaron smiled at her. "I bought the kids a board game. Risk. I think they'll enjoy it. There's nothing that offers good family fun better than competing against each other for global domination."

"Oh, I love that game. Did they do their homework?" *Yeah, right.*

Aaron nodded. "Yes. It's all finished."

Kait crossed her arms. "Did you check it?"

"Yep," Aaron said, smiling.

"How many snacks did they have?"

"Just fruit and whipped cream."

Kait frowned. "Who are you?"

The backyard door opened. Ronny entered and gave Kait a hug and a kiss.

"Oh, my boy. Missed you so much."

"Missed you more." Ronny walked over to Aaron and wrapped his arms around his waist from the side. "Can Dad stay to play Risk?"

Riley ran in. "Please, mommy!"

Kait looked at Aaron and the kids. They all stared back at her with puppy dog eyes and their hands clasped, pleading.

"I feel like I've been set up. But that's fine...If he doesn't mind getting dominated."

The kids cheered while Aaron winked at her.

She rolled her eyes at him. She leaned in and whispered, "Dominated in Risk." She looked at the kids and said, "Set the table. We need to eat, and then you set up the game while we finish cleaning."

"Done," Aaron said. "You'll just have to show me where the sink is."

The kids cheered. Kait smirked.

The eggs were cooked fairly well, and the toast never caught fire. It wasn't hard to do, but given Aaron's less-than-desirable domestic skills, Kait was impressed. After breakfast-for-dinner was over, the four of them sat around the Risk board at the dining room table.

Kait stared at her dwindling number of troops and territories. "I am definitely not dominating."

Ronny threw a cannon on the board and said, "Hey, Dad. Can we have dessert?"

Kait felt her muscles tense. She looked at Aaron, but kept her mouth shut, waiting impatiently for an answer.

Aaron smiled. "You have to ask your mother on that one. This is her house."

Kait nearly choked. "Umm, yeah. You can have one dessert, but that's it."

Riley scoffed. "Come on, Mom. What good is ice cream without cookies?"

Aaron said, "Your mother said one. That's the rule. Too many sweets aren't good for you."

The kids groaned. Ronny said, "Aww, come on, Dad. That's not fair." He crossed his arms and glared at him.

Kait pumped her internal fist. Aaron still owed her a million more of these moments, but this would be the most important of all of them.

After ice cream and Riley's control of the world, which was celebrated with a fitting evil cackle, the kids, of course, ran off without cleaning up. Aaron lifted the board, bent it, and dumped all of Riley's armies into the box that Kait held.

"Thanks for your help," Kait said.

"No problem. It's just cleaning up a game."

Kait said, "No. I meant with the kids and the rules."

Aaron nodded and took a deep breath. "I realized I needed to do a better job of supporting you. I've done a lot of soul searching these past few weeks."

Kait smirked. "Oh, you have one of those?"

"Funny."

"Well, I guess that about does it," Aaron said, putting the cover on the box.

Kait said, "Thanks for dinner, and all of this. It was fun. It almost felt normal."

Aaron smiled that smile. "It felt great." But then the smile disappeared. "It was the way things should've been. I'm sorry I've been the weak link. I wanted to be the cooler parent after the divorce. They spent so much more time with you. I didn't want to waste time fighting and dealing with the consequences of the hard stuff. I realize I was just making it harder for you. It won't happen again."

"Thank you, again." Kait stared at him, waiting for him

to turn and leave, but he didn't. "Why are you looking at me like that?"

Aaron shrugged. "No reason. We should do this again. The kids had a great time. I did, too."

"I think I'd like that," Kait said.

"I should go."

Kait called out, "Kids! Your father's leaving. Come say goodbye."

The kids rushed into the room and wrapped their arms around him, nudging each other for more of his surface area.

"This was so much fun!" Ronny yelled.

Riley said, "It reminded me of the time we played cards on the hotel bed when it rained while we were in Puerto Rico."

Kait smiled on the outside, but the comment stung on the inside. The San Juan trip was the last time the four of them were really together before she and Aaron decided to divorce. Or more accurately, he decided to divorce her.

Ronny still hugged Aaron, but turned to Kait. "Can Dad watch us after school instead of Victoria? I asked him and he said he wouldn't schedule any meetings after two, so he could get us off the bus."

Kait thought for a moment. She looked at the kids and then at Aaron.

He said, "I will be there on time any day you allow."

Will he? "I can't get rid of Victoria. We need her for the summer, and she counts on our hours."

The kids groaned. Aaron's face dropped.

Kait continued, "But, maybe one day a week. I could shift her hours to the weekend to give me a break sometimes." *And date night, if Hunter is still around.* She tickled the kids. "I probably give her more hours than she wants with you two, anyway."

"Hey!" Riley yelled.

"Actually, Victoria can't stay late tomorrow, but I'll be late, so if you're free tomorrow, that would work," Kait said.

Aaron said with a smile, "Done."

"Group hug!" Ronny yelled, engulfing Aaron.

Kait hesitated and stared at the three of them, arms wrapped around each other.

Aaron smiled. "Come on, you're not gonna melt."

She rolled her eyes and joined the hug. Aaron put an arm around her as she wrapped hers around the kids. She smiled, forgetting about what could've been, and just enjoyed the moment.

23

Kait walked into Hunter's conference room/office late the next afternoon, dread wreaking havoc among her internal organs, particularly her small intestine. It would be fitting that their relationship started with a fart and ended with something far messier. She had no idea what she wanted to do with Hunter, at least relationship-wise. She figured he'd want to talk. She probably should've figured out something to say before she had arrived. She would just have to rely on her inappropriate blurting. It always worked so well.

Hunter shuffled some papers, tucking something beneath a stack of random folders and spreadsheets. "Hey," Hunter said, a little too excitedly.

"Hey," Kait said, placing her laptop on the table and sat next to Hunter. She stared at the pile of papers, but couldn't decipher what he had hidden, if anything. "So, let's get right into it. It's tough for me to work late."

"Understood. Well, the results from the group panels are in. We've got logo issues. No surprise there."

Kait pulled up Carl's report on the share drive. "I

reviewed the material. The ingredient data is most troublesome. Even at a twenty percent discount, seventy-seven percent of participants said they wouldn't choose our ingredients over the two leading natural brands."

Hunter shook his head. "We'd get crushed if we lowered our prices by say twenty-five to thirty percent to pick up market share. There's no point in growing if you grow at a loss, at least for an established brand. But this is what people say in a testing room. When they're staring at the prices on a shelf, we know the results could be different. Right?" Hunter scooted his seat closer to Kait and peeked at her laptop screen.

Kait shifted her seat away and then stood up. She nodded, but smirked doubtfully as she paced around the room. She stopped and stared out the window. "Right, but on a weighted-average basis, Mrs. Potts' market share *is* only about eleven percent. Eighty-nine percent of consumers are not choosing your brand and ingredients at current prices. Not to mention the stock's recent action. I think the tribe has spoken."

Hunter chuckled. "Thank you, Jeff Probst. I think Mrs. Potts will be voted off the island at HQ and shut down if we suggest slashing prices so drastically."

"Well, if she won't survive as-is or if you slash prices, then you have to recommend a full product redesign. Sometimes you have to realize you're coming up short and do something about it."

"As daunting as that sounds, I think you're right." Hunter ran his fingers through his hair.

Kait thought for a moment and then sat down. "Would that mean you would stay longer?"

Hunter weighed her words and then said, "It would probably mean that I'd leave sooner and then come back when we need to re-launch." Hunter took a deep breath and exhaled. "So, where do we stand in all this?"

"You're gonna leave."

"But I'll come back."

"Maybe. Maybe you'll be in Europe. Maybe we should... stop," Kait said. Her heart raced. Her small intestine nearly backfired.

Hunter shook his head. "No."

"No?" Kait asked.

"Do you really want to?"

Kait said, "I want what's best for you. Maybe you should take the European job."

"You don't want what's best for me. You don't want to get hurt. Or lose your job. And I don't blame you."

"I do want what's best for you, but you're right." Kait thought for a moment. "I also don't want this to end."

Hunter tapped his lips and said, "I haven't been offered the European job. And I have a lot that's important to me here."

"Here where?"

"Here in the States."

The States. Not Sweet Water. Kait weighed his words. "But you said it's the opportunity of a lifetime."

Hunter shrugged. "It is, but I guess I'll just take it as it comes."

Kait rest her head in her hands. Hunter rubbed her shoulder. She slid away from his touch. "Not here."

"But you're so tense. I know you're stressed about all of this, but just do what I do. Trust that it will work out in both our interests."

"It never works out in my best interest. And you can have any woman you want, so it will always work out in your interest," Kait said, her voice cracking.

"That's not true. I—"

Kait pushed her chair away from the table and stood up. "Since we've decided we're going to recommend a redesign, I think we're done here. I should get home to the kids. Aaron in the kitchen equals a hefty insurance claim."

"Done here, how?"

Kait closed down her laptop and stuffed it into her bag. "Done with the meeting." Without looking at him, she said, "Have a good night. See you tomorrow." She grabbed her bag and rushed out of the office.

"Kait, wait!" Hunter said.

She didn't. She rushed to the stairwell, blasted open the door, and hurried down the stairs, tears streaming down her face.

A thud echoed into the stairwell, seemingly a punch, judging by Hunter's yell of, "Son of a..." But Hunter didn't follow.

As Kait hit the lobby, she thrust her middle finger in Dimitri's face, huffed, and said, "What's wrong with you men?"

24

Kait pulled up to the house. She looked in the mirror and tried to salvage her face amid the mishmash of makeup. She took a moment to gather herself and then got out of the car. She entered the house and thankfully, the smog index was a one. The kids' laughter echoed from the den over the TV. Kait exhaled and walked into the kitchen. Aaron sat at the kitchen table, typing on his MacBook. Papers were straightened. The countertop actually reflected the lights above it.

The kids rushed into the kitchen, engulfing Kait in a hug.

"Hey, guys! Missed you." Kait squeezed them both.

"What happened to your face?" Ronny asked. "It looks like a finger-painting."

Kait said, "Umm, must've been the heat. My face melted."

"Cool!"

Kait and Aaron laughed. Aaron stood up. "We ate, but there are leftovers for you."

"Oh, you didn't have to make me something. And based on last time, it was quite a risky undertaking."

Aaron smirked. "It was the stove."

Kait scanned the kitchen again. "Did you clean up?" she asked, surprised.

"A little."

"Thank you," Kait said.

Riley said, "We made our lunches for school tomorrow."

"And Dad made us pick out our clothes and do our chores," Ronny said, less than enthused.

"Wow. Thank you, Mrs. Doubtfire."

Aaron scoffed. "Do I look like Mrs. Doubtfire? She was like twice my age and most certainly did not hit the gym like me."

"Yeah, but she had a fabulous throwing arm."

Aaron said with a high-pitched voice, "It was a run-by fruiting!" They both laughed.

The kids stared at them like they were idiots.

Ronny slipped something out of Kait's bag. "Mommy, what's this?" Ronny pulled out a folded piece of yellow parchment. It was sealed with red wax. Above the wax and across the length of the letter, in fancy script, it read, 'My dearest Kait.' It was what Hunter had hidden from Kait in his office. It had to be. How had he slipped it into her bag?

"Oh," Kait said. "I don't know what it is. I'll have to read it later." Despite how she left things with Hunter, she had the urge to tear it open, but didn't want Aaron to feel bad. Kait smiled at the kids and said, "You guys go play. I'm going to eat and then I'll join you!"

The kids rushed back to the den.

"That looks old school. Really old school," Aaron said, softly.

Kait changed the subject. "Anything else?" Kait asked. "I *am* impressed."

Aaron said, "Umm, the lawn has been mowed. The weeds wacked."

"I'm pretty certain I pay someone for that?"

Aaron shrugged. "I supervised."

Kait laughed. "Anything else?"

"Nope," Aaron said. "Well, I wanted to ask you something. I was hoping to take you to dinner."

"Just the two of us?"

"Yes. Not like a date or anything. I want to talk to you about the kids and the future. Family planning."

Kait said, "Umm, okay." *When has he ever planned anything?* "Are you dying?"

Aaron laughed. "No. I'm not dying."

"When?"

"Saturday. I already asked Jenn. The kids can hang over there."

"Okay. This must be a big deal. You actually planned something."

Aaron said, "I plan."

"Mmm hmmm."

"Oh, and the kids and I fixed the sink. It was leaking a little at the handle. It's a cool contraption, that sink. Wish I had stumbled upon it sooner."

Kait stood in silence.

"Are you okay?" Aaron asked.

"I'm trying to remember if I had a head injury or something?"

Aaron folded up his laptop. "I'm not sure if I should be offended or not."

Kait said, "Don't be offended. I appreciate all that you're doing. And the kids love having you around."

"And you?"

"I'm happy the kids are happy."

Aaron seemingly forced a smile. "Well, see you Saturday. I'll pick you up at 6:30."

As soon as Kait closed the front door behind Aaron, she rushed to the kitchen and tore open the letter. She scanned it so fast, she had to start over.

Dearest Kait,

You have stolen my loving heart. It all started with a fart and now it stinks when we're apart. Loving you has been my greatest pleasure. Laughing with you (and sometimes at you, I admiteth) is my richest treasure. Bonding over women, oh so slutty. In-between your hands (and legs), I feel like putty (well, some of me is not so putty like... I laugh out loudeth.)

Kait glanced in the kids' direction, fearing they could read it along with her.

I start flipping every time I think about us and skinny dipping. I know you have concerns, foreth I have some, too. But I forget all about them when I'm alone with you. I love my bay breezes, yes indeed. But you're the only sugar that I really need. I'm not sure I could ever wear a kilt, but without you, I might wilt. I don't knoweth where all this goes. In this crazy life whoever really knows? All I know is this... my life is better with you in it, especially when we kiss (with tongue and then we get all handsy...)

Princess Kaitlyn, I wanna be your mansy.

Sexually yours,

Prince Hunter

Kait lay the letter back on the island and took a deep breath. She laughed while tears filled her eyes.

Riley walked into the kitchen. "Mommy, what's wrong?"

Kait wiped her eyes. "Nothing, honey."

"Who is Mrs. Doubtfire?"

Kait laughed. "She was a character from a movie."

"Why did you call Daddy that?"

Kait shrugged. "Just joking around. It was about a man who dressed up as a nanny to spend more time with his kids." *But does he really want us back like the movie?*

"Mommy, I'm confused."

Kait grabbed a tissue and wiped her nose. "Me, too."

"Why can't Daddy come home? This isn't fair." Riley wiped her eyes. "We need him. Every day."

The bottom of Kait's stomach dropped out like a roller coaster. He was the one who left. Why did she have to be the bad guy?

THE NEXT MORNING, Kait sat in her cubicle, pretending to be professional while she read through a report on her computer. Instead of reading, though, her mind tried to make sense of all that was happening in her life. With Hunter. Aaron. The kids and Aaron. At Sutton. Staring down forty years old, her birthday in a week.

"Greetings, Kaitlyn," Hunter said, formally. "Can you get your sister or Aaron to watch the kids Wednesday overnight?" he asked.

Kait looked up to see Hunter standing in her cubicle. She didn't know what to say. Should she address her hasty exit? "Umm, overnight?"

"For work."

"Oh, my first thought was that you wanted to go knife throwing or to forge broadswords."

"How did you know all my date ideas?" Hunter asked. "But seriously, it's to discuss the redesign with HQ, but we should have some fun regardless."

"What's going on?"

"Fred wants us in Austin. I told him what we were thinking, so he wants a more in-depth meeting with him and the broader team. You'll probably also be spending some time with the chefs and chemists."

"It's just wrong that a food company has chemists," Kait said. "But I am excited."

"I know, but we goin' to Austin, baby!"

Baby. Kait didn't know what to say. Was he just going to pretend that their conversation didn't happen? Was he going to ask about the letter? She didn't know how to respond.

Hunter said, "We'll keep up pretenses and cover your hotel room, but you can stay with me at my apartment, if you want. We'll have to be incognito, though, with Sasha joining us."

Kait closed her eyes and swallowed hard. She forgot about all of her issues with Hunter. "Why does she have to be there?"

Hunter shrugged. "Fred asked that she be there. He's, ummm, always enjoyed her company."

"Men." Kait rolled her eyes so hard, they almost rolled down the hallway.

"That's an incredibly broad statement." Hunter changed the subject and asked, "Did you get my letter?"

"I did." Kait looked up at him, but then at the floor.

Hunter crossed his arms and sat back in his chair. "Any...response?"

Kait scrunched up her nose. "Umm, I'm all out of wax. I'm part Brazilian on my father's brother's roommates' side. I go through the stuff like crazy."

Hunter smiled. "That's probably a little T.M.I. But it doesn't actually have to be written on parchment. Or as witty. Text, email, oral are all acceptable methods of response."

"Oral?" Kait questioned, crossing her arms across her chest.

Hunter cocked his head. "Yes. Well, that would be more than acceptable, but I was referring to verbal communication." Hunter stared at her, seemingly waiting for a response.

What should I say? Kait closed her eyes and inhaled deeply. "I loved your letter. I think you are the descendent of a long line of medieval bards. Naughty medieval bards."

"Anything else?"

Kait said, "But it's complicated."

Hunter paused for a moment. "Well, I guess we'll have Austin to figure it all out." He seemingly forced a smile and disappeared.

Kait wanted to disappear as well, but she realized that no matter where she went, her thoughts would follow her. *Austin with Hunter. And Sasha. Mother frigger.*

25

Kait sat with Hunter at the Southwest gate headed for Austin on Wednesday morning. Sasha hadn't arrived yet, which was more than fine with Kait. And if she missed the flight, even better. But then Kait heard the click clack of heels approaching. Sasha bounced toward them with a short black skirt and a tight white blouse, sunglasses on and a coffee in hand.

"Good morning," Hunter said.

"Is it? We're flying Southwest. I don't need first class on every flight, but I'm supposed to fight over a seat?"

"You're a real woman of the people," Kait said. "I love Southwest. The prices are right, and the kids like to pick their own seats."

"Whatever." Sasha sat down next to Hunter and sipped her coffee.

Hunter tried to make conversation as they waited to board, but neither woman had much to say. After they checked in, they waited in the jetway to get on the plane. Hunter was first with Kait and Sasha behind. As they approached the doorway to the 737, Sasha nudged Kait and stepped in front of her.

"Excuse you," Kait said.

Sasha didn't respond. She didn't even flinch.

Hunter led the way onto the plane and grabbed an empty row about a third of the way back in the plane. Kait bit her lip. Not only would she have to sit next to Sasha, but Sasha's power move put her between Hunter and Kait.

"It's frigid in here," Hunter said, putting in a pair of ear buds.

"In more ways than one," Kait said under her breath.

Kait rested her arm on the armrest, but Sasha bumped it off.

"I swear. You're like a friggin' toddler. You know, it's not actually required that you fight over a seat."

Sasha said, "Having the option is growing on me."

"Whatever."

Kait had barely slept the night before and had planned to sleep on the flight. Instead, she watched Sasha like a hawk. Thankfully, it appeared as if the sex bot had been on the prowl the previous evening, which meant she slept more than talked for the two-hour flight.

Once the reluctant trio arrived in Austin, they checked in at the hotel and then headed over to Mrs. Potts HQ. Hunter parked in the employee lot outside a three-story glass building.

"This is where the magic happens," Hunter said with a smile. "Or not, if you look at the stock price and my 401k."

Hunter led them into the building and through security, giving an impromptu tour as they passed important places.

"There's the employee cafeteria. They bring Mrs. Potts straight over from the plant every day for lunch."

Kait said, "Ewww. They serve Mrs. Potts products in the cafeteria?"

"Shhh," Hunter said. "They do, but nobody eats there."

"We won't, either," Sasha said.

Kait raised an eyebrow at Hunter. "Nobody eats there?"

"Should've been a warning sign. I know."

Hunter pointed out a portrait of the original Mrs. Potts. It must've been from the 1960s. She wore a pink dress with a white lacy apron over it, pearls, and a beehive hairstyle. She looked like Jackie O. in front of an oven.

Kait said, "Iconic. It just goes to show you that you don't have to flaunt your tits to be successful." She looked at Sasha. "You might want to write that down."

Before Sasha could respond, a squat man in a blue suit and perfectly-coiffed but oversized grey hair said, "There they are! There's my Sasha."

Sasha forced a smile. "Fred!"

Fred didn't seem to know that Sasha had eyes that he could or should look at. Eventually, he made his way to Kait. He shook her hand vigorously. "I've heard so much about you, Kait. Welcome to Mrs. Potts. Come. Meet the rest of the team."

"Thanks, Fred. It's great to meet you as well."

Once they sat down in the boardroom, eight other people joined them. Senior managers, chemists, chefs, accountants, and even a food compliance expert were there. Hunter would give the presentation with Kait there for support and Sasha there for eye candy, apparently. Then they would break down into smaller groups for in-depth discussions, do a plant tour, and then regroup for a summary.

Kait was pretty happy with how the day went. The presentation was well-received. Kait and Hunter were in a different tour group than Sasha, so it was a home run, really. The worst part was a heated discussion over food dyes, although Kait enjoyed it. She didn't realize red #40 was so riveting. And don't get her started on sodium nitrate and sodium benzoate. Those were the ingredients the customer panels were most concerned about and the ones they recommended replacing. And it was looking like a go. Kait was excited, but she wanted to hear what Fred had to say.

At the end of the day, they all gathered back in the boardroom. Kait looked at Hunter, who smiled at her. She smiled back. He pursed his lips out as if wanting to kiss her. She smirked.

Fred interrupted and said, "Well, you've made a great case. I know the chefs and chemists have their work cut out for them. Not to mention we need the nerds to run the numbers."

An accountant named Greg frowned.

Fred continued, "Let me digest all of this and we'll figure out next steps. While we're on the subject of digestion..." Fred's eyes widened. He clapped his hands, rubbed them together, and looked at Hunter. "Let's take these lovely ladies out for some fine Austin dining. Thank you, everybody."

Everybody clapped, except for Fred and the Sweet Water trio.

"Steak? Seafood?" Sasha asked.

"No, Sasha. This is Texas." Fred laughed. "Barbecue."

"All you can eat," Hunter added.

"Big Belly's?" Fred asked.

Hunter scoffed. "Is there any other place?"

Kait smiled. Sasha looked like she had just sucked on a lemon.

"I'm sure they have barbecued tofu," Kait whispered to Sasha.

Sasha rolled her eyes.

Dinner was spectacular. Kait nearly needed to be rolled out of Big Belly's as her own belly was something the restaurant's founder would likely have been proud of.

"Oh, that hit the spot," Hunter said. "I've only been out of town a few weeks and I've missed it."

"That was so good," Kait said, hoping her waistband would hold.

"I ate pork butt. I don't want to ever speak of this again," Sasha said.

They all laughed.

Fred rubbed his belly, groaned, and said, "This big man's gotta get home to the little lady." He took Sasha's hand and kissed it. "Do come see me again soon, darlin'."

Sasha forced a smile. "Of course, Fred. You know I love our visits."

And he loves other stuff that ends with -its. Fred's eyes found their way down to Sasha's chest and stayed there for quite some time, perhaps as he fantasized about visiting the twins.

Hunter patted Fred on the back. "Well, the missus is waiting."

Fred broke out of his stupor. "Yes. Yes, indeed."

Kait's chest only received a cursory glance, but she was lucky enough to get a hand kiss from Frisky Fred. "It has been a pleasure having you here. You've done some great work with Hunter. You two make quite the team."

"Yes," Kait said, nodding. *Quite the team.* "It was great meeting you, Fred. Thank you so very much for having us and for the opportunity."

"The pleasure is mine." Fred smiled, took a parting glance at Sasha's boobs, and walked away.

"Now what?" Sasha asked.

Hunter asked, "Do you want to see the bats?"

"What do you mean?" Kait asked.

"There's a reason they call Austin Bat City. There are a butt-ton of bats."

"Umm, no," Kait said.

"We finally agree on something," Sasha said.

"Why not? They shit on everyone. It's awesome," Hunter said, laughing.

Kait fantasized about a colony of bats unleashing their business on Sasha's head. Maybe it wasn't such a bad idea, although with her luck, she would be the one getting dumped on.

Hunter waved them forward. "Let me give you a Sixth Street tour then." As they walked by the Roadhouse Bar, Hunter asked, "Anybody wanna run with the bulls? For five bucks and an autographed, lengthy waiver, you can ride a mechanical bull. It's an Austin staple."

Sasha said, "I've always wanted to do that. Sign me up."

"That's the spirit. Sasha embracing her inner cowgirl." Hunter looked at Kait. "How 'bout you?"

Kait shook her head. "Not interested."

"Okay. You're missing out, but whatever." Hunter paid the cover charge for the three of them and led the women inside.

A huge crowd circled around an enclosed and padded bull-riding ring, drinking and cheering a twenty-something male rider. He straddled the bull, holding onto a rope with one hand. A man sat on a chair outside the ring with a joystick that he jostled back and forth. The bull bucked forward then spun 360 degrees and then bucked again. The man bounced from the bull's back, but thrust his hips forward as the bull's head dipped, keeping his seat. The bull's master wiggled the joystick in six different directions within a split second and smirked. The bull sped up, spun, dipped, and bucked. The rider flipped in the air and landed on his back with a thump. The crowd cheered and jeered.

Kait looked at Sasha, gave her a thumbs up, and said, "Good luck!"

Sasha took a deep breath and slipped off her heels by the operator.

Kait frowned. Was that fear on her face? Was the sex bot even programmed for fear?

Sasha entered the ring to cheers and cat calls.

Somebody called out, "Ride me, instead!"

Hunter leaned over to Kait's ear and said, "Don't get too excited. Women are treated a little more gently here."

"That's too bad," Kait said. She leaned up against the ring's border and watched Sasha approach the bull.

Sasha placed her hands on the bull's back, stepped into the stirrup, and swung her long leg over the bull. Her short skirt rode up even higher than normal, prompting cheers. She grabbed the rope with one hand and nodded to the operator.

The operator moved the bull in quarter turns, slowly dipping the bull's head toward the floor. Sasha held one hand above her head and rhythmically thrust her hips forward each time the bull dipped. Kait's mouth dropped open. She had no idea bull riding could be so sexy.

Cat calls rang out from the few men who were able to speak. Some guy next to Hunter elbowed him and said, "That'll get the blood flowin' better than any blue pill."

Hunter laughed.

Heads bobbed to the rhythmic bouncing of boobs. How

could this have gone so wrong? Kait took a deep breath, looked at Sasha, and then at Hunter. "Sign me up."

Hunter did a double take. "You wanna ride? I'd like to see that."

Kait led Hunter to the bull bouncer, nearly tore the clipboard from his hands, and signed the waiver without reading it. She held the clipboard out for him, but his eyes were elsewhere. She looked over to see Sasha thrusting and bouncing in all the right places. She stuffed the clipboard into the man's chest. He grabbed it, but didn't even bother to look at Kait.

"That'll be, umm, five bucks," he said.

Hunter held out a five-dollar bill. Kait stepped past the man and stopped at the ring's entrance next to the operator. The operator slowed the bull down to a stop. The crowd booed, but quickly changed to cheers as Sasha dismounted.

Sasha slipped on her heels and looked at the operator, who was probably a college student at the University of Texas, and said, "Thanks for a great ride."

He gulped and said, "You're welcome."

Sasha leaned over to Kait and said, "Beat that."

Kait took a deep breath. She thought about unbuttoning a few buttons, but she couldn't stoop to Sasha's level.

Hunter said, "Make sure you squeeze your thighs around the bull and you'll be fine. You're good at that."

Kait smirked and then entered to fewer cheers than Sasha.

Somebody from the crowd asked, "How old is this lady?"

"Who cares dude? She's pretty hot."

Kait took a deep breath and mounted the bull. Nothing ripped, which was a good start. Still, Kait's heart pounded. The operator started up the bull as he did for Sasha. Nice and slow. The bull dipped. Kait thrust her hips forward. The crowd cheered a little louder. The bull rotated a quarter turn and dipped again. She threw her hair back as she thrust forward again. Energy surged through Kait's body. The crowd cheered louder still. She looked at Hunter who was clapping heartily and blew him a kiss. Sasha was at the bar, her back to the ring.

Somebody yelled, "Faster!"

"No!" Hunter yelled.

The operator spun the bull a little quicker on the next turn, but Kait held her own. She squeezed her thighs around the bull, remembering Hunter's advice, but the excitement morphed to fear. She tried to smile on the next dip, but anxiety ripped through her.

The crowd began to chant, "Toss her! Toss her! Toss her!"

Kait's eyes widened. She looked at the operator, who seemed swayed by the savage crowd's fickle opinion. She shook her head no, but with the bull speeding up, either the operator didn't notice or didn't care. Kait whipped around in a circle, squeezing her legs around the bull, her screaming drowned out by the music. The rope cut into her hand. Her head began to spin. The crowd blurred. And then cheered as Kait took flight. She soared through the air and then splattered face down onto the padding. Her face stung. Her pride stung even worse.

Hunter cursed at the operator and then hopped over the railing of the ring and helped Kait to her feet. "You okay?"

"Just fabulous. Thank you for the wonderful recommendation." Kait pulled her arm from Hunter's grasp and headed to get her shoes.

"I've never seen that happen before," Hunter said.

As Kait approached, the operator was seemingly very taken by Kait's shoes and refused to make eye contact. The crowd gave Kait one more sarcastic cheer as she stepped out of the ring. Sasha waited for the two of them, her smile wider than Kait had ever seen. Had she gotten that surgically enlarged as well?

"Thanks, a lot," Kait said to the operator.

Hunter grabbed some dude's five-dollar bill as he handed it to the bouncer. "I want a refund."

"Hey!"

Hunter ignored him as he pulled Kait to the front door.

Kait rubbed her eye. Her cheek pulsed. Her pride pounded. Kait stepped down onto the pavement, stumbled and nearly fell. The heat nearly punched her in the face. She felt her hair frizz like corn kernels popping.

"Sorry about that," Hunter said, as he led them back to the car.

"Don't apologize. That was awesome," Sasha said.

"I was talking to Kait."

"Oh, yeah. That was terrible." Sasha's facial expression did not seem to match.

"Do you need ice?" Hunter asked, examining Kait's face.

"No. Let's just get out of here."

"To the hotel," Hunter said with an out-of-place enthusiasm.

It was a quiet ride back to the hotel. At least Kait hadn't had to fight Sasha over the front seat. Hunter pulled up into the circular driveway in front of the hotel.

"Thanks," Sasha said, leaning toward Hunter. "Want to hit the hotel bar for a nightcap?"

Hunter glanced at Kait and then at Sasha through the mirror. "Oh, not tonight. I'm not gonna be in town for long, so I need to catch up on a few things."

"Too bad," Sasha said, getting out of the car.

Hunter grabbed Kait's arm and said, "Can you sneak out? Please. I'd like to be alone with you."

Kait exhaled and nodded. "Yes. I'll head up with Sasha and circle back out."

"Okay. I'll walk you two in and wait for you in the parking lot."

Kait said, "Okay." She opened the door and got out of the car.

Hunter walked with Kait behind Sasha on the way to the hotel lobby. Once they were inside, he said, "Well, I will see you tomorrow at 8:30 to head back to Sweet Water."

Sasha stepped toward Hunter. "Thanks for a great night." She pet Hunter's shoulder down to his chest and then turned.

Hunter winked at Kait. "See you in the morning."

Kait smiled and caught up with Sasha, who walked while typing on her phone.

"Ready to head up?" Kait asked.

"I'm gonna hit the store," Sasha said.

"I'll wait for you."

"No, it's okay," Sasha said. Her phone dinged. She read it and looked at Kait. "You know what? I'm not in the mood for water. I'm gonna grab a drink at the bar."

Shoot. "Okay. Have a good night," Kait said. Not that she meant it. She walked to the elevator and hit the button. She could go up one level and then circle back to Hunter with the stairs and a side entrance. She did just that. She opened the door to the first-floor hallway and peeked around the corner like a poor private investigator and then rushed to the exit door. Her phone dinged with a text, but she left it in her bag. She turned toward the front of the hotel and parking lot and then turned again, facing the front entrance. And then froze.

Sasha stood in front of Hunter, leaned into him, and kissed him on the lips. Kait's knees nearly buckled, nausea spreading quickly. It wouldn't be the first time she had puked while watching Hunter and Sasha together, but the last time was a lot more about the tequila. It seemed like a day passed before Hunter grabbed Sasha's arms and separated from her. He said something to Sasha that Kait couldn't hear. Sasha turned and disappeared. Kait's mind raced, trying to process what had just happened.

Hunter turned, paced in a circle, and ran his fingers through his hair. His eyes stopped on Kait. He froze.

Kait gulped hard. Words flew out so fast, her filter never had a chance. "What the hell was that about? I knew there was something going on with you two," Kait yelled, and then turned away toward the side entrance.

Hunter rushed over to Kait and put his hand on the door, so she couldn't open it. "Nothing. That was nothing."

She turned and wanted to push him back, and not the good, kissing-kind of concussion. "It looked like a lot more than nothing. You were basically sharing her underwear."

Hunter said, "What? That's a little dramatic, no?" He raised an eyebrow. "I would look good in a thong, though."

Kait said, "How do you know she wears a thong?"

Hunter threw his head back. "I don't. I was just making a joke. A bad joke, I admit. Geez. *She* kissed me. I pushed her away."

"After how long? You almost missed morning checkout."

"Kait, please. I didn't count how long. I was shocked. I swear it meant nothing."

"How...how did she even meet up with you?"

"She texted me that she left her sunglasses in the car. I texted you to hold off for a few minutes. Did you get it? Look at your phone."

"So, you wanted time alone with her?" Kait asked, hands on hips, lip quivering.

Hunter's shoulders slumped. "No. I didn't want you and I to get caught. We're trying to keep it a secret, right? She told Josh about us after the camping trip. Read the text. It says that Sasha is coming."

"You're not that good of a kisser," Kait said, monotone. The idea of Hunter doing that to Sasha made Kait shudder.

"Oh, *you* can make jokes?"

Kait said, "I didn't kiss anyone."

"She kissed me. Did you see her kiss me?"

Kait hesitated. "Yes."

"So, you know it wasn't my idea. How can you blame me for what she did?"

"I don't know," Kait said, shaking her head. "I'm just angry."

"Can *we* just kiss and make up?" Hunter asked, stepping toward her.

"I cannot kiss you until you are disinfected."

"I will gargle with Lysol at once." Hunter stared up at the sky. "This was not how I wanted things to go." Hunter grabbed her hands. "We were going to meet my parents for dessert at Mama Sugar's. I was going to show you my apartment. Maybe another thing or two."

"I don't want to see two things. Wait. What? Parents?"

Hunter nodded. "I want you to meet my parents."

"Don't you think that's something you should've told me?"

"I'm telling you now. Do you need to mentally prepare or something? They're nice people. My mom smells like mothballs. My dad uses words like shucks and reckon."

Kait just stared at him.

"What's wrong?"

"I don't know," Kait said.

"Do you wanna come with me or not?" Hunter said, throwing his hands up.

Kait shrugged. "Why don't you go with Sasha?"

"Why are you doing this?"

I don't know.

Hunter continued, "I told her to leave. If Aaron kissed you unsolicited, would you think I had a right to be mad at you?"

"How would she know you didn't want her? You're always joking with her. You went to dinner. You play tennis together. She calls you for brunch."

"Who's the middle sister from *The Brady Bunch*?"

"Jan, I think," Kait said, her brow furrowed. "Why?"

"You're like Jan Brady, always bitching about her pretty, older sister. Marcia, Marcia, Marcia."

"Oh, she's prettier than me?" Kait knew she was, but he wasn't allowed to think so.

"That's not what I meant. That was how Jan felt. Why am I forcing this when you don't want it?" Hunter asked. "I didn't ask Sasha to meet my parents. And I wouldn't have asked you if you didn't mean something to me."

"Yeah, but for how long?"

Hunter threw his hands up and yelled to the sky, "I wish I could find that woman I spent the weekend camping with! I'm not sure she exists in the regular world!"

"What's that supposed to mean?"

Hunter ran his fingers through his hair. "What do you want Kait? I don't know how to do this with you."

"I don't know what to tell you. Just tell your parents I don't feel well. Because that's the truth. I feel sick."

"If that's what you want."

Kait said, "It is."

Hunter gulped. "Okay. I will, umm, I guess I'll pick you up for the airport at 8:30."

"I'd take an Uber if that didn't mean you'd be alone with Sasha." Kait turned, tore the door open, and stormed into the hotel.

"What...just...happened?" Hunter muttered, as the door surged toward his face and slammed shut, an inch from his nose. He didn't follow her. Again.

26

Kait bolted the door behind her. She didn't even bother to get undressed. She climbed into the bed and sobbed. No matter how many tears she expelled, they kept coming. At least it was somebody else's comforter this time. And the pain never left. Helpless. Hollow. Hate. She hated Sasha, but she hated herself even more. *What a joke I am. I knew this would happen and I still let it happen. I'm so weak. Worthless.* She rolled over and stared at the blurry ceiling. She did this for what seemed like hours, until she drifted off to sleep.

A knock at the door jolted Kait awake. She sat up and looked around. It was 8:03 a.m.

"What the—" Kait looked down at her wrinkled clothes and attempted to straighten them, to no avail. She stood up and walked to the door, the knock persisting. "Friggin' housekeeping." She leaned in and peeked through the peep hole. Her heart nearly imploded. Hunter stood on the other side of the door. "Damn him." Even his nose hair was perfect. Her hair, nose or elsewhere, was not. "Just a minute."

Kait rushed into the bathroom and stood in front of the mirror. Her hair looked more like frizz bomb shrapnel. Her eye shadow and mascara were smeared across her face like she was a clownish *Braveheart* warrior. She wet her hands and hair and pulled it back into a ponytail, and then washed her face as quickly as possible.

"Kait?" Hunter called through the door.

A minute later, Kait arrived at the door and opened it. She stared at Hunter, her chest tightening.

He looked her up and down. "Did you sleep in that?"

"No. I just wrinkled it all up and put it back on this morning."

"Okay, stupid question. Can I come in?"

Kait stepped aside and closed the door behind Hunter. She walked into the room and started tossing her stuff into an open suitcase on the luggage rack. Hunter followed her.

"Can you sit so we can talk?" Hunter asked.

Kait turned and sat on the bed.

Hunter paced back and forth behind her, seemingly not sure what words to use. After a moment, he said, "I don't know how we got to where we are, but I didn't want to end up here. I barely slept last night. I couldn't shut my brain off." He took a deep breath. "I don't want to hurt you."

Too late.

Hunter continued, "But the truth is that I'd be lying if I said that a part of me didn't enjoy Sasha's attention. Everybody wants to be wanted. But you have to believe me that I have never felt anything for her like I have for you. I don't want to be with her. I want you with all my heart."

Kait hung her head in her hands. "I...I just don't believe that. I feel like I'm always going to be looking over my shoulder, wondering what younger, prettier woman is going to catch your eye." *Like what happened to my mother.* "And that's without wondering whether I'll even see you again after we're done with Mrs. Potts."

Hunter fell to his knees in front of Kait and grabbed her hands. "Sweetheart. I am not too good for you. I think I'm blessed to have you in my life. How can I make you understand?"

"Tell me what we're doing. Are you taking the job in Europe?"

Hunter shrugged. "It hasn't been offered. I'm just living my life as it comes."

Kait asked, "Assume it's yours. Will you take it?"

"I don't know."

"I can't do this. I'm not strong enough." Kait wiped tears away.

"So, be stronger."

Kait sniffled. "That's not how it works."

"How do you know? Have you tried?" Hunter asked.

"I've tried my whole life. I'm never strong enough or good enough."

"I don't believe that," Hunter said.

"So, I'm a liar?"

Hunter hung his head. "No, but..."

"What time is it?" Kait asked through tears. "We have to get Sasha and go. We'll miss our flight."

"Sasha texted me last night."

Oh, God. "And?"

Hunter stood up and paced in front of her. "She left already."

"Finally, some good news."

He rubbed his face and closed his eyes. "And I'm not going back to Sweet Water."

Kate frowned. "Since when? Why aren't you coming back?"

"Since now. You don't seem to know what you want or who you want to be. It's not gonna work if you're jealous and insecure all the time. I'm telling you I love you. Why don't you believe me?"

"I...I don't know."

Hunter wiped a tear from his eye. "I need to unplug. To get away for a few days. I just...I don't...I'll be in touch," Hunter said, deflated. Shoulders slumped, he walked toward the door.

Kait stood up. "You'll be in touch? Is this a business relationship?" She shook her head, confused.

Hunter turned and said, "It's always been a business relationship. And I guess a fling to you. Goodbye, Kaitlyn." Hunter opened the door and left. Tears welled up in Kait's eyes. She wanted to call out, but didn't. Or couldn't. She wanted to chase after him, but for some reason, her legs didn't move. She just watched him go, tears streaming down her face.

KAIT WENT THROUGH SO many tissues on the flight home, she thought she might get charged for them. Surprisingly, she still had some tears left by the time she returned home. Ronny and Riley greeted Kait as soon as the door opened. She fought back those remaining tears.

"Mommy," they said, in unison.

"It's so good to see you guys," Kait said, dropping to her knees and engulfing the kids in her arms.

Riley said, "Mom, you've only been gone for like two days."

"I know, but kind of a lot's happened since then. What's

exciting in your world?" Kait scooted back and smiled through tears.

"Are you crying, Mommy?" Riley asked.

"Yes. I'm just so happy to see you. So, tell me. What did I miss here besides you two?"

"School was kinda boring. Not much else going on," Ronny said.

Riley said, "Dad sold his motorcycle."

Kait said, "Oh, wow. That's big news. Good. I hated that thing. We fought about it all the time."

Riley frowned. "Why did you hate it?"

"I don't think they're safe. And he bought it on a whim. Barely knew how to ride it. I didn't want him to die and for you two to grow up without a father."

Kait's head throbbed. She stood up and winced.

Ronny asked, "Are you okay?"

Kait laughed nervously. It was a loaded question. "I have a headache. I just need some medicine."

"Don't worry, Mommy," Riley said, heading toward the kitchen. "I'll get the chocolate."

Kait laughed through tears. "I love you, guys."

27

Friday morning was a joy. Kait lay in bed until the last possible second, analyzing every mistake she had made since meeting Hunter. She knew this would happen. She knew! And she still fell for him. How could she not? He was amazing. But still, it was her fault. She had learned nothing from Aaron. He was out of her league. And he told her he didn't do serious? How stupid could she be?

Kait willed her way through the morning routine, fueled by the life-saving combination of coffee beans and hot water. She slinked through the stairwell and the hallways to avoid any and all human contact en route to her cubicle. It was a beautiful day outside, so Josh would be gone by 2 o'clock, leaving Kait with about five hours to endure. Could she manage? It was doubtful. The pain too strong. Her thoughts too scattered.

She wanted to stay in her baggy sweatpants and Aaron's torn 'Save Ferris' t-shirt, her hair a rat's nest, double fisted with pizza slices, like she had after her divorce. But she could barely admit what had just happened. Her friends would know something was up if she didn't show up to work. Maybe she could just put on a good show for them.

Kait tossed her laptop bag and pocketbook on her desk and slumped into her chair. *I don't want to be here.* She just wanted to snuggle up with Hunter and forget all that had happened.

But how would she get through the day? People would want to know what happened in Austin—Carl and Josh from a business perspective and her friends from a personal one. Her biggest challenge would be Shelly and Taylor, who she couldn't avoid. Even if she could, they knew where she lived. She had already avoided a bunch of The Circle's texts. Texts like this:

Could she hide under her desk a la George Costanza from *Seinfeld*? Kait's phone dinged from within her pocketbook. Her pulse quickened. Could it be Hunter? She opened her pocketbook, removed two travel tissue packs, and checked her phone. It was not Hunter, but apparently, she had won a free singles cruise.

Great timing as usual, life. She leaned back in her chair. She wanted to call him. Or at least text him. She wanted to say the words, 'I made a mistake. I miss you. I want you. I need you.' But she couldn't. They just wouldn't come out. *Why not?*

A darkness hovered over Kait, like clouds cutting off the sun before a storm hit. She frowned as she studied a curious shadow on her desk. Two shadows, actually. Kait looked up to see Sasha's boobs in her cubicle, along with the rest of her.

Sasha stared down at Kait, who stared back, her gut flaring up.

"Hunter's supposedly leaving. We may lose the account after Mrs. Potts," Sasha said, bitter.

I think I'm gonna puke. Kait frowned. "Leaving...where? Mrs. Potts?"

Sasha scoffed. "Leaving the country. Apparently, they made him an offer last night for that job in Europe."

"What?" Kait asked, confused.

"Yep. He's going to hand the project over to Tammy. She'll see the product redesign through." Sasha smiled at Kait.

"You talked to Hunter?" Jealousy surged up within Kait.

"No, Tammy called me this morning. He took a few days off."

Kait stared at her desk, numb. Would she ever feel again? She didn't think she would ever recover from Hunter.

"I don't know why you're so shocked. Splash and dash. Remember? I warned you," Sasha said with an I-told-you-so attitude.

The numbness morphed to anger. Kait stood up, but was nearly bounced back down by Sasha's boobs. "You know what, Sasha? I am *so* sick of your attitude. Of your arrogance. You're lucky I didn't knock you the frig out after you kissed Hunter when you *knew* we were together," Kait said, her chest heaving. "You knew because you reported it to Josh."

Sasha didn't say anything as they stared at each other.

Kait couldn't catch her breath, but continued anyway, "And you're so upset we may lose the account? I lost Hunter. And maybe if you hadn't tried to take him from me, maybe, just maybe, we wouldn't be on the verge of losing the account. Take some responsibility for your actions. For once."

Sasha spat, "It's not my fault you couldn't get him to stay. That's on you."

Kait stepped toward Sasha. "In one of the hundred times you look at yourself in the mirror in the next hour, maybe try to look a little deeper than the Botox and the Instagram pouty lips. You undermined me every step of the way. *You* could've cost us the account. *You* may have cost us Bountiful." Kait looked at her watch and then back at Sasha. "What are you waiting for?"

"What are you talking about?"

"Isn't it about time you run off and tattle to Josh?" Kait

grabbed her pocketbook and pushed past Sasha. "I'm done with this friggin' place." She stormed off down the hall.

Kait turned the corner and nearly slammed into Josh.

"Kaitlyn, whoa! Where are you going in such a hurry? How was Austin?"

"Ask your pet, Sasha. I'm done with this place," Kait said, without stopping. She opened the stairwell door, walked through it, and slammed it behind her. Dimitri was about to get a beatdown.

28

Kait woke up on Saturday morning and rolled out of bed. It was quiet. Too quiet. She walked into the hallway. Both kids' doors were closed. Were they actually still sleeping? What time was it anyway? Kait shuffled to the kitchen, no sign of the kids, and turned on the Keurig. It whirred to a start. She didn't know what to do with herself. She was tired of sulking, but had nothing to keep her busy.

Kait's stomach growled. She had barely eaten all of Friday. She opened the cabinet and pulled out two packets of oatmeal from a box and poured them into a bowl. "Nice and healthy," she said to herself.

She was about to close the cabinet, but did a double take instead. Next to the oatmeal stood a bag a chocolate chips. She tore the bag open, grabbed a handful of chocolate chips, and sprinkled them into the oatmeal. Then she grabbed another handful and popped them into her mouth like a shot. She made coffee and went to the fridge for some milk. She topped off her mug and returned the milk. She grabbed the chocolate syrup and squirted a bunch into the coffee. She shrugged. How could that be bad? Chocolate had antioxidants and flavonoids.

She sat down at the kitchen table, eating her oatmeal and chocolate chips, or perhaps it was more chocolate chips than oatmeal, while staring out the window. What the heck was she gonna do all day? Did the kids have any sports? They were all done for the spring season and travel hadn't started for the summer. And then it hit her. She had dinner with Aaron tonight. She sighed. What soul searching had he done? Maybe she should do some of her own.

A door from the hallway clicked open and then Riley appeared in the kitchen a few seconds later. Kait turned with a smile.

"Morning, sweetheart."

"Good morning, Mommy," Riley said, rubbing her eyes. "What time is Aunt Jenn coming?"

"A few hours before dinner."

The extent of Kait's morning and afternoon consisted of breathing air and inhaling chocolate until Jenn pulled up at the house at about three. Kait opened the door for her while the kids packed a bag.

"Hey, sis," Jenn said, walking up the stairs.

"Hey. The kids need a few minutes. They're packing up. Can't live without certain toys for twenty-four hours."

"Sounds like you and Buzz," Jenn said, laughing.

"Buzz is my best friend."

Jenn frowned. "That's hurtful." She called out to the kids. "Bring a nice outfit. We're going to dinner tonight." She sat down on the couch and said, "What's going on?"

Kait sat down next to Jenn, took a deep breath and willed the tears back into their ducts. "Hunter and I are over. I think he's taking the European job."

"I'm sorry, Kait. You *think* he's taking the job?"

"I haven't talked to him. We actually broke up before then."

Jenn rubbed Kait's hand. "What happened in Austin?"

Kait shook her head, confused. "I couldn't talk about it. And I don't really know. We were struggling before that. Then Sasha kissed him in Austin. I lost it and blamed him for it. The next thing I knew, he was telling me that he wasn't coming back to Sweet Water."

"You will get through this," Jenn said. "I know that probably doesn't help to hear that."

Kait chuckled. "No. No, it doesn't. But I have no other choice, do I? I have to endure this. My pitiful love life. Oh, God. And I turn forty next week. Monday, actually."

"I wasn't gonna remind you," Jenn said, laughing.

"Thanks, little sis. Your time will come."

"A whole two years," she said, laughing. "So, what do you think this whole thing with Aaron is about?"

Kait shrugged. "I really don't know. He's been different. I feel like he's gonna drop a bomb on me, but I have no idea what it could actually be. He never would've taken me to Cuts when we were married, had it been open. I think he's going to give me a dose of poison and counter with the antidote of Cuts' chocolate cake."

The kids walked into the room, each of them with a backpack and a duffle bag stuffed to the brim.

"Are you guys shipping off to war?" Kait asked.

"What?" Ronny asked.

"Nothing," Kait said, laughing.

Jenn stood up and said, "Well, it'll be nice to get dressed up and take your mind off things."

"So, yoga pants and my glitter sneakers?"

"Umm, no. It's Cuts. You don't have to wear sequins, but something nice."

"What is going on?" Kait asked. "Do you want me to be with...?" Kait looked at the kids. "You know."

"No." She scoffed. "I want you to be happy." Jenn kissed Kait's cheek. "Promise me you'll try."

"I promise."

KAIT WALKED towards Aaron's car. She wore a navy and white striped short-sleeve dress. It was casual and flowy, but smart with a midi belt. She held it as it blew in the breeze.

Aaron stood up out of the car. "I was gonna knock."

"I was ready. It's no problem. It's not a date." She certainly wasn't ready for that, if ever.

Aaron smiled. He looked like a model. He wore white linen pants and a tight blue, V-neck t-shirt with sunglasses hanging from it. "You look nice, by the way. And we match." He pointed to his shirt.

"Thank you. As do you."

Aaron nodded to Kait's car. "How's the Honda hotrod driving?"

"Like a dream. It's coming apart at the seams, but the gas mileage is amazing," Kait said, laughing.

Aaron walked around to the passenger side, following Kait.

"Not a date, remember? And you never opened my door even when it was," Kait said.

Aaron opened the door for her anyway. "People change."

Kait slipped into the car, Aaron joining her a few seconds later. He started the car and threw it into gear.

Kait eyed him sideways. "So, what is this all about? Why do we have to go out to dinner to talk?"

"We don't, but it's hard to have a serious conversation

with the kids around. And we've always enjoyed nice meals together. And wine."

"You can't tell me now?"

"Nope."

"So, you're gonna wait until I have a few glasses of wine?" Kait asked. "This makes me nervous."

Aaron laughed. "Not yet. Don't get crazy."

Kait stared out the window.

Aaron asked, "What's wrong?"

Kait forced a smile. "I'm okay. It's nothing that concerns you."

"Okay."

Kait turned to Aaron. "Can you give me a little morsel or something? Why are you being so mysterious? I feel like you're going to drop a bomb on me."

Aaron turned "I don't want to spoil it."

"Are you gonna become a monk or something? Or divorce me again? Isn't that what double jeopardy is for? Don't I have legal protection against that?"

Aaron laughed. "I thought double jeopardy was when Alex Trebek gave you twice as much money for your right answer."

"That's the daily double on *Jeopardy*."

"Oh. Well, I'm not divorcing you again." Aaron pulled the Charger into the Cuts parking lot.

"And Cuts is expensive. Are you gonna make me pay my own way?"

Aaron laughed. "Your meal is covered."

A valet waited for the car to stop and then opened Aaron's door.

"Welcome, sir," the valet said, handing Aaron a ticket.

"Thank you." Aaron took the ticket and held out his arm for Kait, waiting for her. "The name's Colby."

The valet nodded to another valet by the door. "Colby."

Kait put her hand on Aaron's inner elbow, not wanting to fully commit to the whole arm-in-arm thing at a date place.

"Do they always take your name here?"

"No. I just like to pretend I'm James Bond." He gave his best Bond face. "The name's Colby. Aaron Colby."

Kait shook her head, laughing.

Aaron led Kait up the stairs and into the restaurant. Kait headed for the hostess stand, but Aaron headed in the opposite direction. Kait nearly busted a heel trying to keep up. "Where are we going?"

"We've got a table out back on the patio. We'll check in there," Aaron said.

"Okay," Kait said, following along through the restaurant.

Aaron stopped in front of an oversized glass door that led to a stone patio. He pulled open the door and held it for Kait. "To the left," he said.

Kait walked out onto the patio, turned, and stopped dead in her tracks. A line of people stood before her and yelled, "Surprise!"

Mother frigger. Kait's mouth dropped open. She scanned the crowd, but then the crowd surged toward her. Riley and Ronny led the way, followed by Jenn, Shelly, and Taylor. They engulfed her in a ginormous hug.

"We totally got you!" Aaron said.

"So much for your soul searching, mister," Kait said with a smirk.

"Happy birthday, girlie," Jenn said, as she hugged Kait, sharing a private moment among the crowd. "Forty is the new awesome. Fresh start. New you."

Kait laughed. "Yeah, because it worked so well the first time."

Jenn whispered, "Oh, stop. You can't just give up."

"I didn't give up, but..." Kait shook her head, staring at the floor. "I'm forty years old. I couldn't make them stay in my thirties. How is going to get any better?"

Jenn said, "Let's not worry about that now. And aren't you glad you didn't wear yoga pants?"

Kait looked down at her dress. "The jury's still out, but I do kinda look good in this."

"Kinda good?" Shelly asked.

Kait shrugged. "That's the best I can do right now." She looked around and saw her mom standing on the edge of the crowd. Jackie was Kait, but with grey hair. Kait walked to her, arms outstretched.

"Happy birthday, baby."

"Thank you." Kait turned to Jenn and said, "Thank you for doing this and for bringing the kids here. You're the best sister anyone could ask for," Kait said. "I wouldn't know what to do without you."

Jenn said, "Really? Because you never seem to do what I tell you."

"Touché."

"But seriously, the party was Aaron's idea. I mean, I paid for it, but it was his idea."

"What else is new," Jackie muttered. "Stupid dick."

"Mother!" Kait said. "The kids."

Jackie shrugged.

"He's changed a lot. Anyway, it's the thought that counts," Kait said.

Jackie rolled her eyes.

Jenn laughed. "I should've given *him* the idea and he could've paid for it."

"Just bill Billionaire Ben a few extra hours." Kait hugged

Jenn. "I feel so loved. The timing didn't work out too well, but I do really appreciate it."

Jackie asked, "Is your father's tramp coming?"

Jenn huffed. "Mom, can you please just call her by her name?"

"I'd have to care to know it. I just hate feeling second best."

"You're not second best, Mom," Jenn said.

It runs in the family. "She's here with Dad." Kait nodded to her father, Phil. He stood at the back of the patio, a fit sixty-six, tan and grey. The tramp stood beside Phil; a solid thirty years younger than him.

The three women stared in their direction.

Kait thought of Sasha. She said, "Fake hair, fake boobs, fake lips."

Jenn added, "At least the upper ones. She's too young for vaginal rejuvenation."

Jackie said, "She's younger than you both. It's disgusting. I think I'm gonna stuff a beef kebab down her throat."

Kait said, "I think she's vegan."

Jenn said, "And with those lips, I'm not sure it would be the first time."

"That's disgusting," Jackie said.

Kait nodded. "Yes, but culinary violence is totally acceptable."

"It is if she stole *your* husband."

Jenn shrugged. "Maybe I should introduce her to Russ?"

"Will you stop?" Kait said. "And don't blame this all on her. Dad was the one in a committed relationship. I should probably say hi to him and the rest of my guests."

Jackie said, "Keep an eye out for the kebabs."

"Will do, Mom."

Kait shook her head and made the rounds, welcoming

everyone. At the end of the line, she found Shelly and Taylor. She smiled and waved them off. "I already said hi to you."

Shelly smiled, pity on her face. "Are you okay? We missed you yesterday. Jenn told us what happened."

Kait thought for a moment. Pictures of Hunter flashed through her mind. "I'm not okay, but I will be."

"A more important question," Taylor said. "Drinks? What do you want?"

Kait smiled and said, "I'll have a bay breeze."

"You sure?" Shelly asked.

"It's just a drink."

They shuffled Kait over to the bar. "Birthday girl approaching!" Taylor yelled to the bartender.

After appetizers and salad, a waiter moved a chair to the middle of the patio and handed Jenn a microphone. Jenn turned to face the tables of guests. "May I have the birthday girl here?"

Kait rolled her eyes and stood up. She walked over to the chair, the crowd cheering. Thoughts of the mechanical bull rode into her mind. She plopped into the seat; at least thankful it didn't appear to be an ejector seat. Kait stared back at the crowd.

"How about another round of applause for the birthday girl?" Jenn said into the mic. The crowd obliged.

Somebody yelled, "Time for a little humility!" Somebody else yelled, "Roast her good."

Kait whispered, "I've had forty years of humility."

Jenn said, "There will be no roast. This is a toast. This beautiful young woman is turning forty." Jenn wiped a tear from her eye. "This is gonna be short," she said, sniffling. "Even though she doesn't give herself nearly enough credit, we all know that she is an amazing woman, mother...sister...

and friend." Jenn took a deep breath and looked down at Kait. Her voice broke, "You need to know that with every fiber of your being, because it is the truth."

Kait smiled, holding in tears.

Jenn grabbed her drink from a nearby table. "I'm going to start sobbing if I say anymore." She held up her glass. "To Kait, my amazing sister."

"To Kait!" Everyone cheered. Glasses clinked.

Shelly and Taylor yelled out in unison, "Arriba!"

Kait laughed, stood up, and hugged Jenn, both of them crying.

Aaron headed toward them and said, "Sit down. You're not done."

"Oh, God," Kait said, sitting down. "I'm gonna need another drink!"

Everyone laughed.

"Should I smash it?" Jenn asked, ready to break the microphone.

"No. I'll survive. He might not..."

Aaron took the microphone from Jenn and smiled at Kait.

Kait laughed. "Really? You've roasted me our whole relationship."

Aaron said, "Which is why I'll be doing something different tonight." He looked at Jenn. "Jenn missed something—"

"I did not," she said, laughing.

"You did," Aaron said, turning to Kait. He paced in front of her. "I had a minor roast planned, but I'm going to detour. Jenn didn't mention how amazing she was as a wife. It was my fault that it didn't last. And I'm terribly sorry for that. The pain I caused you. And the kids. The pressure. The extra burden." He took a long slow breath and exhaled. "For treating you like you weren't important. Weren't good enough. I hate myself for what I did to you. To the kids."

Kait took the napkin from her drink and wiped her eyes. The entire patio was dead silent.

Aaron knelt down on one knee, rested his arm on Kait's leg, and looked up at her. "I want you back with all of my heart. I love you for loving me even when I didn't deserve it. But more important that, I love you just because you are amazing. I will do anything. Anything. I'll sublet my place. Or I'll just leave it empty. I don't care. I sold my motorcycle. You were right. It was too risky. You and the kids are the best thing that ever happened to me. I was too into myself. Too insecure. Too selfish to realize it. You've always given me and the kids one-hundred percent commitment. But I didn't give you the same. Not even close. And I want to spend the rest of my life making up for it."

Kait's lungs nearly ceased operation. She saw spots. Her equilibrium was anything but. She didn't say anything. Couldn't say anything. She looked over at Jenn and her friends. They had no answers. She looked at Riley and Ronny. They held hands, their smiles as wide as she'd ever seen them.

Aaron held the mic up to Kait's still-open mouth. "What do you say?"

Kait looked around at the crowd. Every eye was on her. Every droplet of moisture in her mouth had evaporated. She swallowed hard, preparing to speak. With a full filter breakdown, her words blasted through the microphone, "Holy fuck."

The crowd gasped. The kids' eyes widened. Taylor fist pumped and whooped.

Aaron whispered so only Kait could hear him, "Is that a good holy fuck or a bad one?"

Kait stood up and frantically searched for an exit.

"What's the matter?"

Kait hustled toward a gate between two plants in the corner of the patio. "This isn't the place to have this discussion."

Aaron followed. "Let's talk outside then."

Kait pushed on the gate, but it didn't open. She rattled it and prepared to kick it down, but it opened before she raged on it like poor Dimitri. Kait surged through the door with Aaron close behind. The gate slammed, which seemed to open the floodgates on the patio. Chatter erupted.

Aaron grabbed Kait's elbow. "Please wait. Talk to me."

Kait stopped, gathered herself, and turned to face Aaron as they stood on a stone path halfway to a gazebo and another outdoor seating area. Waiters shuffled back and forth around them.

Kait looked into Aaron's eyes, attempting to control her emotions. Anger. Frustration. "Did you think you could guilt me into getting back together with you? Why would you do that in front of our kids, my family, everyone we know?"

Aaron looked down. "I swear to you that was not my intention. I did not plan to say all those things. They just came out. I *do* want to get back together with you. That was the soul searching I was talking about. I was going to ask you, but not like that. I was just telling you that to get you here for the party. Please believe me. I want this. The kids want this. But I...I'm such an idiot." He looked up at the sky. "I already need to apologize to you. I can't do anything right. I ruined your birthday. God dammit."

"You didn't ruin my birthday."

Aaron looked down at Kait. "Really?" he asked, surprised.

"Well, you kind of ruined it. But I wasn't really all that

excited about it, anyway. And you don't need to apologize. If you're being honest and I do believe you, you've never treated me with more respect." Kait looked away and wiped a tear from her cheek. "Which is what makes this so difficult." She looked back at Aaron. "My answer is no. I don't love you." *I love Hunter.* "It won't work if I just pretend for the kids' sake."

Aaron didn't or couldn't speak for a moment. "When did you stop loving me?"

Kait hesitated. "I'm not sure that I ever was in love with you. And I don't think you ever loved me. I craved your attention and affection. Your approval. I lusted for you, but I don't ever think we were in love. We never had that true connection." *Like the one I have with Hunter.*

Tears welled up in Aaron's eyes, as he nodded, biting his lip.

"I'm sorry," Kait said.

"Don't be sorry."

Kait wrapped her arms around Aaron and squeezed.

A motorcycle revved in the distance.

Kait let go of Aaron and said, "Don't even think about it."

Aaron laughed and wiped his tears away. "I'm so getting a new crotch rocket."

Kait looked at him with a frown. "Penal enlargement surgery is very dangerous." And then laughed.

"Hardy har har."

"Are we good?" Kait asked.

Aaron took a deep breath. "I am not that great, but we are good. I meant what I said. I am changed and whether you love me or not, I plan to be the best father I can be, and best co-parent-er. Is that a thing?"

"I get your drift. And I appreciate it."

Aaron nodded to the party. "Are you gonna head back in?"

"No." Kait eyed a waiter and said, "I'm gonna go eat my feelings in the gazebo." She looked at the waiter and said, "It's my birthday." And then she grabbed a plate of chocolate cake from his tray.

The waiter stopped and stared at her for a moment. "Umm, okay. Happy birthday? I guess I'll just grab another piece."

"Make it two." Kait grabbed a second slice of cake from the tray.

"Okay," he said, turning back to the restaurant.

"You want me to stay?" Aaron asked, smiling.

Kait smiled sheepishly. "No. I just want two pieces."

29

Kait headed to the gazebo, plopped into a chair, and took a forkful of cake. A big forkful. Like a quarter of the cake. It was glorious. She swallowed it and sighed. She looked up to see her trio approaching, Jenn leading the way. Kait took another bite. Jenn sat down next to her, Shelly and Taylor a few feet across from her.

"Sweet Water Circle Talk," Shelly announced.

"Do we really have to announce it every time? Do you take meeting minutes?" Kait asked.

"Are you okay?" Jenn asked.

"What happened?" Shelly asked.

Kait stared at Jenn. "Did you know he was gonna do that?"

"No. Just the party. I know he wanted to say something, but he told me it would be light."

"That was heavier than Sasha's tits," Taylor said.

Sasha. Hunter. Kait had actually forgotten for a short while. She took a bite of cake. "I told him I didn't love him. I love Hunter." She leaned her head back and stared at the roof of the gazebo. "I'm gonna be single forever. An asexual being with a lifetime supply of batteries and lubricant. Just me and Buzz against the world."

Jenn said, "Being single isn't so bad, right, Shelly? Plus, being married's not that great, either."

Shelly said, "I'm not single. I'm celibate."

Taylor asked, "Is it celibate if it's not by choice?"

"I'm waiting for the right one." Shelly crossed her arms, annoyed.

"You actually have to look," Jenn said.

Kait laughed, but it was more frustrated than fun. "I love it how you all pull my strings, but you're seemingly unhappy and Shelly, you're single, and neither of you do anything about it. And I don't even know what to say about Taylor."

"Hey!" Taylor said.

Kait ignored her. "I knew this would happen. I knew I would fall in love with him and be left with a broken heart."

Jenn said, "Because that's what you focused on. Everybody's been burned by love. Everybody's failed." Jenn leaned over in front of Kait. "Look at me."

Kait did as she was told.

Jenn continued, "Why don't you deserve the best that life has to offer? You're a great mother. You're smart. You're funny, sweet, beautiful. The list goes on." Jenn put her hand on Kait's shoulder. "So, tell me? Why don't you deserve the best?"

Kait thought for a moment. "Well, I'm—"

Jenn interrupted, "No. The correct answer is I *do* deserve the best that life has to offer. Look at how far you've come in just a short time."

"You're the tableside guac, baby," Taylor said.

Kait scoffed. "But how do you know that?" She looked at Jenn. "I think you got all the confidence genes."

Jenn stood up and stared at Kait. "Faith is a decision. Beliefs are a decision. Do you recall the only time The Circle failed?"

Kait said, "Of course. Bobby Moran. You were in love with him in high school. And then, just poof, he was gone. You were devastated, but you never told us what happened."

Shelly added, "You never let us help you. I don't know how many times I tried to get you to tell me what happened or why."

Jenn said, "I'm sorry that I didn't tell you two and Mom. It may have been horrible at the time, but it was the best thing that ever happened to me."

"So, what happened?" Kait asked.

Jenn took a deep breath. "He embarrassed me. Every day. And I didn't know it. He would tell me how corpulent I looked, or in French class, that I was embonpoint. I thought he was complimenting me until I noticed more and more kids laughed around us when he said it. I looked the words up in the library during lunch and started sobbing. He was calling me fat and I was, no pun intended, eating it up, and thanking him for it."

"That's horrible," Kait said, rubbing Jenn's arm.

"Do you know how humiliating that is? Do you know how much that crushed my self-esteem?"

Kait nodded. "I remember. We called it the Dark Ages."

Shelly said, "You were miserable."

"I was. And I gained another twenty pounds. I was heavier after that than I was when I got pregnant with Coop. I became even more corpulently embonpoint." Jenn laughed.

Kait asked, "What changed? You lost all the weight and have been a confident force of nature ever since."

"I hit rock bottom. I ate a gallon of ice cream in the

Wawa parking lot. With a plastic spoon in the winter. Do you know how hard that is to do? I felt disgusting, and I cursed Bobby for making me feel that way. I decided then and there that I would never let anyone else determine my self-worth, but me. And I decided that no matter how I felt at any given moment, I was worthy, no matter what." Jenn stood in front of Kait and jabbed her finger into her shoulder. "And you need to do the same."

"The moment you came into this world, you were good enough," Shelly said.

Kait stared at them, tears streaming down her face.

Aaron drove Kait and the kids home. Kait stared out the window, trying to make sense of everything that had happened. She caught a glimpse of Riley in the sideview mirror, arms crossed, eyes boring into the back of Kait's head. She turned to see Ronny bopping his head and singing under his breath. She chuckled.

"What's so funny?" Riley spat.

Kait turned and said, "I was just thinking about how different you two are, but how I love you just the same. Infinity times infinity."

"That's a lot," Ronny said.

"That's not a number," Riley said. "And I hate you."

Aaron looked in the rearview mirror. "Don't speak to your mother that way. If there's anybody you should hate, it's me. Us not being a family is my fault."

"No, it's not. She can change that."

Kait said, "Don't hate anyone. I'm sorry that you're upset, but Daddy and I are never getting back together. We will both always be there for you. We will both get along and treat each other with respect. But we won't ever live together. He and I will never be together."

"You're laying it on pretty thick there," Aaron said. "I think they get the point."

Kait shot him a look.

"But your mother is right. This might not be the perfect family, but we will make it work. We'll make it work great."

Riley huffed and stared out the window.

Kait took a deep breath and exhaled.

Aaron pat her arm. "She'll come around."

THE SUN SHONE through Kait's bedroom window as she lay there on Sunday morning. It warmed her face. She thought of waking up with Hunter, snuggled in the tent. Her heart ached. She missed him. *I want to wake up with him every day. Why didn't it work? Because I wasn't good enough. No. I didn't think I was good enough.*

Ronny surged into the room and belly flopped onto the bed. "Good morning!"

Kait wasn't sure she agreed. "Good morning, my lovely." She smiled sheepishly. Riley wasn't there. She was probably still mad. Kait rolled over and hugged Ronny.

"I love you, buddy boy."

"You're crushing me, Mom!"

Kait laughed. "You really know how to make a woman feel good about herself."

"Huh?"

Riley's voice whispered from the doorway. "Can I come in?"

Kait looked over at her. "Of course, baby girl."

Riley climbed up on the bed and then onto Kait. "I'm sorry, Mommy."

Kait squeezed her tight. "You don't have to apologize for anything. It's okay to be upset."

"I don't really hate you."

"I know."

Riley said, "I was angry, but we just want you to be happy."

Kait wiped a tear away.

Ronny asked, "Why are you crying?"

"It's okay. They're happy tears. I have everything I need right here, and I love you both so much."

30

Kait sat at her desk on Monday morning, staring hopelessly at the screen. A logo of a cleavage-less Mrs. Potts smiled at her. She was a real woman. A proud grandma offering Kait a tasty meal.

A week earlier, she would've been excited. With new recipes and a marketing campaign built around the improvements, Kait was certain Mrs. Potts would be reformed. But without Hunter, it wasn't the same.

And she could kiss her promotion goodbye. She had basically told Josh to shove it and walked out pretty much before work even started on Friday. He would forgive her, but probably bring up her lack of professionalism and tell her to stay in her lane. She was tired of staying in her lane.

She picked up her phone and called Hunter. With each ring, her anxiety gauge ticked up. She was kind of relieved when his voice mail kicked in.

"Hey, it's me. I just...wanted to talk to you. Quickly. I know you're upset. I know you're unplugging, but there are...things to say." Kait hung up the phone and stared at it. "I love you," she whispered.

"The feeling's *not* mutual," Sasha said, standing in her cube.

Kait stood up and stared at her. "You have something to say, Sasha? You should know that I knocked the crap out of Dimitri."

Sasha laughed. "I've always thought you were funny."

"Yeah, but you always seem to be laughing at me, not with me. Why do we always have to be at war?"

Sasha nodded. "I'm sorry. I shouldn't have joked about your feelings for Hunter that way. And you're right. I haven't been very nice to you. *And* you're right about what you said the other day. I was angry, because it was true."

Kait stood arms crossed. "I'm listening."

Sasha thought for a moment. "I see that you really care about him. And I know that he really cares about you. I'm sorry it didn't work out."

"You warned me."

Sasha shook her head. "Because I didn't want it to work out."

"How do you know he cares about me?"

"Because he bitched me out for kissing him and then again for disrespecting you. A lot."

"A lot of bitching or a lot of disrespecting?"

"Both."

Kait's mind raced. He had stood up for her? Hunter was always so defensive of Sasha.

Sasha continued, "So, maybe this little tidbit will be a small step to repairing what I've done. He picked Tanya to replace him. He didn't pick Dave."

"So?"

"He's much more qualified...and a lot hotter. There's probably a reason he didn't want Dave around you. Come to think of it, I might give Dave a call. We can double date."

Kait laughed so hard, her side hurt. Sasha rolled her eyes and then joined in. Kait stopped laughing and said, "Thank you for that. I really needed it. I don't think we'll ever double date, but even if we did, I'd actually need a date."

Sasha chuckled.

"What's so funny?"

"You seem to think that you actually need to find someone new when you had the perfect guy."

Kait shook her head. "The key word being 'had.'"

Sasha shrugged. "If that's what you think, I guess you'll never know for certain. Good luck with that." She turned and walked away, but turned back. "Or I could tell Josh that you need to head back to Austin to meet with Tanya for a day or two to get her up to speed on the project. I'm sure we could find the money in the budget. You did land the account."

"That's really...nice. You would do that for me?"

"As long as you don't tell anyone." Sasha smiled and then strutted away.

Kait sat beside Jenn in the front passenger seat of Jenn's white Lexus SUV. Shelly and Taylor lounged in the backseat as they idled curbside at the airport drop-off.

"All of you didn't have to come to drop me at the airport. I could've driven myself or taken an Uber."

"We're here to support you," Jenn said. "That's one of the perks of being in the Sweet Water Circle."

"Do you need us there? Please?" Shelly asked.

"I wanna ride some bulls," Taylor said.

Kait laughed. She wasn't sure if said bulls were literal or

figurative. "Thank you, but I'm forty years old. I need to do this on my own."

"We're only a call or a text away," Jenn said.

"Are you sure about this? I don't trust Sasha. Her boobs are filled with venom," Taylor said.

"And she has a lot of storage capacity in there," Shelly added.

Kait asked, "What's the worst that can happen?"

Taylor shrugged. "You die in a plane crash?"

Kait laughed nervously. "Oh, geez. Not what I meant. The worst case is that he says no, which he already has. Josh knows I'm going. I think she was actually trying to be helpful. I think the sex bot has a virus or something. Plus, Hunter apparently put her in her place."

"What if he does say no?" Jenn asked.

"He already has said no. We can't break up twice." Kait looked at Jenn and then at Shelly and Taylor, and said, "Thanks for supporting me."

Shelly smiled and said, "We wouldn't let you do this alone, plus if he doesn't take you back, I'm taking my shot."

"Yeah, right," Kait said. "I'd almost welcome you taking your shot."

Jenn looked at the clock on the dashboard. "You should get going. Good luck."

"Git 'er done," Taylor said. She peeked between the seats. "Maybe lose a button or two on the blouse. Let the girls do some of the work for you."

Jenn rolled her eyes. "Just be you."

31

Kait landed in Austin just before nine, the sun setting as she connected with her Uber driver, a Honda Civic seemingly older than her own. She had fifteen minutes before she got to Hunter's apartment on West Street. Fifteen minutes to figure out what to say, which was a problem, because the two-hour flight produced very little. She almost hoped the Honda broke down. If only she could rub some grime on the spark plugs. She sat in the back seat, regretting not slashing a tire on the way into the car to give her more time.

She had a whole one-word script worked out by the time she arrived at Hunter's high-rise building. It was 'Hi.' It could work. It worked for Jerry McGuire with the whole 'You had me at hello' thing. Or should she go with a more exciting 'Hey,' and maybe throw in some finger guns to spice things up?

Surprisingly, she hadn't come up with any additions before finding herself in front of Hunter's apartment door. She knocked and stepped back. She pat down her blouse. She usually checked her buttons to make sure she didn't have any soldiers slacking on the job, but this time she wondered if Taylor was right. Should she lose a button or even two? No. She wasn't Mrs. Potts or Sasha, for that matter. She didn't need the girls to sell Hunter on what she had to offer.

Hunter didn't answer. She knocked again and then put her ear to the door, listening for signs of life. Nothing. She called his phone. Voicemail. Was she wasting her time? Should she head back to Sweet Water?

She whispered, "I'm not willing to give up. I'm not willing to settle for something less than what I want and deserve with Hunter." She paced in a circle. "This is nuts. What am I doing? I can't do this. He dumped me. He's going to Europe." She turned to leave, but turned back to the door. "No. I can do this. I am so tired of feeling powerless. I *will* do this. I refuse to let life happen to me. I refuse to not see my value! Just decide. Just friggin' decide, Kait! I am worthy." She said it a little louder, "I am worthy." She yelled, "I am worthy!" Energy surged through her with a force she had never felt before in her life. "Yes!" Kait pumped her fist. She nearly kicked down the door, but footsteps squeaked down the hall toward her. She turned to see a balding man in a bathing suit with a towel over his shoulder staring at her like she was a lunatic.

"Everything okay?" he asked, eyebrow raised.

"I have never been better. And, how are you on this fine evening?" She fixed her hair and smiled.

"Umm, good. Are you looking for Hunter? He's down at the pool, swimming laps."

"Thank you," Kait said, and took off running. She stopped and turned around. "Where's the pool?"

The man smiled. "Take the elevator to the lower level and it's out the back."

"Thanks!"

Kait rushed to the elevator and caught the doors as they were closing. She hopped in and pressed the button to the lower level. The ride broke her long-standing record of longest psychological elevator ride, even beating out the time she peed while pregnant.

The doors opened. She followed the signs to the pool and burst through the doors. A few people on lounge chairs stared at her. None of them were Hunter. She scanned the pool. It was empty. Where was he?

She heard footsteps behind her. She spun around to see Hunter's abs heading toward her, along with the rest of him, as he dried his hair with a towel, seemingly unaware that Kait was staring at his ripplingness.

Hunter threw the towel over his shoulder and ran his fingers through his hair. He looked at Kait and then away. And then he froze. His head rotated slowly toward her. "Kait? What...What are you doing here?"

"Hi. Hey," she corrected, but omitted the planned finger guns. It was the wrong occasion. It was clear to her at that moment. She waited, hoping that was all she had to say, and they would wrap themselves around each other. But he didn't say anything. He looked as confused as she was.

Kait said, "I was in the neighborhood. I had a butt-ton of Chinese food, but a bunch of hipsters threatened to beat me...at skee-ball if I didn't give it to them."

Hunter laughed. "I don't believe you. Hipsters don't eat Chinese food and you could take out about a dozen of them, just spinning them and tossing them by their beards and/or man buns. There would be flip-flops and beard oil flying everywhere. I would've heard about it on Reddit."

Kait nodded. "I knew I should've gone with an organic quinoa salad or something."

"Do you want to go for a walk and talk?"

Kait pointed to his fish-pattered swimsuit. "In that?"

"Have you seen some of the outfits around here? Is this really worse than all that flannel? I mean, it's June in Austin. Why are they wearing long-sleeve flannel?" He shook his head, smiling. "I gotta get out of here."

"I heard that you are," Kait said, softly.

Hunter nodded and said, "I was offered the chief marketing officer role for Bountiful's European division. It's the job of a lifetime. I would be the likely successor to Jim Hanlon as CMO for the whole firm. And I have the work we did on Mrs. Potts to thank for that."

Kait stared at her shoes. "Oh."

Hunter said, "I'm taking the job."

"I understand."

They both stared at each other. Kait knew she needed to say something of substance, but what? Should she use the finger guns to stall in like a hold up or something?

"So, come with me," Hunter said. "The kids can come, too. They can go to one of the best private schools. They can experience all the great cities of Europe. We can go to Paris or Rome for the weekend. It will be the experience of a lifetime."

Whoa. Kait took a step back. She hadn't expected that. A million questions and concerns rushed through her mind. It seemed impossible. She whispered, "I'm sorry. I can't go. I can't take the kids away from their father. Their lives."

"Wait for me then."

Kait scoffed. "Wait for what? I can't just put my life on hold. It's a permanent job. You may never come back. And I'm either good enough for you to stay or not good enough at all. So, go. Or don't. I don't mean to be harsh. I love you and will always love you, but I deserve the man who will stay. I can't pay you any money, but I can match your deal of a lifetime. I offer my love and commitment to you, boundless, forever. I can write it on parchment if you like." She shrugged. "The royal herald's horse was stuck in traffic. The horse doesn't count as an occupant in the HOV lane. This place is just weird."

"I'll write city hall." Hunter took a deep breath. "I don't know what to say. My company needs me. I'm not sure you do."

What now? Kait stared at Hunter's feet and then looked up at him. "Did anybody ever tell you that you have Hobbit feet?" *Oh, God. Not that.*

"No, but thank you for that."

"I'm sorry. I like Hobbits. You still make me nervous after all this time. Where was I?" Kait thought for a moment and then looked up at Hunter. "You're right. I don't *need* anyone, you included. But I want you more than anything I've ever wanted, and I can't imagine ever wanting anything more. I could meet a billion men and not find one who fits me better than you."

"I worked so hard for this." Hunter looked away and said, "I made a commitment. I signed the contract an hour ago. I'm sorry. I can't change it now."

Kait pursed her lips, nodded slowly for a moment, and then said, "I understand. I'm sorry. I was so terrified of you breaking my heart that I screwed everything up. But I just couldn't leave things as they were. I had to know that I gave you everything that you deserved. I never gave you that. And I never gave myself that, I guess."

"You just did for both of us."

"But, too late, it seems," Kait said.

Hunter seemingly forced a smile. "Do you want to stay... with me...tonight?"

Kait thought for a moment. She looked up at him and sighed. “More than anything, but I can’t. I won’t.” She walked up to him, lay her hands on his chest, and kissed him on the cheek. “Goodbye, my love.” She turned and walked away. Every fiber of her being urged her to look back, but she didn’t.

32

Kait sat next to Taylor and across from Shelly in her office. Jenn was on the speakerphone. Kait stared out the window, having just told them the story of Austin.

"Hold your head up high, girlie," Shelly said. "You'll get through this."

"We'll get through this together," Taylor said. "Let's get drunk this weekend and maybe *we'll* get together."

"I'm through it already," Kait said, with a chuckle. "And you're not my type, T."

"I'm everybody's type."

Shelly said, "Well, you done good. You can't control what other people do. You made your case. That's all you can do. And Taylor, you're in charge. I'm leaving for Europe at once."

"Very funny. But I agree. If he doesn't see my worth then he's not right for me, as much as I do love him."

"We love you, girlie. And we're proud of you," Jenn said.

"I'm proud of me, too." Kait stood up and headed for the

door. "You really are the best friends I could ask for. Even you, T."

"I'm taking that as a compliment."

"It is," Kait said, laughing.

Kait left Shelly's office. On her way back to her cubicle, she passed Sasha in the hallway.

Sasha asked, "How was Austin?"

Kait stopped to talk. "Not good, but good. If that makes any sense." It was surreal chatting with Sasha in the hallway.

Sasha chuckled. "It does, but it doesn't. I think you're wrong."

"Of course you do," Kait said.

"I think it's all good." Sasha smiled and walked away.

Kait frowned. *What the heck did that mean?*

She turned the corner into her cubicle and stopped short. Hunter sat in her chair, feet up on her desk.

Kait jumped back. "What are you doing here?"

He sat up. "I had an interview," Hunter said.

"Huh? Where?"

"The smoothie place downstairs. I'm a wiz with goji berries."

"That's just weird."

Hunter laughed. "I didn't take the European job, or I resigned, I guess. I had another once-in-a-lifetime opportunity to lock down."

Kait nearly hyperventilated. "How much do...they pay at the smoothie place...unless you've always been passionate about goji berries?"

"I'm sorry. I lied. I got a job here at Sutton. I talked to Josh last night. I took a 6 a.m. flight this morning." He shrugged. "What can I say? The pit sniffers have grown on me."

"Oh, is that the only reason?" Kait's heart rattled her rib cage.

Hunter stood up. "And I told Josh we would be together, company policy or not."

"You and the pit sniffers?"

Hunter laughed. "No, me and you."

"What did he say? He forbade it." She crossed her inner fingers.

"He gave me the thumbs up. He told me no humping in the focus group room." He shrugged. "Apparently, they have cameras in there."

"What?" Kait shrieked.

Hunter cracked up. "I'm kidding. He said I had a nice ass, though. Totally unrelated to any security cameras."

Kait exhaled. "Well, I can't argue with that." She spun Hunter around. "I missed that skinny thing."

"Not at the office," Hunter said, laughing. He turned back around to face her.

Kait asked, "What if he said no?"

Hunter said, "It was worth the risk. And then I would've challenged him to a cage match to the death."

Kait laughed, but then took a deep breath.

Hunter stepped closer. "What's the matter? Have you... moved on already?"

Kait shook her head. "No. I'm just upset."

"About what?"

She crossed her arms. "You're gonna come back here and attempt to win me over and you're not even wearing a kilt?"

Hunter laughed and then whispered in her ear, "How about you meet me at the hotel, and I wear nothing?"

Kait raised her hand in the air and yelled, "Check, please! But wait a minute. How can I believe you? You lied to me."

"What are you talking about?"

"You said you don't do serious."

"I'll show you serious." Hunter looked down the hall and then grabbed Kait around the waist. He pulled her in and kissed her. Kait let go of everything and kissed him back. The chair spun and smacked into the desk. She fell back, knocking over a picture, which tumbled to the floor with a crash.

On the other side of the cubicle, Carl muttered, "Holy Christmas."

Kait and Hunter parted. They both looked over to see Carl peering over the partition.

"This is above your pay grade, Carl," Hunter said. "Sit down and plug your ears. If the cubicle is a-rockin', don't come a knockin'."

Kait smacked Hunter on the arm playfully. She looked at Carl and smiled sheepishly, "Sorry."

"It's okay." His head disappeared below the cubicle while he muttered, "I gotta get a girlfriend."

Hunter's eyes widened. "Oh, by the way. You have an office now. And we're heading our own team together."

Kait frowned, "What are you talking about?"

Hunter smiled. "My job here. Our job here."

"I have to work with you?" Kait looked up to the ceiling. "My once-promising career is tanking."

"First of all, it's actually your team. I told Josh you have the right to fire me at any time."

Kait smiled. "You better play your cards right. I won't hesitate to pull the trigger on that now that I'm a very powerful woman."

"That you are." Hunter continued, "And second, what are you talking about? Your career isn't tanking. We've carved out a niche. We're going after Auntie Mae's next. Have you seen the ass they put on her? It's just waiting for us to plunge right in."

Kait shook her head, smirking. "There will be no plunging. And wait. They put her butt in the logo?"

"Yes, she's in mid twerk. The slogan is something like, 'Oatmeal's back...and it's big.'"

Kait said, "Well, I don't know if there's anything to improve there. That's advertising mastery."

"So, let's take the morning off. It's 9:17, anyway. I'm exhausted."

"I hope you're joking, mister."

"What did I tell you about me getting serious?" Hunter asked.

"I'm not sure that helps your position here."

"So, let's go to my hotel and figure out a new position."

Kait could feel her panties disintegrating on the spot. "I, umm, think that *could* work. We may have to experiment a lot."

"If I have to."

KAIT STRETCHED GROGGILY in her bed on Saturday morning. Her hand grazed over skin that wasn't her own. She squeezed.

"Owww," Hunter groaned. "Purple nurples are the worst alarm clock. I prefer lower-body stroking."

Kait snuggled onto Hunter's chest. "I bet you do."

"Do you want to try again?" Hunter asked.

"Maybe tomorrow. The kids are with Aaron all weekend. I've got things to do today."

"Am I on that list? The kids are gone. Hence, plenty of time for the stroking alarm clock."

"You're already awake. I think it would be redundant."

"Respectfully disagree." Hunter sat up. "What *are* we doing today?"

"Can't tell you specifics, but throw on your hiking thong. I need you today. There's something I need to accomplish. We need to accomplish together."

"I hope you need me every day. And I think we accomplished a lot last night. Plus, my hiking thong is in the wash."

Kait kissed Hunter's neck. "I want you every day." She slipped out of bed and walked across the room naked.

"That's good enough for me." He lifted the comforter and peered underneath it. "And suddenly I'm feeling very ambitious to add to last night's accomplishments. And the ambition is growing by the second."

Kait laughed and said, "I'm on a mission for a different type of personal growth." She looked back to see Hunter's own impressive personal growth. She rushed back into bed and climbed onto him. "Maybe both kinds could work."

Hunter moaned, "It already is..."

KAIT LED HUNTER through the same hiking trail that they had taken on their camping trip. The trees above them blocked out most of the sun, but the heat still permeated the forest's shield. Kait wiped sweat from her face as she turned and stopped to face Hunter. She adjusted her backpack and took a sip of water from the canteen on her shoulder.

"You good?"

"I need a break," Hunter whined, and pursed out his lips.

"You want me to make out with a whiny baby?"

Hunter raised an eyebrow. "Yes? And why couldn't we put bay breezes in the canteens?"

"Who's to say I didn't?"

Hunter pointed to Kait's canteen. "You've been drinking out of that the whole way? Without me?"

Kait smiled and slipped off her backpack. She opened it and pulled out a large rambler bottle and shook it. Ice and bay breeze swished and clunked around inside.

Hunter said, "I didn't think it was possible to love you more than I already did, but you just leveled up in love." He leaned in and kissed Kait, reaching for the bottle.

She held it away from him. "Not yet."

"Come on. Where are you taking me?"

"You'll see."

Kait grabbed Hunter's hand and pulled him forward. They hiked down the path. Water crashed in the distance.

Hunter's eyes widened. He broke out into a dance. "We goin' skinny dippin'. We goin' skinny dippin'."

Kait said, "We're going to the falls. And no promises on skinny dipping." She led Hunter to the small path that led to the cliff across from the falls. Kait dropped her pack and canteen.

"We're jumping?" Hunter asked, surprised.

Kait unbuttoned her shorts and let them fall the ground around her boots. "Does that answer your question?"

"Not sure. I have many answers to give you while you're pantless."

Kait shook her head, smiling, and continued to undress. Hunter watched with much interest. She pulled off her shirt, revealing a red bikini.

Hunter scoffed. "How can you ask me to wear my hiking thong when you didn't?"

"Let's see. Take 'em off." Kait nodded to Hunter's shorts. "Hurry up already. I thought it could mark the start of our journey together."

Hunter's shorts dropped to the floor. He took off his shirt, turned around, and pulled his boxers up, revealing his cheeks like a sumo wrestler. "See?"

"Please don't do that ever again," Kait said, laughing.

"So, we both skipped out on the hiking thong. I like it better when you're unprepared." He shrugged. "But this is still pretty good."

"Pretty good?" Kait took out the bay breeze bottle and took a swig. "*This* is pretty good." She handed the bottle to Hunter and turned around. She smacked her butt. "This is spectacular."

"I will not argue with that, my dear." Hunter looked over at the falls. "You ready or do you need some more booze?"

Kait took the bottle from Hunter and capped it. "I don't need booze to take this jump with you. Let's save the booze to celebrate."

"If we survive."

Kait cocked her head. "Really?" Kait laughed and pulled Hunter by the hand to the ledge. She felt her pulse throb in her neck. She took a deep breath, turned to Hunter, smiled, and said, "Ready, Bay Breeze?"

"My name is Hunky Hunter. And yes. I will follow you wherever you go, regardless of how likely it is that your top falls off when you get there."

"What?" Kait shrieked. She thought for a moment and then shrugged. "Good things have risks." She interlocked her fingers in his, stood on her tippy toes, kissed him, and then said, "Three, two, one, jump!"

Kait and Hunter jumped off the ledge, hand in hand, their adventure just beginning.

THE END

DON'T FORGET to check out Jenn Reinvented, book two in the Sweet Water Circle series!

A NOTE FROM GRAYSON

First and foremost, thank you for reading my book! I hope you loved it. I had so much fun writing Kait's journey.

I have to tell you that the stairway scene was based on true events! A few people have told me they thought it was a little over the top (and they might be right—I may have added a few farts to the story), but it actually happened—and thankfully, not to me! I guess it's true, life is stranger than fiction sometimes or at least makes for good fiction...

If you join my newsletter, I'll share with you a few more fun stories about the making of this book and the rest of the Sweet Water Circle Series. You can do that here: https://graysonavery.com/kaitbonuses/

Perhaps most important, though, I firmly believe that Kait's story is true for so many of us. As for me, writers often struggle with confidence and I was no different earlier in my life. I didn't write my first novel until I was forty, although I had the writing bug for almost twenty years prior to that. While this is my first book written as Grayson Avery, I have been a successful children's humor author under a different pen name for the past few years. I know with certainty that our beliefs are just decisions we make. We consciously or unconsciously choose to believe limiting things about ourselves that just aren't true. Where are you doing this in your life? What decisions can you make about yourself that will serve you better? Find your Circle and help make each other better. And if you don't know who the Taylor is in your group, it just might be you!

I wouldn't be the man that I am today without some strong, confident women in my Circle. And you're lucky for that because you might never heard about hiking thongs without them! Be well and happy reading!

Messages **Grayson Avery** Details

Do you want to join my newsletter?

What do I get?

Ummm, awesomeness.

I'm intrigued.

You get free bonus content, discounts, the pleasure of my company and inappropriate humor.

Sign me up. I need that.

Join at GraysonAvery.com/KaitBonuses

https://graysonavery.com/kaitbonuses/

A SHAMELESS PLEA

If you loved this book (and why wouldn't you? Only non-awesome people don't.), can you share it with like-minded friends? In the off chance that you hated it, please feel free to recommend this to people you don't like as a punishment. My hope is that you won't realize that they are awesome and will love the book.

Also, for the awesome people, I would also very much appreciate if you could leave a review wherever you bought Project Kaitlyn or on Goodreads.

You can also follow me on Facebook, Amazon, Goodreads, or Bookbub (that's the first time in at least ten times I've type Bookbub correctly. For some reason, the k is usually a b...(I blame it on Sasha.) Thank you!

ABOUT THE AUTHOR

Grayson Avery is the author of The Sweet Water Circle Series, a romantic comedy series that focuses on childhood friends in their 30's and 40's as they help each other navigate the stormy waters of dating, marriage, divorce, and a whole lot of inappropriate, naughty, and downright hysterical situations.

Grayson enjoys piña coladas, but not getting caught in the rain, and may or may not be the inspiration for Hunter's bay breeze obsession. He has never worn a hiking thong, but doesn't judge those who do. However, he urges wearers to do so responsibly.

He also wonders if Taylor might be his long-lost sister and how inappropriate the conversation would be should they ever unite.

facebook.com/GraysonAveryAuthor
amazon.com/author/graysonavery
bookbub.com/authors/grayson-avery

Made in United States
Orlando, FL
10 June 2022

18659904R00157